SAVING ANGELINA

Saving Angelina

PETER TINUCCI

Copyright

Acknowledgements

Acknowledgements

I attempted to be as accurate as possible in regard to the streets, stores and buildings that existed during the time period this story takes place. I did quite a bit of research into Tucson history for this. Tucson was an interesting city in the 1970's and is very different now.

I want to thank my wife, Irma, for understanding my writing notes and spending time in front of my desktop computer writing.

And I want to thank Jacob, Jordan and Jade, my kids, for their continued support and ideas that have contributed to this novel.

Also, I would like to thank the many people to whom I discussed parts of the story obtaining insight on Tucson during the time period this story takes place.

Chapter 1

Sept 1975

After High School graduation Angie needed to readjust because she no longer needed to be studying every day. She read more books on engine swapping and auto repair in general. This didn't fill much time or really occupy her mind. She read more crime novels but these didn't take much time or occupy her mind either. She needed something more complex to keep her mind occupied as she always wanted to be learning something and did not care to sit idle. She thought about that and remembered that her mother had told her that she would always be looking to learn. And it would frustrate her when she could not find what she sought. Now she could understand what her mother said. Sometimes she felt anxious when she could not find answers to what she would seek. She would become anxious when she couldn't think of something to search for and learn. At times she would go to the library to look for books. But when she began looking, she looked for something that would stick out, something that caught her interest. At times she would find something interesting but mostly she found nothing. She continued to think about what she could do to keep occupied.

She worked at her father's shop, Dom's Automotive and Performance Center, from opening to closing Monday through Saturday. She continued Martial Arts training on Monday's and Wednesday's from 6 PM to 9 PM. She also did her work-outs every day after work except for the nights she was training. However, she now had quite a bit of time to fill.

The weather had been warm, in the upper 80's to upper 90's and clear to partly cloudy. It was beautiful weather for this time of year as it is the end of the monsoon season.

Angie visited with her friends a few evenings during the week. They got together and went shopping, watched TV, went out to eat and talked. One time while they were together and talking Angie jumped as if she just had a shock. This was just like when you get a big static shock. Her friends noticed this time. Usually, she was able to cover these up but not this time. Gina asked, "Are you OK Angie? You looked like you just got shocked."

"I am fine Gina, thank you. There are times I get a vision of something popping into my head. It does not seem to mean anything however."

"What do you mean a vision?"

"I just saw a distressed adolescent girl that is all. It probably does not mean anything. I was just startled, that is all." Angie replied.

"That's so weird. You just see stuff like that?"

"Yes, it is just a picture and no one I know. I just think it is some memory of something I saw in the past." She was becoming slightly apprehensive about these visions. She thought that this girl resembled herself but she wasn't certain. The visions didn't show her anything other than a distressed young adolescent girl. But she couldn't think of anything that had happened in her life that could contribute to something so traumatic. Outside of the incident with Mike she could not think of anything. She felt as though she couldn't have asked for a childhood any better that she had. She kept thinking about this. She had good parents that always supported her and helped her whenever she had a problem. They were always there for her to listen or explain things, so it couldn't be her parents. She thought about her Grandfather Joseph and Grandmother Kristina and could not think of a time that she had been angry at them. She thought the same about her aunts and cousins. She thought this couldn't be it. What could be causing her to see these visions she wondered. The more she thought about it the more she felt that this couldn't be her.

One Saturday afternoon at closing time Angie's Grandfather Joseph stopped by to talk to her at the shop. "Hello Grandfather." She went and gave him a hug. "What brings you here? Car trouble?"

"Hello Angelina, I came to see you."

"You came to work see me? Why?"

"Now that you are working full time, I wanted to have a discussion about building a portfolio."

"Grandfather, have you been reading my mind? I had just been thinking about this and thought I would visit you to discuss this."

"Is that so?"

"Yes Grandfather. I know you have done very well investing and I know that is how you and Grandmother became wealthy. I have admired your ability to invest since I learned what that means. I thought that maybe you could assist me with this. I know you have been assisting Father and he appears to be satisfied with how he is doing. But I would not know where to begin. I want to build for my future, possibly buy my own house and maybe retire early."

"That is wonderful Angelina. I did not know you had thought this way. If I had known that I could have been working with you already. You never cease to amaze me."

They went into the break room and sat down. He went over some strategies and explained that she would need a broker to buy and sell for her. He explained how to watch the market and what to look for to determine when to buy and when to sell. Also, he told her about buying stocks that pay dividends. He also suggested that he could show her when she decides to begin. He suggested that she could come to his office once a week after work and they could begin. She told him that she would open an account at the bank and each pay day she could put a portion of her pay into it. Then she would use this for investments only. They agreed on an amount for the deposits. Then she would go to his office and he would begin to show her how to get started.

Angie decided that Tuesdays would be perfect because she trains on Mondays and Wednesdays and received her pay check every Friday. Angie chose the following Tuesday to begin.

Joseph was impressed. He left thinking how forward-thinking Angelina was. As he drove home, he thought that he would surprise her and take some money out of one of his accounts for her to get started. He thought a gift of $1000 would be sufficient to make her first investment.

When Tuesday came Joseph went to his bank and withdrew $1000 to give to Angie when she arrived. He thought that he could go with her to the bank to open an account for her. About 5:00 the doorbell rang. Kristina went to answer it. "Angelina! This is a nice surprise."

"Hello Grandmother." She gave her a tight hug. "I am here to see Grandfather. He is going to teach me about investing."

"That is wonderful Angelina! I did not know you had interest in investing."

"I have admired Grandfather's ability since I knew what it meant to invest and since I am working full time now, I have the means to begin." They spoke while they were walking towards Grandfather Joseph's office.

"I am impressed! This is another surprise! Your Grandfather will be a good teacher. Do you know he has been helping your father invest?"

"Yes Grandmother, I have known since he began. I have been waiting for the time I would be able to begin as well."

Kristina knocked on the door. "Yes, you may come in." Joseph said.

Kristina walked in along with Angie. "Hello Angelina. Come here. I set a chair for you here next to me so you can see what I am doing."

"I will leave the two of you." Kristina left and closed the door behind her.

"Angelina, I have decided to give you some money to help you begin investing." He opened his center desk drawer and pulled out an envelope and handed to Angie. "This is for you to deposit when you open your account."

"Thank you, Grandfather. You are so generous." She opened the envelope. "$1000!" She immediately stood and hugged him and gave him a kiss on his cheek. "I cannot believe this! I opened a new savings account after work Saturday and trans-ferred some money from my existing savings account. Here is my passbook." She handed it to him.

"$1500? I wasn't aware you had saved so much."

"I have been saving a little here and there since I began working. I only have my car, insurance, gas and registration and whatever I need for spending for the week. The rest I have been putting in my savings account. I believe Father pays me almost as much as the seasoned mechanics. He told me I was well worth every penny. I left myself about $800 in my other account in case I need something. I am very serious about investing. I would love to be in a position such as you and Grandmother later in life."

"Angelina, you have impressed me again. Now you have another $1000 to add. I believe you will do well."

Joseph worked with Angie for about an hour and he showed her some stocks to begin her portfolio. These were stable ones such as AT&T; Kodak; IBM. He started an account with the broker he uses and explained what she should watch and how to determine what to buy. It was almost equivalent to a class in school. She loved this. She had many new things to learn, which was something that she felt she needed.

Joseph could not be prouder. "You know your father has told me quite a bit about your grandparents. I believe they would be proud as well, Angelina. When I think about it, I find it incredible. Just you alone, your grades throughout school, your hard work at you father's shop, your racing and your ability to defend yourself and your overall attitude, I almost cannot believe it."

Angie had tears in her eyes. She looked up to her grandfather for as long as she could remember. He was always strong and she believed a good role model. She admired him for his ability to manage money. "Thank you, Grandfather, I am proud of you as well. You and Grandmother have always been wonderful role models for me. I need to leave for today. Thank you again for your help and for your gift. I love you so much!"

"I love you as well." They hugged. She left and closed the office door as she went out. She looked for Kristina so she could say goodbye.

"Angelina, you're leaving already?"

"Yes Grandmother, I need to get home for dinner. Mother is holding it for me." They hugged each other. "I love you Grandmother."

I love you as well sweetheart." Kristina hugged her back.

Angie also has been thinking about projects she could do related to her passion for cars. She felt that any project could teach her something new, particularly if it was something that they haven't done at the shop yet. She still craved new knowledge and since she was not studying for school, she needed another way to learn. One thing she thought would be nice would be to add air conditioning to the CUDA. Now that she is using it as her every day driver and driving it quite a bit more than when she had been going to high school, air conditioning would be a benefit on the 100+ degree summer days and through the monsoon season as well. She discussed this with her father and the guys at the shop and they all thought this could be a nice addition for the car. "A Panther Pink HEMI CUDA with air would be sweet." Eric said. (Eric was the 5th mechanic Dominic hired)

Dominic talked to many of the racers and some of the guys that came into the shop for performance parts. He told them that he was looking for a junkyard CUDA that had factory air conditioning. It didn't take long before Dominic received a list of a few junk yards that had CUDA's.

Dominic contacted the junk yards and chose one recommended by a racer friend because he said this place will guarantee to gather every part required. Dominic made a deal for all of the necessary parts including the dashboard, ducting, wiring, compressor, condenser hoses and all of the other pieces needed to convert a non-air conditioned car to an air conditioned car. They would remove all of the necessary parts, package and ship the parts to the shop.

Angie spent quite a bit of time at a Plymouth dealer parts department looking through parts books to determine what all of the parts were and where they would go and how they fit together. The exploded drawings helped her the most. The only issue was that HEMI cars did not come with air conditioning so they would need to modify the brackets for the compressor. The parts they ordered from the junkyard were from a 440 CUDA.

Since Angie was working every day now, she was getting to know the regular customers. And there were racers that came in often to buy parts or to get advice on modifications. Usually, they talked to Dominic but a few wanted to talk to Angie since she had been running so well at the track.

Every so often one of these guys would ask Angie out on a date but she always politely told them that she wasn't interested in dating at this point. One guy, Rich, asked, "Angie, would you like to get together sometime?"

"Rich, I am flattered that you asked but the truth is that I am not interested in dating now. But thank you for asking."

The next time Rich came in he asked again but differently, "Hello Angie, would you like to go somewhere after work to just talk cars? I would like to hear about how you launch so hard. I'm really not looking for a girlfriend. I would just like to be friends."

"As I have said many times Rich, I appreciate the offer but I have definite plans for the next few years and they do not include any male friends or boyfriends. I do not want to be tempted which could significantly alter my plans. I trust you can understand this."

"I guess, if you say so." He was disappointed. But he honored her wishes although he didn't understand. He walked away wondering what plans she could have that would keep her from having a boyfriend. He did however talk about this with a few of his friends. They all told him the same thing. A few of them had asked her and they had been turned down as well.

One day Rich was looking through the books in one of the racks as Angie was standing at the counter filling out some paperwork. She appeared to get what looked like an electric shock. Her demeanor changed immediately. She looked at him oddly and he took that as she needed help. He told her he would help her to a chair. She sat and looked lost in thought for a minute.

"Are you OK Angie? Should I get you father?" Rich asked.

After a minute or so she said, "No, I am fine thank you. It was just an odd feeling." She stood, "Thank you Rich for helping me to a chair. I get these sometimes but I do not think it is anything to worry about. I need to get back to work if you will please excuse me." She left him and went back into the shop.

Angie thought to herself that she hoped these visions do not happen too often. She saw a distressed young lady, but they could be any young lady anywhere. She thought it was maybe because she did not sleep well the previous night. She shrugged it off and continued to work.

The shop had been very busy lately which kept all of the mechanics busy. She found that when she was very busy with a job that required her to concentrate, she didn't have these visions. She thought about this for some time. She determined that when she wasn't thinking of much, she would have these visions. Maybe she could control the visions by doing or studying about something enough to keep her mind occupied. She thought that this may be the key to control when she has these visions, especially since she has been getting these at times where she may need to explain herself.

In about a week and a half the crate with the parts from the wrecked CUDA arrived. Angie and Dominic carefully laid everything out on the floor and Angie cleaned all of them. Angie, Dominic and Eric (besides being a mechanic he is also a fabricator) took the compressor to the CUDA and looked at how the brackets would need to be modified to fit the HEMI. They took measurements and cut the brackets and Angie would then need to make sketches of the pieces that needed to be fabricated. Eric would then show her how to make them and weld them together. Angie remained at work after closing a few nights to clean and paint some of the greasier pieces, make the sketches and verify the measurements for the pieces for the compressor brackets. She had stayed late a few evenings in the past and also the last few nights so Dominic was not worried that she would have any problems. On Friday every-one had left and she was the only one in the shop. She verified that all of the doors were locked and then locked the last one when Dominic went home. Earlier, she had parked the CUDA just inside the overhead door and had the hood open to take measurements. She walked over to the CUDA a few times to work on the cardboard cutouts of the new pieces for the cardboard compressor bracket template that she had made. The last time she was walking over to the CUDA she happened to look around and she felt a little spooked. She looked around again. The shop looked normal except that there was no one else there. She saw movement in the corner of her eye in the shadows the she thought appeared to be two guys. But when she looked, there was nothing there. She whispered to herself, "What is spooking me tonight? I have not felt this the last few times I stayed alone." She took the cardboard pieces and fitted them over a few studs that stuck out and they fit. The other pieces fit just as she had versioned. She thought, "That was not that difficult." She picked up the pieces and closed the hood. She turned to walk back to the office and she felt chilled, just enough to make her shiver a little. She had not realized that the shop was damp and she had an eerie feeling. "Snap out of it Angie," she said to herself. "There is nothing here that is not here during the day. Maybe I am just tired." She walked back to the office and shut off the shop lights as she passed the switches. She stopped and looked back and said, "Nothing there." Then she realized she had said that out loud. She shook her head back and forth as she walked into the office.

It was about 9:00 PM when Angie had finished putting everything away, closed and locked the office and stopped in the bathroom. She finished, washed and dried her hands. As she was reaching for the door knob, she hesitated and felt a bit of fear and thought, "What is wrong with me?" She shook it off, shut off the light and opened the door. She walked out and almost walked into one of two guys that had just broken in looking for things to steal. This shocked both her and them. Immediately the guy that was behind her grabbed her around the arms and the other was going to punch her to try and knock her out. She used the first guy's hold on her to lift her legs and kick the other guy in the face. She kicked him quite hard with her right foot. He stumbled backwards across the room into the chairs next to the table. Then he fell on his back and some chairs fell over him.

She moved her head forward and slammed it back and hit the nose of the guy holding her. He screamed and let her go. She knew this causes quite a bit of pain and usually makes the eyes water. Angie turned and kicked the guy that just let go of her in the chest and he fell backwards and skidded out through the break room door. This knocked the wind out of him. He was gasping for air. She turned to see the other guy start rushing her. His nose was bleeding. He tried to punch her and she blocked it, grabbed his wrist and pulled then slammed her forearm into the guy's arm and broke it. This is a classic Aikido move. He screamed in pain and stepped back a few steps in shock.

The other guy caught his breath, got up and pulled out a bowie knife, "So you're the karate girl. You can't be that good. I saw the news. I know it was all bullshit. They're two of us you lose, ha ha." He swung the knife trying to cut her stomach but she quickly stepped back and kicked his arm in the same direction that he swung the knife then stepped forward and grabbed his head to make him continue to spin and at the same time kicked out his left leg. He fell hard and screamed then didn't move. He fell on his knife and she thought it had killed him.

Then Angie turned and the second guy had recovered somewhat from the broken arm enough and screamed, "You killed him! Now you are going to die." He reached into his jacket pocket and pulled out a revolver and Angie kicked his arm to the side with a forward roundhouse using her right foot just as he fired the gun and he shot the wall. She spun around and as she came around, she cocked her elbow and snapped it back with all of her strength and hit him directly in his left temple. His head slammed against the wall knocking a big hole in the drywall. Then he bounced the opposite direction and fell over slamming the other side of his head hard on the edge of a table. It made a thud sound gashing the skin and tipped the table over. He landed with his arms limp and his eyes wide open. Blood was running out of the gash.

Angie ran to the phone and dialed 911. The 911 operator said, "Hello 911 what is your emergency?"

"This is Angie Tucci at Dom's Automotive and Performance Center 847 N. Stone; I am being attacked by multiple armed guys that broke in. Please help." Then she slammed the receiver down. When she returned to the guy that stabbed himself, she found that he had pulled out the knife and managed to stand. He looked at Angie and raised his arm with the knife and she got in position and did a 360 degree reverse roundhouse to the side of his head. He went down slamming the side of his head on another table edge so hard that it cracked the plywood top. As he fell the hand that he was holding the knife hit the floor and twisted. It stabbed him again as he fell. Blood was running out of the gash in his head and from the knife wound. She was positive he was dead now. She thought it was over and began to relax and realize what just happened. She began to shake and her legs were beginning to feel like jelly.

Angie heard sirens and made her way to the light switches for the shop and turned the lights back on. She was startled when she saw a third guy running towards her from the back door. She immediately focused and ran towards him, jumped and did a side kick to his face. His head snapped back and he fell backwards onto the floor and skidded a few feet. Just as she landed, he sat up, shook it off and started to get up. Angie thought that he must have been high on something because this should have at least stunned him. She ran a few steps towards him then jumped and kicked him in the face again before he was on his feet and he went down again, this time much harder and when his head hit the floor it sounded like a bowling ball hitting the floor. She landed past him and as she turned, he sat up, shook his head a little and stood. He reached into his jacket pocket and began to pull out a gun. The instant she saw the gun she spun and did a 360 reverse roundhouse to the side of his head and made certain her boot heal hit him right in the temple. His eyes went blank and he fell over like a bag of potatoes and slammed the other side of his head on the corner of the battery charger. He hit it so hard that it bent the wheel bracket on that side of the battery charger and it tipped over. He landed on the floor with a kind of slapping sound. The battery charger made a bang when it fell over on the floor. He didn't move. Blood was running out of his head from the gash he received from hitting the battery charger. She had been working with her sensei on this kick since the incident with Mike almost a year ago and has perfected it. Her spin is incredibly fast, her body tight and she now can deliver a lethal blow to whatever she targets.

Just as she was doing the 360 degree reverse roundhouse Lieutenant Edwards came through the back door where the guys had broken in. He witnessed Angie spin and hit the guy and he saw him going down. She turned around and jumped into her stance again ready to attack. Lieutenant Edwards said out loud, "Angie, its Lieutenant Edwards. Angie it's me." Angie took small steps towards Lieutenant Edwards to take aim at him. She was full of adrenalin and did not recognize the Lieutenant. She was in her stance her eyes were wide open and had her right hand in a fist cocked back to her side and her left hand in a fist just in front of her face. She was gritting her teeth and was growling. She looked as though she is ready to kill. She wasn't going to let anyone even touch her. Lieutenant Edwards screamed, "Oh Shit!" and then louder, "Angie it's Lieutenant Edwards," He screamed louder each time, "Angie, Angie, Angie!"

Finally, she heard him and focused on his face. When she was certain it was him, she relaxed and all of her emotions came out at once. She ran to him and started crying. She put her arms around him and put her head on his shoulder, "Sir," She cleared her throat, "Oh God it was dreadful." She was shaking. "I believe I killed them, oh God!" She was sounding almost as if she was getting hysterical. She started shaking and her legs felt like jelly. Lieutenant Edwards had to grab a hold of her to keep her from falling. He holstered his gun and grabbed her with both arms. He had to remember that she was a girl that just had her 19th birthday. He always thought she spoke and acted as if she was much older.

Three more officers came running in when they heard the Lieutenant screaming. "Go check up front and this purp right there." He pointed at the last guy Angie killed.

The officers ran to check out each guy. Each came back and told the lieutenant that the guys were dead. They were all shocked. They said two still had guns in their hands and one had a large knife and it appeared that he fell on it. They didn't understand what happened.

Lieutenant Edwards was still shocked that she was only 5' 6" and maybe 110-115 lbs. as he walked Angie to a chair and got her to sit down. "What took so long Lieutenant?"

"Angie, I got the call and was here in about one minute. I was right down the street."

"One minute? It felt as though it took forever sir. I did not know if there were any more. When I turned on the shop lights the third one was running at me. I was ready to engage whoever rushed me." She was talking through her tears, "Oh, I wet your shoulder from my tears, I am very sorry, sir." She reached her hand to wipe it off as if the wetness would brush off. She was trying to stop sobbing.

"Angie that is the least of my worries, besides you needed someone to console you at that moment. It's alright, don't worry about it."

Then they heard a loud screaming engine and a vehicle skidding to a stop. Lieutenant Edwards had told dispatch to call Dominic when he received the call.

They heard Dominic unlock the front door and he and Lizzy both came running in and they immediately saw the two guys lying on the floor in the break room that appeared dead. There were officers all around. Chairs were everywhere; a couple of tables were knocked over and there were blood puddles around each guy's head.

Through her tears Lizzy tried to scream but it was muffled from her crying, "Angie, Angie." She gasped as she turned towards the shop, she saw another man lying on the floor in the shop and it was obvious his head was bleeding profusely. Even from the front of the shop she could see the blood puddle growing. She gasped out loud, "Oh no!" and was beginning to get hysterical. Then she saw Angie with Lieutenant Edwards. Angie looked up and saw Dominic first and screamed Father! She jumped up and ran to his arms. Then she saw Lizzy. She said, "Mother!" and let go of Dominic and fell into her mother's arms. Angie had tears in her eyes again. They both asked Angie at the same time, "Are you hurt?"

Angie wiped the sweat off of her forehead with the back of her hand, then wiped her hand on her pants and said through her tears, "I do not believe I am. These guys broke in while I was in the bathroom and I walked out almost into them."

Lizzy was frantic and looked at Angie and started to check her all over looking for cuts or a gunshot. She checked her arms, her chest and her legs as if she was doing a pat down as the police do but found none. "You are not hurt?"

"As I said mother, no I am not." Her voice was shaky and distressed.

"I do not understand, what happened and who killed these men?"

As they were talking the fire department and ambulance had arrived and there were firemen walking all around and the captain officially pronounced all 3 guys dead.

"I did mother." She cleared her throat. "I was attacked and I reacted, just as I did last year." Her tears began again as the realization that she just killed three men was sinking in.

"I do not understand, they had guns and a knife what did you use to defend against those?"

"I used my training mother, martial arts."

"Just martial arts? That is it? Against guns and knives?"

The Lieutenant walked up to them. Dominic looked at him shocked and said, "Lieutenant, what happened to you sir?" His hair was soaked and he had sweat dripping from his head and his shirt was wet. It was a particularly damp night as this was the end of monsoon season, and everyone had been sweating but he was soaked. He looked as though he just run in a marathon.

"I was just confronted with something I hope I never have to see again Dominic."

"What was that sir?"

"Angie."

Dominic frowned and said, "Angie? I do not understand."

"I came running in just as she kicked the third guy and I would swear he was hit by a truck. This guy flew over to the side." He looked at Angie with perplexity, "you can't be more than 110 or 115 pounds? Then she turned and got into this position," he hesitated and swallowed, "and was ready to kill. The look on her face and the position she was in, her arms, hands, her legs, it was obvious she had her muscles all tensed up and she was gritting her teeth and growling. It made me think about the new Joe Singso martial arts movie I just saw last Sunday. And the sight of her scared the shit out of me. I hope I never have to face anyone like that again. I was about ready to turn and run, and I had my gun drawn."

"I will take that as a complement sir." She had stopped crying. "I was not aware there was a third attacker until I turned on the shop lights. I had no way of knowing if there were any more attackers. I am very sorry I scared you. I was concentrating on the next threat and I will not back down in a situation such as this until I know it is safe sir. Thank you again sir."

"Angie I am relieved that you are alright." Lieutenant Edwards began "I am glad you finely recognized me when I came in. You were a scary sight. I am still shocked that you defended yourself against three armed purps and didn't get hurt. You will need to sit with me and give me a description of what happened."

"I can do that now if you wish." Angie was finally calming down.

"Give me about 10 minutes to keep the media out of here first." He walked towards the back door then went outside.

Angie stood there and waited with Lizzy and Dominic.

Just as always, the TV reporters showed up. But the lieutenant was not allowing them into the shop. He had gone outside to make a statement. He made a brief statement to the gathered reporters and then explained that this was a crime scene and no one would be allowed inside. He then put an officer at the door to keep them out. When he walked back, he asked Dominic, "Could you lock the front door just in case anyone tries to come in please Dominic?"

"Yes sir." Dominic said and he went to lock the door.

Since she had no school on Saturday's Gina was watching an old late night horror movie on TV when a special report broke into the movie she was watching. The same reporter that covered the incident with Mike came on. *"We have a developing story here at Dom's Automotive and Performance Center, 847 N. Stone."*

Gina jumped up and said out loud, "Oh my God, not again! Angie!" She put her hand over her mouth as she was staring at the TV.

"We were just informed that there was a break in," he looked off the camera, *"what, say again,"* he looked back at the camera, *"three armed thieves attacked Angelina Tucci while she was working late."* There was someone feeding the reporter information and he didn't appear to believe. *"I am told that the three armed thieves were killed by,"* he looked away again, *"Who? What? Are you sure? OK, OK, no one is going to believe this."* He turned to the camera again, *"they were killed by Angelina Tucci as she defended herself."* He turned again, *"She what? Really?"* He turned back to the camera, *"She defended herself using her martial arts training. She is 19 years old and has been training since she was 7 years old. That's...12 years. I have been assured this is what happened. We will keep everyone informed as we obtain additional information. This is Brian Atkins for KDLT news"* He sounded shocked as if he didn't believe it.

Gina was at first horrified. Then when she heard Angie killed the three men she screamed, "Way to go Angie!" But then thought that she could be hurt.

The camera man signaled that the camera was off. Brian Atkins didn't believe what he was told by one of the crew. He went to look for him and asked him where the information came from. He was a little worried that he just told a lie on a live broadcast. The crew member said he got the information from a Lieutenant Edwards. He said the lieutenant came to the door and made a short statement and also stated that no one would be allowed in the building and put an officer guard then went back into the building.

Gina knew it was late but she called Sherri anyway. Fortunately, Sherri answered the phone. "Hello," Sherri sounded as though she had been sleeping.

"Hi Sherri this is Gina. There was just a break in at Angie's dad's shop. It's on the news now."

"My God, what happened? Angie was involved, wasn't she?" Sherri said.

"What? How do you know that? Are you watching the report?"

Sherri said, "No, I fell asleep while I was studying."

"Well, the news said she was working late and three armed men broke in to steal things. Get this, Angie killed all three while defending herself! They didn't say anything about her though so I'm worried that she might not be OK."

"What? I hope she is OK. They didn't say anything else?" Sherri asked.

"No, the news broke into the show I was watching and didn't say a whole lot. I had to call you first. I know you have some kind of connection with her." Gina said.

"What do you mean a connection?" Sherri asked.

"I don't know, you seem to be connected somehow. I can't explain it but I see it." Gina said.

"You're right, there is something. I don't understand it. It's odd, just before I fell asleep, I was thinking about Angie and what she did to Mike and the thought came into my head was she will need to use it again. She is OK Gina; I know she is. That's so weird. That just popped into my head." Sherri said.

"See I told you. I need to call Denise and Paula. I can call Karen and Janet too. Gina said.

"I'll call Karen and Janet. You will be on the phone all night and they might not appreciate getting a call this late. I've known them longer it will be harder for them to get mad at me." Sherri said. "I'm glad you called Gina, thank you."

"You're welcome, Sherri. I'll call you if I hear anything new. OK? Gina said.

"OK Gina."

Sherri called Karen and Janet. She explained what Gina told her. Janet had been up watching the same old horror movie as Gina and saw the news break. But she was afraid that Angie was hurt again. Sherri assured her that she was not hurt. Then Janet asked how she knew. Sherri told her it just popped into her head.

Lieutenant Edwards returned and he, Angie, Lizzy and Dominic went into the office. Dominic went and grabbed a couple of chairs from the break room so they could all sit. Then he closed the door.

"Angie, tell me what happened here tonight." Lieutenant Edwards asked. He had his notepad and a pen.

"Sir, I was here late making sketches for a compressor bracket for the CUDA. I had measured and cut out a pieces of cardboard to do a trial fit. I had been in and out of the shop four or five times. I finished and closed the hood then turned off the lights and walked back here to the office. When I was certain I was finished I cleaned up, closed and locked the office door and went to the bathroom in preparation to leave. As I walked out of the bathroom, I almost walked into one guy. Then the guy that was behind me grabbed me around my arms and I used him as a support to lift my legs and I kicked the other guy in the face. He fell back into some chairs onto the floor."

Just then Angie had another jolt and got a blank stare. She still saw the same distressed girl. The girl was obviously very scared. This was only for a few moments.

Lizzy said, "Angie are you OK? What is wrong?"

Angie snapped out of it and said, "It was just another one of those odd memories again mother."

Angie got back to the description as fast as she could to avoid more questions. She was feeling self-conscious about her visions. "Ah, where was I," she thought for a few seconds and continued. "Then I moved my head forward and then back as hard as I could and hit the guy that was holding me in the nose. He immediately screamed and let go of me. I got into my stance and kicked him in the chest and he fell backwards onto the floor and skidded through the break room doorway. I turned to find the other guy getting ready to punch me and I blocked the punch grabbed his wrist and pulled his arm into my forearm which broke his arm. This is a classic Aikido move. He screamed and stepped back. I turned to find the other guy had pulled a knife and said he was going to cut me. He swung and I stepped back and kicked his arm in the same direction that he swung then stepped towards him and grabbed his head and twisted it as I kicked out his left leg. He spun and fell over onto his knife.

"I turned and the other guy was pulling out a gun so I kicked the hand he had the gun in and he shot the wall. I followed through spinning and cocked my elbow and hit him in the temple as hard as I could. His head smacked the drywall and made a hole." She looked at Dominic, "There is a hole in the break room wall from his head Father," Then she looked back at the Lieutenant, "then he bounced away and fell and banged his head extremely hard on the edge of one of the tables and he fell to the floor with the table. This guy was bleeding profusely from his head and was not moving.

"As I turned around the other guy was still on the floor so I ran and called 911. When I came back the one guy had pulled the knife out of himself; stood up and raised the knife. I did a reverse 360 degree roundhouse to his head and he fell over and his head also slammed onto the edge of another table so hard it cracked the plywood top. This split his skin and he was bleeding profusely. He ended up falling on his knife again.

"At this point I thought it was over so I went and turned on the shop lights and saw a third guy running at me. I ran at him and jumped and did a side kick to his face and he fell and skidded a few feet. Then he began to stand up and I did it again. When I turned around, he was standing up again and was pulling out a gun. When I saw the gun, I did the reverse 360 degree roundhouse that you witnessed Lieutenant."

"Angie that is quite a story. And it is unbelievable that you didn't get hurt. I have what I need, all of you can go home now." Lieutenant Edwards said. "Are you sure you are OK Angie? You didn't get bumped in the head or anything? You just had that strange thing happen."

"No sir, I just get these weird visions in my head sometimes but I do not believe them to be anything." Angie replied.

Dominic said, "I will need to stay to figure some way to lock the back door. They obviously pried it open to get in and likely damaged the lock and striker. I cannot leave it open all night. Lizzy," he tossed her the keys to the truck, "you and Angie can go home in the truck and when they are finished here, I will figure out how to keep the door closed and come home in Angie's car. We cannot move it now because the fire truck, ambulance and the news trucks are all out there. And I will need to clean up the blood again. I don't want any customers to come in tomorrow and see blood puddles."

Angie gave Dominic her keys and hugged him. Lizzy hugged and kissed him and said, "See you soon honey." They left.

Dominic began cleaning up the blood puddles as soon as the bodies were removed. When everyone left, he found some pieces of 2 x 4 and some long bolts, large flat washers and nuts. He cut the 2 x 4s' to fit the door jamb then drilled through the wood and the door. Then he put the bolts through the holes in the door and put nuts on to hold them. He closed the door and pushed the 2 x 4's over the bolts and put a large flat washer over each bolt then put on the nuts and tightened them. This held the door closed.

Then he opened the overhead door, started and backed out the CUDA then closed and locked the door. He drove home.

As Lizzy and Angie drove home Lizzy asked, "Angie, how are you feeling now? I would think what you had to do must be very distressing."

"Yes Mother, it was. I keep running this through my head in the attempt to determine if there may have been a non-violent method of handling these guys but I cannot think of anything. I was thrust into an impossible situation that required instant reaction. The whole experience is very concerning and troubling for me. I know this will be causing rushing thoughts tonight and I will not sleep well."

"Angie, I feel terrible that you were in that situation. We can sit and discuss this when we are back at home. We will then have each other's full attention. I do not feel that this is something we can discuss reasonably while I am driving."

"I agree mother. I have many thoughts already running in my head and I feel as though my head will explode if I do not at least share these."

"We will be home directly honey. I would not wish this on anyone."

Soon they were home, Lizzy parked the truck in the garage. She pushed the garage door closer button and they went into the house. Then they went into the Arizona room. This room is always soothing to each of them because of the closeness to nature. They sat down and Lizzy waited for Angie to begin.

"Mother, it worries me that I did not feel anything was about to happen. I usually get a feeling particularly when something intense or negative is about to happen. I did not feel anything. An instant prior to Mike hitting me I felt dread. It was almost as though I was being warned. But there was not time to react before he hit me. But today I did not feel anything." Then Angie looked in thought for a minute. "Mother,"

"Yes, dear."

"I just remembered. The last time I walked to the CUDA to check my work I had a strange feeling in the shop. I got spooked. It was an odd feeling because I never have been spooked in the shop. Then I thought I saw two figures in my peripheral vision but I looked and there was nothing. And as I was walking back to the front of the shop, I felt a chill but it was an eerie chill, something comparable to how you feel while watching horror movies. It made me shiver. And when I turned off the shop lights, I found myself saying out loud, 'Nothing There.' It was a strange feeling"

Lizzy reached and took one of Angie's hands and squeezed it. "Is it possible this was your warning? I did overhear Maria say that it can be different each time."

"I do not know mother. It would seem very odd for those feelings to be a warning, although I believe anything is possible. Possibly the two figures I saw were a premonition."

"At that point I had completed my sketches and templates, put them away and closed and locked the office door. I remember thinking of having something to eat, taking a shower and going to bed."

"The thought just came to me about that thing that happened while you were explaining what happened to Lieutenant Edwards. You said it was an odd memory. What exactly did you see? Maybe these episodes were in the back of your mind. Is it possible all of this is connected?"

Angie thought for a minute. "Maybe that is it. I have not said anything mother but lately I have been feeling these jolts quite a bit, I do not know any other way to describe it. I feel something that feels much like an intense static shock, then I see visions of a distressed young girl. I somehow know that she is 10 to 12 years old. But that is all, just a distressed girl. It kind of feels as if it is a memory but I do not know. I cannot think of any time I saw anything such as this in the past or in a movie so I do not think it is from memory. It is very strange."

"I do not know what to tell you. If you keep having these episodes we should go and talk to the doctor. It is possible you have a chemical or hormonal imbalance. This possibly contribute to your insomnia."

"Maybe. But these images are so clear just as if I was watching television. They are very realistic as though I could reach out and touch this girl. I am standing there and this girl is sitting on the floor with her kegs bent up and her arms around them. She has her head down on her knees. The light is shining down on her and everything else around her is black. She is sitting on a dirty concrete floor and I feel that it is hot as it would be in a garage. I do not see anything else. I do not see how this could be from a chemical imbalance."

"And going back to what happened today, when I begin to fight, I just react to the danger. I do not feel anything until after it is over. It is if my emotional mind shuts off and I automatically fight. And when it is over all my emotions come at once. I do not want to be in situations such as this mother. I know that I had to fight to survive and had no choice but it is still distressing knowing I killed 3 men. And I feel terrible that I killed them. These are thoughts are running though my head now and I am convinced that these thoughts will keep me awake tonight. I always have running thoughts but these are very distressful."

Lizzy took Angie in her arms and hugged her tight. "Angie, I do not enjoy hearing that you have been in situations such as this. This is distressing to me as well as your father. I do not know if there is anything I can say that will help." Tears began to run down her cheeks. She felt as though she couldn't help Angie and this would be the first time. Usually, she could at least help by explaining or giving her things to think about but she knew nothing about this.

Angie could feel her mothers' frustration and uncertainty. She didn't know how she could but she did and somehow knowing this made her feel better. "Mother, I can feel your frustration and uncertainty and I understand. I do feel much better. I am not certain what you did but it definitely has helped. I love you mother, more than I know how to express." She hugged her back tight.

"I love you just as much honey."

"Mother?"

"Yes?"

"I hope we never lose this. I do not know how I would survive. Our talks, particularly in the past year, have helped me immensely."

"You likely do not know that they have helped me as well Angie. You and your father are my life and my world.

Chapter 2

Johnny was sitting drinking a beer in front of the TV and saw the news report about Angie fighting and killing the 3 guys that broke into her father's shop. He became very angry. He gulped the last of the beer he was drinking and threw the bottle across the room.   He instantly obsessed about this. He couldn't think about anything else. He thought, "Why should this girl get attention when I am the champion? Who the hell is she?"

He lived in a small apartment that was above his mother's attached garage and because of this his mother usually heard when he pounded on the floor or walls. Since Johnny had a volatile temper, she would hear him often. He always said the noise was from practicing his Karate. Sometimes he would hit or kick things and they would crash to the floor and break. Then he would be angry that things broke and pound on the wall.

Johnny competed in Karate matches along with a few other guys from the Dojo where he trains. Recently Johnny has been winning championships as far away as LA. He has a place in his apartment that he set up kind of shrine with his trophies. He has his trophies, pictures and newspaper articles set up in a display. He looked at himself as "the" champion. He felt that no one was better than he was since he hadn't lost a championship in almost a year. He has a few friends that compete as well and feel somewhat like Johnny. And one of the guys that Angie killed at her father's shop turned out to be the brother of Johnny's friend Andy. Andy had just found this out and hated her for that. He didn't hold back when he talked to Johnny about it.

Johnny was jealous of Angie's fighting and how she has been on the news and they talked about her martial arts fighting. "This is the second time, dam it! First was when that Mike kid was going to kill her and just now." He thought he should have been on the news because he is better. He continued, "Why does she get to be on the news? I am the champion and won lots of tournaments. I even have trophies. How can she think she is so good? Bitch! I need to show her. It should have been me on the news." He didn't care that she was attacked by three guys with weapons. "I could fight guys like that easy."

Johnny's friend Andy was angry because Angie killed his brother. It didn't matter that he tried to rob her father's shop and then was going to kill her. He edged Johnny on. He wanted to see Angie get beaten. Johnny wanted to beat her and Andy wanted revenge. Johnny beating her was just a beginning he thought.

Andy said, "Maybe I can get a chance at her too. She's a girl and how good could a girl fight? It should be easy to kill her. She killed my brother that bitch."

"They are talking about a killer like she is some kind of hero. Why is the news doing this?" Johnny said.

Johnny talked to his cousin Denny the next day. Denny lives in St. Lewis, Missouri. He used to live in Tucson but his mom moved to St. Lewis to be with her new boyfriend. Denny wasn't working so to continue to have a place to live he moved with his mother. Johnny used to see him all of the time but not anymore. But he does visit him occasionally.

Denny didn't work in St. Lewis either. He joined a gang and made his money from theft mostly. He had dogged charges many times. And he is a suspect in a murder case. Johnny told him, "There's this girl that is in the news stealing the limelight from me. And it's the second time. She also killed my boy's brother."

"You're gonna do sumptn bout it right?" Denny asked him.

"Yea, I'm gonna do something. I got an idea but I gotta plan."

When Denny was living in Tucson he and Johnny would get in trouble for fighting. Johnny always bragged about being a champion and that led to fights. The police knew them well because the two of them put a few people in the hospital because of fights.

Johnny was at his Dojo the next week and his Sensei was watching him spar with another student. He was becoming aggressive and it appeared that he was hitting full force. He kicked the other student and the student fell back and slid on the mat. His Sensei screamed, "Johnny stop. You kick too hard. You stop."

Johnny sneered at him, then turned away. The other student got up, engaged him again and was able to kick Johnny. Johnny got angry and kicked him back full force. It was obvious he was hurt. His Sensei screamed Johnny, stop. Come here." Johnny walked over. "Johnny, you fight here for training not competition. Go change, you no spar more today."

Johnny was very angry now. He thought, "Who the hell is he to tell me how to fight, I am the champion." He changed, grabbed his things and left. It was evident he was angry. Everyone there could see it. A few students at the Dojo were becoming afraid of him. He was always arrogant but now he is beginning to fight as if he was competing.

He got into his car, pounded the steering wheel and said, "Dam bitch, now I got in trouble because of her." This was all he could think about. He continued obsessing about it. The more he thought about it the angrier he got.

Chapter 3

The next day Sherri was helping her mother prepare dinner. "Mother could I talk to you about something that is bothering me?"

Her mother could see that Sherri was anxious and wiped her hands and pulled out a chair from the kitchen table and sat down. "OK Sherri, let's talk now, I am listening." She sat and focused her attention on Sherri.

Sherri also sat. "Mother, last night there was another thing at Angie's father's shop. Angie was there alone and was attacked by 3 armed men. The news said that she killed all three with her martial arts training."

"Again!" her mother exclaimed. "Is Angie alright?"

"This is what I need to talk about mother. Yes, she is alright but I didn't talk to her and they didn't say anything in the news report."

"How do you know then Sherri?"

"It is very strange mother. Last night the thought came to me about the fight Angie had with Mike and then I knew she needed to do it again. I fell asleep on the couch while I was studying. Gina called to tell me about the news report and she said that they didn't say anything about Angie. I replied that she was OK and I was positive that she was. It just came to me like a premonition but afterwards." Sherri was upset and somewhat afraid. "Mother, I don't understand this. What's happening to me? How could I know this? I'm afraid mother."

"Sherri, you know that you have had some kind of connection to Angie since she was attacked by that guy. Maybe this is that connection. Can you remember any other times anything like this has happened?"

Sherri thought for a minute or two. "I can't think of any time. I have had dreams that I think came true and I remember a few times I turned on the radio in the car and the song I was thinking of was playing but nothing like this."

"Well, maybe you have some ability to sense certain things. Or it is possible you could be a little precognitive."

"That scares me mother. I don't know if I want that. What if I see bad things? I don't know how I would handle that." She was beginning to cry and her mother reached out and took her into her arms and rocked her.

Her mother talked softly, "Sherri, I don't believe this is something to fear. I believe this is something you have been blessed with. I have read that when people begin to recognize that they have this kind of ability the first thing they feel is fear. I believe this can be a very scary thing to feel sweetie. But I do not believe it is something to fear. I understand that is how you feel and there is nothing wrong with that. If you continue to be fearful, I will help you find someone to discuss this with. I want the best for you sweetie. I want to help you any way I can and I believe your father will feel the same."

"Really mother? I was a little afraid to tell you this."

"Your father and I always tell you that you can come to us with anything. We will always do what we can to help. We have never criticized or teased you for anything you needed to talk about."

"I know you always say that. I love you mother. Thank you for listening. I do feel a little better. You know, Angie always tells me that her parents say the same thing. She says she can always talk to them about anything. I know I can trust you and father as well. But this feeling is just scary."

I love you too. I could not love you more sweetie." She hugged Sherri tight. "You could ask Angie about this. Maybe she has feelings like this too. And from what you say about her I believe you will be able to trust her just as you do us."

"I didn't think of that mother. That is a good idea. Thank you. I will talk to her."

Chapter 4

Angie Adds Air-Conditioning to the CUDA

The next day, Saturday, Angie felt that everything was back to normal, she wanted to get back to the air conditioning installation in the CUDA. That afternoon Eric showed her how to make the required parts for the compressor brackets. They cut these out of 3/16" steel plate, drilled holes and deburred each of the pieces.

Next was setting them up to be welded together. Sometimes this can be tricky but, in this case, it was fairly easy. They bolted the new pieces to the engine and put the top part of the original bracket on and held it with some vice grip pliers. Then they fitted a gusset to the back and used another clamp to hold it in place. Once this was done the pieces could be tack welded. They did have a 225 amp AC/DC Arc welder at the shop. Eric showed Angie how to set up the welder and choose the settings. The welder had a chart on a plaque on the side that gave basic settings and he explained that as she learns she will get better at choosing the settings. He also explained about electrodes and said that they mostly use 1/8" E-6013 at the shop. He gave her a quick description on how arc welding electrodes are marked and the uses of each. Then he proceeded to show her how to tack weld the pieces together. First, he put the ground clamp onto the bracket, then made a few tack welds. They had two welding helmets so she could actually watch. At this point they took the compressor and mounted it on the modified bracket. One piece required a slight amount of tapping to fit the compressor but basically everything fit together well. When everything was lined up, he finished tacking the pieces together. Then he turned off the welder and they took the compressor off of the bracket and the bracket off of the engine. They went over to a bench that was set up for welding and he showed her how to weld the entire bracket. He suggested she grab some scrap steel and practice welding.

When the bracket cooled Eric knocked the slag off and they took it over to the blast cabinet and bead blasted it. The modified bracket was ready to be painted. Afterwards Angie painted it semi-gloss black with a rattle can. When the bracket was dry they placed it with the other A/C parts that Angie had already cleaned, blasted and painted.

Angie decided that next Saturday afternoon they would begin to disassemble the dashboard on the CUDA and begin to swap out the heater assembly and wiring with the A/C pieces. The week passed and Angie had no visions.

Friday night Angie got together with her friends at Tucson Burger. They ate and talked and Angie had no jolts. They discussed what happened at the shop the past Friday night. They were happy that Angie wasn't hurt and they talked about how she felt afterwards.

Saturday afternoon Angie and Eric spent about 4 hours and finished everything inside of the car. Eric showed Angie how to cap the evaporator connections to keep dirt and moisture out of them.

The following Saturday they would install everything under the hood, leak check the system; pull a vacuum and charge it with refrigerant.

The week past again without any jolts. Angie met her friends at Tucson Burger again. She did not have any jolts and for the most part ha forgotten about it.

Saturday came and they installed the hoses, dryer, the modified compressor bracket, idler pulley and compressor. Then they disassembled what was necessary to install the condenser in front of the radiator and connected the hoses. At this point they did a pressure check and the system held pressure. Then they put on the vacuum pump.

All they had remaining was the crankshaft, water pump and alternator pulleys. When they took the pulleys from the 440 CUDA they found they would work without modification. They just removed the original pulleys and replaced them with the pulleys from the 440 CUDA. Each air conditioning pulley had 3 groves compared to the two groves of the non-air conditioning pulleys. They went to the stock area and pulled a few belts and tried them and one size fit perfectly. They adjusted the belt tension and they were ready to charge the system.

Since they had kept all of the refrigerant lines and pieces capped off, not much moisture had been absorbed. This was evident because they were able to pull a good vacuum quickly and it remained under vacuum with the pump turned off. Eric went and looked up how much refrigerant the 440 CUDA used and grabbed the charging scale and the bottle of R12 refrigerant.

He spent some time with Angie teaching her how to use all of the refrigerant tools and how to charge the system. He let Angie disconnect the vacuum pump and connect the hose to the refrigerant bottle. Then he set the scale on a cart and pushed it next to the CUDA. Then put the refrigerant bottle on top it. Next, he showed Angie how to bleed the hoses and set the scale. The CUDA used 3 lbs. 6 oz. of refrigerant. He showed Angie which valves to open and had her watch the scale reading. When it was close Eric closed the valve completely and let everything equalize. Then he cracked the valve open and closed it at 3lbs. 6 oz. They were finished. All that was remaining was to disconnect the refrigerant bottle and the gauges and put everything away. They re-connected the battery cable.

After they connected the battery cable and put the caps on the refrigerant taps on the lines, he asked Angie to start the CUDA and turn on the A/C. The compressor clutch locked and the compressor started spinning as he watched the sight glass. As the system ran the bubbles disappeared and the air from the vents began to get cold. Eric grabbed a large fan and put it in front of the car blowing into the grill. He glanced at the thermometer and it was 79 degrees in the shop. He had Angie turn the A/C to high and gave her a thermometer to put into one of the vents in the dash. After a few minutes it read 38 degrees. The system was complete and working correctly. He asked her to shut off the car.

They cleaned up and they both locked up and went home. Angie now probably has the only Panther Pink HEMI CUDA with factory air conditioning.

Chapter 5

The following Monday afternoon towards the end of the day someone drove up and parked in front of the shop in a 1967 427 Impala SS. Dominic was at the front counter and looked up through the window. He thought "Sweet!" and waited to see who it was. As he was watching Enzo and Maria got out and walked in.

They walked in, "Hey Dominic. Look what I just bought. Pretty sweet huh?"

"You just bought it?" he asked as he looked at it through the window. "Marina Blue 427 4 speed. Wow!"

"It has a 12 bolt 4.11 posi too." Enzo said.

"It looks good with Cragar SS wheels. Wow, I never thought I would see you buying a muscle car Enzo!"

"He wanted to keep it a secret until he actually made the purchase big brother." Maria said.

"It is a beautiful car. I need to call Angie. She will love it."

"I will go and call her Dominic." Maria said.

"Alright."

Maria walked in to the shop. Angie turned and saw her. "Aunt Maria! What brings you here?" She took off her gloves and walked over. She gave her a hug.

"Enzo and I came over to show you and you father our new car."

"You bought a new car?"

"Well, it is new to us. It is a 1967."

"1967 what?" Angie said as she walked in front with Maria. "Hello Uncle Enzo." She went and gave him a hug. Then she looked out the window. "You bought an Impala SS? Sweet!" She almost ran out to see it. Enzo, Dominic and Maria followed. "A 427? 4 speed? How cool! And Marina Blue! I love this color. Is it OK to look under the hood?"

"Be my guest." Enzo said.

Angie opened the hood. The engine and engine compartment was almost spotless. "It has headers! And air! How does it sound?"

Enzo tossed her the keys. Angie opened the door and started it. "Sounds like it has turbo mufflers and large pipes. Does it have a cam? Sounds like it." Angie knew how most muscle cars sounded stock.

"That is what they told me, 2 ½" turbos and the whole system is 2 ½" and it has a bigger cam. Has a nice lope. It is the 385 horsepower 427."

Angie shut it off, got out and closed the door. "This is sweet Uncle Enzo! I love it."

"Enzo has been looking for something such as this for a while but there was not anything that excited him until this car became available.

"I did not know what I wanted. But I did want something that Bella and Rosa could ride in comfortably. I looked at lots of cars but none of them were exciting. The closest was a '68 428 Catalina with an automatic but is just was not sporty looking." Enzo said.

"I can see that. The Impala is a looker." Dominic said.

"We do not want to keep you from work. We just stopped to show it to you. See you soon Dominic."

Maria went and hugged Dominic and Angie. Bye big brother and Angie." Maria said as she followed Enzo out.

Chapter 6

Angie got together with all of her friends the following Friday night. They decided to meet at the Tucson Burger on Oracle and Wetmore. They have been going to this one because it is the one closest to where they all live. The main topic was what happened at the shop. They were relieved that Angie was alright afterwards. They talked about this for a while. They wanted to know how she killed the guys. She described what happened. She also told them how she scared Lieutenant Edwards.

Gina said, "You scared him? A cop?" and began to laugh. But then she realized how Angie would have looked.

They were all happy that she didn't get hurt but understood that it must be difficult to know you killed someone. Gina said, "I think I would freak out if I killed someone. How do you deal with that Angie?"

"I meditate and when I go to bed and I tell myself that I had no choice and I did this to defend my life. It usually takes some time before it stops bothering me." Angie said.

"I don't know how you do it." Gina said.

Then Gina remembered what Sherri said on the phone that night. "You know when I called Sherri that night to tell her about the news, she knew that you were alright Angie. It was the strangest thing. She said it was weird how she just knew."

Sherri was a self-conscious about this. She blushed and looked a little scared.

Angie noticed and said, "Did any of you not ever get a feeling about something before it happened?"

"You mean like knowing you are going to do well on a test and you do?" Karen asked.

"Yes, something such as that would not be much different, would it?" Angie asked.

They all thought for a moment. They all agreed that it was something like that and the discussion about this ended.

Gina said, "You know, nursing school is completely different than high school. I didn't like high school and didn't like studying. Now I don't exactly like school but it is specifically for my future so I am studying a lot. It's not that I like to but more that I have to. It's weird. And I worry when I don't do well on a test. In high school I didn't care at all, I just wanted to pass.

Angie said, "Gina, it appears that you are becoming responsible. You are taking responsibility for your future and it shows in your changed perspective."

"I guess. It's still very hard. Sometimes I feel like the classes are going too fast. There is so much I need to learn and remember. And this is only the beginning of school."

Sherri added, "I completely understand Gina. It is different but difficult to explain. It is different than high school and a lot harder. I have so much to read and study. I have wanted to go into business administration for a while but I didn't think it would be this hard. I guess I never really thought about it."

Karen said, "My new job is hard too. I mean I am a clerk and casher at the Shoe Store over there" she pointed because it was next store, "but there is so much to learn. I never expected work to be like this. I feel embarrassed when I don't know how to do something or if a customer asks me something and I don't know the answer. A couple of times I felt like I was going to cry." See looked as though she was going to cry.

Janet put her arm around her and said, "Karen, you just started this job. You have to expect you need time to learn. Don't be so hard on yourself. What does your boss say?"

"He says that I shouldn't worry and I will learn. He did say I was doing pretty good."

"See, you are being hard on yourself." Janet said.

"Well, maybe." She didn't look convinced.

Janet said, "I start next week at JC Penney's as a clerk. I will be working in the women's cloths department. I think learning to use the cash register is going to be hard. They showed me that at my interview. I kind of scared me cus there are so many buttons. It's scary just thinking about starting this job. I never worked for anyone before and I am afraid of making a mistake and getting embarrassed or feeling stupid."

"See, that's how I feel." Karen said.

"Like, My job at the Doctor's office isn't bad. I check in patients and make appointments for people." Denise said. "They pay me too."

Gina asked, "You get paid? You don't work for free?"

Everyone laughed.

"I mean the patients pay me for their appointments. No, I don't work for free. I'm not stupid. Geez."

"I just started my job at a law office. Right now I just do filing and get files they ask for." Paula said. "I feel a little uneasy working there because of all of the lawyers. I mean, it sorta feels like I am in trouble for something. The first few days my legs kind of felt like jelly. Before I got this job I was never in a lawyer's office.

"Do you get to see what the cases are about?" Janet asked.

"No, I'm not supposed to look at them. But I hear them talking about some cases. I don't really understand what they are talking about."

"I felt like that when I started the job at the shoe store. I was there with my mom buying shoes a bunch of times but working there is different. It's kinda scary. It feels funny walking through the doors to the back." Karen said.

"I did not have those troubles working for my father. I had been going to work with him for a long time previously. I did not feel much of a difference when I began to work for him. I had a much different situation. But I can feel for each of you." Angie said.

Just then Angie jumped a little as if she was just shocked. Gina saw it, "Are you OK Angie? I looked like you just got shocked."

"That was very strange. It felt as if I was just shocked. Maybe I touched something on the table?" She knew it was more but didn't want to say. She saw just a flash of the same distressed young girl in her head. She didn't say anything because still she didn't know what it meant and she thought that her friends would think it was strange. Especially since this happened around them once before.

Denise was fiddling with her rings and remembered she just got another. "My mom just bought this for me. See." She showed it to everyone. "She says it is a promise ring to remind me that she loves me. It's sterling." It was a plain thin ring but on the top it was split with the split parts wrapped around each other.

"That's pretty Denise." Karen said. "That was sweet of your mom."

Sherri said, "That is a very nice ring, Denise. You should feel good that you mother gave you something like that, I would."

"I was surprised. She told me this way I wouldn't forget that she will always love me. It made me cry. My family doesn't say I love you so much."

"That is so sweet Denise." Angie said. "Do you talk to your mother a lot?"

"I don't know. Sometimes, I guess. I don't know maybe not. Like, when we met you the first time. I went home and cried.

My mom tried to talk to me but I couldn't. I was so embarrassed. I guess not always."

"That makes me feel sad Denise. I do not know how I could survive without the ability to talk to my mother. I discuss everything with her." Angie said.

"I don't talk to my mom much. She is too weird." Gina said.

"Why do you say that, Gina?" Angie asked.

"She always tries to tell me how much harder it was when she was my age. I feel like she wants me to feel sorry for her."

"Do you think it is possible she is trying to show how she dealt with the same feelings? Not everyone knows how to express themselves well. Is it possible that this is her method of trying to help you. Possibly she is saying how it was hard for her as well as you."

"I don't know. Maybe. It just makes me feel like she is saying I have it easier that she did."

"Well, I believe all of us have some things that are easier than our parents had but we also have things that are different enough that another perspective can help. Do you think that she may not know any other way to help you?"

"I never thought of it that way Angie. I always felt like she was putting me down." She thought for a minute. "I guess seeing it from that point of view, maybe that is her way to try to help me." She was sitting there thinking. "I never thought of it like that. Maybe I should talk to her about this. See, this is what you do. You make us see things differently. Just like you did the first time we met you."

"This is what my mother and father do with me Gina. It always stimulates me to think about what we discuss."

"Yea, that's what you do." Paula said. "You make us see things from a different point of view. Maybe that's how you inspire us."

"It is interesting that you came to that resolve. I learned this from my mother and father during the incident with

Mike. I determined that this is what they do with me. They continually show me a different point of view. My mother has explained that when we look back on past experiences, we will see them from a different point of view as well and this is how we learn from mistakes or poor choices."

"Your mom is smart." Denise said. "My mom never said anything like that to me."

"Me neither." Janet said.

"Same here." Karen said.

"Denise, maybe if you had told you mother about how you felt and how embarrassed you were it is possible she may have said something to help you. Sometimes it is difficult to admit something to my mother but I always end up telling her and she always tells me something that helps me feel better." Angie said.

Denise said, "Maybe. I don't know."

This whole time Gina was thinking. "Maybe I should talk to my mother. This is making me think. Maybe Angie is right, this is the only way she knows to help me."

Then Gina said, "I really need to go. I have a test in the morning and I still have to study."

Paula said, "Oh man, I have an invoice from my dad's print shop to drop off to my aunt and uncle. I was hoping we could stop there on the way home."

"That's all the way in Sam Hughes. I don't have time for that, I have to study. I'm sorry Paula. I really have to study. Its weird hearing myself say that but I need to pass this test."

"I promised my dad we would drop it off. Now what am I going to do?" Paula said. She looked somewhat distressed.

"I can drive you there Paula." Angie said. "It will not take very long."

"Angie, I would really appreciate it. Thank you."

Everyone sad bye. Denise and Gina left along with Sherri, Karen and Janet.

"Come Paula." Angie said. They went to the CUDA and got in.

"Wow, your car is really nice Angie. I never really saw it this close." Paula said. They put on their seatbelts and Angie started it.

Paula was startled at how it sounded and felt inside. Angie pulled out of the parking lot and turned right onto Oracle. She accelerated a little hard. Paula grabbed the armrest and tensed up. "Where is your aunt and uncle's house?" Angie asked as she glanced at Paula. "Oh, I am sorry, I did not think you would be scared."

"I'm just not used to a car like this. I'll tell you when to turn when we get there. My dad has a fast car too but I have only ridden in it a few times."

"What kind of car does your father have?"

"I don't know, it's purple and loud. The name is something like Devil or something."

"Is it a Demon?" Angie was showing some excitement. She loves muscle cars.

"Maybe that's it. It has a little red devil guy on a sticker on the front fender. He keeps it in the garage and doesn't drive it much. Turn left at Speedway." Angie turned. "Take this to Olsen and turn right." Angie turned. "It's 4 blocks down. 720 on the right. Just pull into the driveway. Right here." She pointed.

Angie pulled into the driveway and stopped and shut off the car. They got out and walked to the front door. Paula rang the doorbell. "My Aunt and Uncle are nice." Someone unlocked the door and opened it. It was her Aunt Mary. "Hello Paula." She reached out and hugged Paula. "Who is this lovely girl?"

"Aunt Mary, this is my friend Angie. Angie, this is my Aunt Mary."

"I am pleased to meet you Ma'am." Angie said as she held out her hand.

Aunt Mary took her hand lightly, "I am pleased to meet you as well Angie. Please come in." She held the door open until they were both in and closed it.

"I have an invoice for Uncle George." She reached into her purse and took out the invoice and handed to her aunt.

"Thank you, Paula for dropping it off. Angie, what kind of car is that? I never saw a pink car before. I'll bet George would want to see it. He is into cars."

"It is a HEMI CUDA ma'am."

"George," Aunt Mary called.

He came into the front room. "What is it? Oh, hi Paula." He went and hugged her.

"Uncle George, this is my friend Angie. Angie this is my Uncle George."

"I'm pleased to meet you sir." Angie held out her hand.

George took her hand lightly and said, "It's nice to meet you as well."

"I thought you might like to see Angie's car." Aunt Mary said. "It's a HEMI CUDA, whatever that is." She looked at Angie, shrugged her shoulders and said, "I don't know anything about cars."

"Really!" he looked at Angie. "A HEMI? I never saw one. Do you mind if I go look at it?"

"No sir I do not mind. I can show it to you if you like." Angie, Paula, Aunt Mary and Uncle George went out to see the car.

"This is really nice Angie. And Panther Pink! I never saw one this color. And it has a shaker, cool!" Uncle George said.

Angie opened the hood. "Would you care to hear it sir?"

"I would love that."

Angie opened the door, got in and started it and revved it a little then let it idle. It definitely had a strong lope.

"You have modified it haven't you?" George asked.

"Yes sir, I swapped the cam, the heads have been pocket ported and had a 5 angle valve job, the carbs are modified, the distributor is recurved and it has headers. My best time so far is 12.35 at 123 miles per hour."

"You drag race? Really?"

"Uncle George, Angie's dad owns Dom's Automotive and Performance Center. Remember I told you."

"She is the one?" He looked at Angie. "I would never guess. You are very beautiful. And you work on cars?"

"Yes sir. I work on cars. In fact, I added factory air conditioning to this car with parts from a wreck."

"This has air? I was about to ask; I didn't know you could get air with a HEMI."

"You cannot. The air conditioning came from a wrecked 440 CUDA." Angie said.

"You put it in? It looks like it came that way. I'm impressed." Then he looked at Paula, "Have you told Angie about your dad's Demon?"

"I just did on the way over here. Well, I told her he had a purple devil car." Paula said.

"Angie, her dad has a 1971 Demon 340." He looked at Paula, "You should show her Paula." George said.

"I guess. We need to go now. Angic was nice enough to drive me over here so I could drop off the invoice. I don't want to keep her too long. I'm sure she has things to do. She's always very busy." She hugged her aunt and uncle.

Angie said, "It was a pleasure meeting you both and I enjoyed talking."

Angie and Paula got into the car and left. "Your Aunt and Uncle are very nice Paula."

"Thanks. I don't know why I didn't tell you about my dad's car. I guess I don't think about it." Paula said and thought for a minute. "You know, Denise's dad has a yellow muscle car. I just remembered. I only saw it once though. It was in the garage."

"Really? I will ask her about it. This is a surprise although many people have muscle cars." They got to Paula's house and

Angie pulled into the driveway. Paula's dad was in the garage doing something with his Demon. He turned to see what the car was that sounded so good. He didn't know who it could be. Then Paula got out then Angie. He walked over to the CUDA to see it.

"Hi dad, this is my friend Angie. Angie, this is my dad."

"It is a pleasure to meet you sir." Angie raised her hand.

Paula's dad took her hand and lightly kissed the back. "It is a pleasure, Angie. Are you a model?"

"No sir, I am not a model. I am an auto mechanic."

"No, you're not, really?"

"Dad, she works for her father. He owns Dom's Automotive and Performance Center on Stone."

"Really? She's the karate girl? Her?"

"Yes sir." Angie said.

"I'm shocked. This is your car?"

"Yes Sir. It is a 1970 HEMI CUDA."

"A HEMI? Really? Could I see it?" He was very excited.

Angie opened the hood. "This is so cool. It even has the shaker!" He was looking under the hood. "This car has air? They didn't offer air on HEMI cars. How do you have air?"

"I bought the pieces from a wrecked 440 CUDA and installed them on my car. We had to modify the compressor bracket but everything else fit perfectly"

"You did it? That's amazing! It looks just like it came from the factory. You did a great job!"

"Thank you, sir. Could I see your car?"

"Sure. It isn't anything compared to a HEMI though." They all walked over to the garage. "It's just a Demon 340."

"Just a Demon 340? These are fast cars. I see you have added headers and an intake."

"Yes, it has a hotter cam and I added a 3.91 LSD Dana 60."

Paula was lost. She had no idea what they were talking about. She thought they could be speaking in another language and she would understand just as much.

"Could I hear it" Angie asked.

"Sure." He pulled the keys out of his pocket got in and started it. It ran and sounded sweet. It had a strong lope.

Angie said, "It sounds sweet sir. I am certain it is fast. The Demon 340's run very well at the track."

He shut it off. "Thank you, Angie."

"Thank you for showing me your car sir. I need to be going. It is late and I still need to do my daily work out. Paula, I enjoyed meeting your aunt and uncle and your father." She and Paula hugged and she left to go home.

Chapter 7

One morning Jack came in and told Dominic about a car he was looking at to buy. "Dominic, I am getting tired of the Bell Air I have been driving and have been looking at some newer cars. I particularly want air and I have been thinking about something that has more performance. It seems everyone has been buying some kind of muscle car and I am feeling the bug." Jack had been driving a 1962 Chevy Bel Air hardtop with a 283 and powerglide.

"What exactly are you looking for?"

I found a car but I would like if you would come along to see it. It is a 1969 Pontiac Catalina Station Wagon. It was originally a 400 with a 3 speed manual but the guy swapped in a 428 HO and a 4 speed. It has also been modified with a cam and headers, exhaust and it has Cragar SS wheels."

"That sounds interesting. Just let me know when you would like to go and look at it."

Jack arraigned to look at this car in the afternoon right after lunch. He and Dominic went to see this car. It wasn't far. They met the guy and looked at the car.

This car was quite nice. The 428 engine swap looked as though it came from the factory and the air conditioning was cold. It drove and rode well. It had a strong lope. The guy said he had put in a Ram Air IV cam and 4.10 gears in the rear axle. It also had Hooker headers and a custom exhaust built with 2 1/2" pipes and turbo mufflers. It was Liberty Blue Poly which looked good in the sun.

Dominic told Jack that it looked like a great car. The guy wanted $4500 for the car and Jack offered $4000. The guy thought for a minute and said how about we split the difference and said $4250. They agreed and Jack bought the car.

The guy signed over the title and Jack drove it back to the shop.

When Jack pulled into the lot behind the shop everyone looked. It was a little loud but sounded good. They walked to the door to see who it was. Angie went out right away. She thought it sounded sweet. "Uncle Jack? Whose car is this?"

"It is mine, I just bought it."

Dominic pulled into the lot and parked.

"Really? I never really thought about a station wagon as a muscle car but this looks really cool with the Cragars." She was looking at it. "It has a 4 speed? Really? In a station wagon? How cool is that?"

Jack opened the hood. "It is a 428 HO with a Ram Air IV cam and headers."

"It has A/C as well! This is so cool Uncle Jack!

Eric had come out to see it as well. "This is cool Jack! And it really sounds sweet! I never saw a station wagon with bucket seats."

The guy that I bought it from said he special ordered it in 1969. It came with a 290 horse power 400 and a 3 speed on the column. He put in the 428 and 4 speed." Jack said.

"We should get back to work everyone." Angie said.

Chapter 8

Jason
October 1975

Sherri had enrolled at U of A and was studying Business Administration. One day while she was studying at one of the tables in the Student Union, she met Jason. He stopped at the table where she was sitting reading one of her textbooks.

"Excuse me miss, do you mind if I sit at this table?"

Sherri said, "No, I don't mind."

"Thank you miss." He replied. "My name is Jason. I'm studying history, what are you studying, if I may ask?"

"I am taking the Business Administration curriculum. My name is Sherri. I am pleased to meet you."

"I'm pleased to meet you as well Sherri. I have to confess, I came over here to meet you. You are very beautiful and attractive."

"Thank you for the complement, Jason." She was blushing.

"Would you like to meet here after your classes finish today? We could have coffee and talk. Maybe get to know each other somewhat. I would very much enjoy your company."

"Ah," Sherri was a little surprised. She never thought that she would meet anyone there. "Sure. I finish at 3:00 today."

"That's great! My classes end at 3:00 as well. We can meet right here, OK?"

"Alright. I will meet you here then."

"It was nice meeting you Sherri."

"It was a pleasure, Jason." He walked away.

Sherri was surprised that Jason acted like a gentleman. She didn't expect to meet anyone at school that was so polite. He was attractive, fit and tall with short black hair and brown eyes.

They met after classes and talked for almost two hours. Sherri liked him quite a bit. Jason asked her out to dinner on Saturday night and she accepted.

They began to meet in the Student Union and soon they began to date. She fell for him hard and thought he could be her true love. He was courteous and had very good manners much like Angie. They went out on dates many times and she really liked him. A few times she asked Angie to go along so she could meet him. She told Angie that he is polite and opens doors for her and treats her like she is that special person. Sherri told Angie she couldn't believe she met someone with qualities like she has been learning from her. After some time, she decided she needed to tell him that she was raped in high school.

One night they went up "A" mountain to watch the sunset Sherri built up enough courage to tell Jason what happened to her and her two friends.

"Jason,"

"Yes."

"There is something I need to tell you about myself. I am a little afraid."

"I don't believe there could be anything you could say that you need to be worried about."

"Well, um, the first week of high school last year, ah."

"Go ahead Sherri, you have nothing to worry about."

"The first week of school last year I was raped at knife point by one of the jocks." She watched his face as she spoke. "He raped my two friends as well. Then he didn't get in trouble. He got away with it because his father was the Tucson City

Manager. Afterwards we were treated, well actually almost ignored. No one would talk to us. They said if it was really rape, he would have been arrested." Sherri had tears in her eyes. It still bothered her to talk about it, especially since she was telling Jason and worried that he would not understand. "A few girls kept teasing us saying that we didn't want anyone to know that we wanted it so we said it was rape. I was very depressed from this."

"That was terrible. It must have been very hard to go to school." He put his arm around her and hugged her.

"Then I became friends with a girl that had just transferred to my school and she helped me to get past it. That is my friend Angie. We talked a lot about it and she listened. I'm not sure what she did but after knowing her for a while it became easier and it didn't bother me as much."

"Well Angie must be a good friend. I am glad to hear you have someone you can talk to. I would like to meet her some-time. What does she look like?"

"Well, she is a little taller than I am, she has long straight blonde hair with light skin and blue eyes. She is also very fit."

"She sounds pretty."

"She is, most people think she is a model." Sherri said.

They had been dating for a while when Jason introduced Sherri to Bradford, his best friend. He was polite just as Jason was. Sherri thought he was very nice and when Jason suggested she introduce him to her friend Angie, she agreed. She knew that Angie didn't want a relationship but she thought if she met Bradford, she may change her mind.

One day Sherri said to Angie, "Jason has a friend that I think you may like. He is very proper and polite and he speaks well. So, I thought maybe you would like to meet him. His name is Bradford."

"Well, maybe. I still have trouble trusting guys since Mike and the three guys that broke into the shop. If he does have manners such as you say I may be willing to at least meet him." Angie said.

Angie put it off for a few weeks because she did not have the time. She had been working late a few days each week learning more about how the business is run; practicing welding and with training on Monday's and Wednesday's she really had no time.

She listened to Sherri talk about Jason and Bradford quite a bit. Angie heard the excitement in Sherri's voice and it made her happy that Sherri found someone. Angie then decided to meet Sherri and Jason for dinner one night before meeting Bradford. She felt that if she thought Jason was genuine it is possible Bradford would be as well.

They met at El Corral Restaurant on River Road. It had rained hard during the afternoon and the damp monsoon smell was in the air. The sun was setting and the humidity was beginning to rise. It was cooling off as it was getting dark. The lights reflected off of the pavement as if polished from the rain. Angie was sweating and she felt beads forming on her forehead. She thought it was a little odd because she usually doesn't sweat much unless she is working hard. Angie rolled up the windows, shut off the car, got out, locked the door and walked in. Her sweater was damp from the high humidity so she was a little chilled by the air conditioning in the restaurant. She shivered. She had chosen a long sleeve sweater for tonight and she was happy she had made that decision. Sherri and Jason were sitting at a table already. Angie asked the hostess and she brought her to their table. Jason stood.

"Angie, may I present Jason and Jason may I present Angie." Sherri said.

Angie put her hand out and Jason took it and kissed the back of it. "I am pleased to meet you, Angie." Just as Jason touched her hand, she felt an intense rush of negative feel-ings shoot into her hand and up her arm. It felt like a rush of electricity unlike anything she had ever experienced. She almost pulled her hand away but she controlled the urge. She had something flash into her mind's eye for an instant but she could not quite make it out. It appeared to be a dead girl. She thought, "How could that be?"

"I am pleased to meet you as well Jason." Jason walked around the table and helped Angie with her chair. "Thank you, Jason. That is very gentlemanly of you."

"You are very welcome, Angie. I hope I am not being too forward; you look very beautiful tonight, Angie."

"It is not too forward Jason, thank you for your comple-ment. It feels nice to be in the company of someone with good manners." Angie was impressed. But she had felt dreadful vibes just from touching his hand and she saw a glimpse of a vision that did not make sense. Her feeling was that he was not who he was portraying himself to be. She didn't understand the feeling but it was very strong. So much so that she had to struggle to keep smiling throughout dinner and resist the urge to stare at him.

They talked about many things. Sherri explained how she and Jason met and got together at the Student Union after classes. They talked about Angie's job as a mechanic.

"Angie, I wonder, how you keep your hands clean and soft doing what you do for a living. I could never guess that you work on cars."

"That is an impressive observation, Jason. No one has asked that of me. I wear gloves all of the time and I wash my hands often. I also use hand cream many times throughout the day. I always try to look my best and that includes my hands."

"I still can't get over you working in an auto repair garage, especially since you don't have cuts and scrapes and dirt ground into your hands. And, you do not appear to be the type to work on cars. I think that's great! And you speak very well. That is very uncommon." Jason said.

"Thank you, Jason. I learned to speak properly from my parents and my family. I believe speaking well and having manners shows respect for yourself and others. What is it that you do for a living Jason?"

"Right now, I am a full-time student. I inherited my parent's house and enough money to get an education. My plan is to obtain a degree and use that to find a decent job. I want to have a future better than my parents had."

"Your parents have both passed? I am very sorry Jason." Angie said.

"Yes, both passed together. They were found fatally shot in the desert almost a year ago. No one has been able to determine what happened. But fortunately, I was 18 at the time and was able to inherit the house and their assets."

"That is disheartening." The thought came to Angie that he had no emotions while telling her this. He said it matter of factly, as if he was giving someone an address for something. She thought that was odd. She would expect someone that had lost both parents to murder would still be upset while telling someone. I feel for you Jason. I understand how difficult that must have been. My father and aunt lost both of their parents by the time he was 17 and my aunt was 16. They have told me their story many times. So I understand how you must have felt."

All through dinner her mind was focusing on the vision she saw when Jason took her hand. Although she thought she saw someone dead in the vison she could not be certain.

"Thank you, Angie. That is kind of you. Sherri told me that besides working at an auto repair shop you also drag race."

"Yes, it has been my dream since I was quite young. My car was a gift from my parents for my 18th birthday and I never guessed that they had that planned. I had been under the belief that my mother did not approve of me having a car before I graduated but I found that she had decided it was something I earned. I kept my grades high throughout high school. I had a straight A average every semester. Because of this and the hard work I had been doing at my father's shop she changed her thinking. I feel fortunate that I have parents that have the means for that." Angie noticed that she had a cold sweat, was shivering because of it and she didn't understand why. It wasn't that cold in the restaurant. Then she noticed that her hands were sweaty and shaking.

"Well, you are fortunate. And you must be smart if you had an A average throughout high school. I am impressed. Sherri mentioned that you did well but she didn't tell me that."

Angie was also hearing something in the tone of his voice that made her feel uneasy. "Jason, what is it that you are studying at the U of A?"

"I am studying history. I believe I would like to be a teacher, possibly High School History."

"Why did you decide on history and not some other subject such as mathematics, reading or composition or possibly something else?"

"I have found history to be incredibly interesting. I feel drawn to it."

"I understand. It is a wonderful thing to have the opportunity to follow your interests. You are fortunate."

At this point their food was served and they began to eat. Angie and Sherri had Filet Mignon and fries and Jason had a large Prime Rib and a baked potato. Angie continued to feel as if there was something about Jason that was not right. She was almost feeling repulsed by him. She tried to put it out of her head but the vision continued to linger in her thoughts. She also could not shake the feeling of dread.

They talked about many different things while they ate but nothing made Angie feel any better about Jason. If anything, the feeling became stronger. She found herself constantly looking at him but tried not to stare.

They finished and the waitress brought the check and Jason grabbed it immediately. "Since I invited you Angie, I should pay. This is how I was taught. You don't mind, do you?"

"Not at all Jason, I feel that you are a gentleman. Thank you, I appreciate the gesture." Angie was beginning to feel that she needed to distance herself from Jason. This feeling was unlike anything she had felt in the past. She was feeling extremely uncomfortable and feeling that she should run far away from him.

Jason paid the check and said, "It was nice meeting you Angie. I believe Sherri has a good friend."

Angie stood and said, "I feel the same for Sherri. It was nice making your acquaintance Jason."

Sherri and Jason stood and Angie walked around the table and gave Sherri a hug and said, "I had a nice time tonight. I will say good evening to you both." She turned and left.

When she got into the CUDA and closed the door she exhaled a sigh of relief. She thought, "Now I can finely relax." Then thought, "Why do I need to relax?" She thought about this during the whole drive home. She also realized the cold sweat was gone but she kept thinking about the image that flashed in her head when he touched her.

Chapter 9

Jason & Bradford

The following day Angie talked to her mother about the previous night. "Mother, do you have a few minutes to talk?"

"I always have time for you honey. What is it?"

"Last night I met Sherri and Jason for dinner at El Corral Restaurant."

"Yes, that was what you said you were going to do. How was your time with them?"

"That is what I wish to discuss. I was feeling anxious as I drove up and when I walked into the restaurant. I broke out in a cold sweat. Then Jason stood and took my hand and kissed the back. The instant he touched my hand I felt a huge inrush of negative feelings. So much so that I needed to work hard to keep from pulling my hand away. It was almost like the feeling of electricity shooting up my arm. I also had an image flash in my head but not long enough to really see it. I thought I saw a dead girl but I cannot be certain. I felt as if he was not what he appears to be."

"He was very polite throughout dinner and insisted on paying for dinner because he had invited me."

"That was gallant and he sounds as if he is a nice guy otherwise."

"I don't know mother. What I felt when he touched my hand and something in his voice caused me to feel as if he is not a nice guy. Almost as if he is acting to cover up something. I felt such dread. And the image that flashed in my head, I did not really see it fully but I feel as though it was of someone dead, someone that was recently killed. Then when I left and got into my car I felt as if a huge weight was lifted. I felt relieved."

Lizzy said, "Do you feel that these could be genuine feelings or could it be that since you share that strong connection with Sherri that you may be overprotective of her?"

"I am not certain Mother, either could be possible. Sherri also has told me that Jason has a friend, Bradford, to whom they desire that I meet. She also said that he is polite and well-spoken but I feel very hesitant, almost fearful."

"You will need to decide if your feelings are genuine or not and not be swayed by your feelings about Jason. This is one thing you will need to determine for yourself, which feelings are genuine and which are not. And you will need to learn to identify the difference. I wish I could tell you but this is something you must determine for yourself."

"I understand mother. These feelings were very strange and I have never felt anything such as this. I feel concerned, almost concerned enough to warn Sherri. But I would not know what to warn her about. Thank you for listening. I love you."

"I love you as well Angie" They hugged.

Angie felt uneasy and skeptical about meeting Bradford but she ended up telling Sherri that she had decided to meet him anyway. She decided that the only way she was going to learn if her feelings were genuine or not was to go.

Angie called Sherri. "Hello Sherri, how are you today?"

"Hi Angie, I am fine, thank you. And you?"

"I am fine, thank you Sherri. I called to tell you I have decided to meet Bradford but I am not in a place to become serious with anyone or to begin dating. The incident with Mike a year ago and the three guys at the shop are causing me to be wary. My trust for guys has been strained."

"I understand. Maybe the right guy could make a difference."

"That is possible but I will just need to wait and see." Angie said.

"I wanted to tell you that I finely told Jason about the rape in high school. I was afraid but I felt it was time to tell him."

"What happened? What did he say?" Angie asked.

"He was very sympathetic and it appeared that he got tears in his eyes. Then he hugged me hard. It felt so good. You know, I feel like I am falling in love with him, like he is my true love."

"I am very happy for you Sherri" Angie strained to say this without sounding as if she was forcing herself. But the feeling of dread felt much stronger now.

"Thank you, Angie. I really trust your opinion."

"I will always be here for you Sherri. I will talk to you soon, bye." She hung up.

Now Angie felt that she was betraying Sherri's trust. She felt bad because she hadn't told her about her feelings yet. But she couldn't determine that her feelings were genuine. She felt if she said something and it caused Sherri to break it off with Jason and her feelings were not genuine, she would not be able to forgive herself.

A few days later they talked and decided to meet at Jason's house the following Saturday afternoon. The week went past without incident until Friday night.

Friday night Angie woke around 3 AM from a nightmare. She sat up. She was breathing hard. She had been walking past some Palo Verde trees and they became alive. The crooked branches reached out and wrapped around her arms and legs. When she looked at the trees they now looked as though they were wicked witches. She struggled to get free but could not. As she was struggling someone walked up and said, "Now that we have you, we can do what we want. Just like all of the others." And laughed a sinister laugh. This is when she woke. The person that spoke was just a figure with no features, but was male. She found that she was sweaty just as if she really fought to free herself. She panicked and sat up and quickly pushed the blanket off of herself. She looked at her arms and legs because the dream was so realistic but there were no marks and she realized it was just a dream. She was shaken up quite a bit and her heart was pounding. She laid back down but it took some time for her to relax and get back to sleep.

The next afternoon after work, Saturday, Angie prepared for meeting Bradford and dressed in nice designer jeans, a nice sweater and her favorite cowboy boots. While Angie was getting ready Sherri arrived at Jason's house. Bradford was already there and they went into the living room to wait for Angie. Jason asked, "Sherri, Angie is still coming, isn't she?

"Yes, of course she is."

"Are you sure?"

"Why do you think she isn't coming?"

"Bradford has been stood up many times before and he is hoping it doesn't happen again."

"Angie will be here Jason, you can always count on her." Sherri was somewhat apprehensive. She felt that something wasn't right but tried to put it out of her head because she wanted to believe she trusted Jason. This was the guy she was falling in love with. Even so, she began to have a feeling of dread. And there was something about Bradford. She felt as though he was acting very suspicious but she thought to herself, "He is Jason's best friend, how could I not trust him? I trust Jason, don't I?" She continued to think about this. "Why am I thinking this? Is there something to worry about?"

Jason spoke and it shocked her out of thought. "Would you like some cola Sherri? Bradford?"

"Sure." Bradford said.

"That would be great. I'm really thirsty, thank you, Jason." Sherri replied. She noticed Jason giving Bradford an odd smile. She was wondering what that meant. "Could they be planning on doing something bad?" She thought. "What am I thinking, this is Jason. Why am I thinking this?" She knew she sensed something off but didn't want to believe it. Her heart was pounding and she had a cold sweat as if she was in danger but she didn't want to believe Jason would do anything bad.

Jason went into the kitchen to get some cola for everyone and he gave a glass to Sherri, one to Bradford and he took one. They sat and Jason talked about what he knew of Angie to Bradford. Sherri began drinking. She drank quite a bit quickly because she had been very thirsty. Jason and Bradford had their cups as well. After a few minutes Sherri said, "I'm feeling woozy like I am going to pass out. This is strange. Jason and Bradford started to laugh. Sherri said, "I don't understand why are you laugh..." Sherri passed out. Bradford grabbed her and Jason grabbed the glass so it wouldn't spill. Jason put the glass down and they carried Sherri to the back of the house and went into a secret room they had built. They had closed off the back part of a large bedroom and made the front look like a small office. She was out cold. They laid her on a bed and took off her shoes and clothes then tied her wrists to the headboard and her ankles to the bed posts with ropes that were already there. Now she was lying on her back completely naked and tied down spread eagle. She had no idea that Jason put something in her drink. Jason and Bradford left the room.

After a short time, Sherri started to come to. She found her legs and arms were tied to the bed posts. She became completely terrified and began to struggle to get loose. She didn't see anyone in the room. She didn't know where she was, even though she had been at Jason's house many times. Just then the door opened and Jason walked in. "Good you are awake." He said.

"What are you doing? Why did you do this?" Sherri said in a panicked tone.

"Why? Because you're a slut. All women are sluts. You had sex with that jock in high school and now we are going to rape you. We're also going to rape that friend of yours Angie. She is going to be a lot of fun because she is a virgin. We are going to do some things you probably never imagined too." Jason said and laughed.

Sherri was panicked, "I thought we had something. I thought I was falling in love with you." Sherri said through tears. "You can't do this to me. You can't hurt Angie." She was crying now.

Jason went over to her and held her head. He said, "Calm down Sherri, I know you are going to love this. Too bad none of the others did." Then he put a piece of duct tape over her mouth so she couldn't scream. "Calm down sweetheart. It will be fun. Then we are going to strangle you both and burry you in the desert. No one will ever find you. They haven't found any of the others yet, he-he and they never will." He enjoyed telling the girls what they were going to do to them. He got a rush from them being panicked before they even began.

Sherri tried to scream but the tape muffled it. She was beyond terrified now. She kept struggling but eventually gave up. She laid there with her eyes wide open and her whole body shaking.

Bradford was in the living room waiting for Angie. Jason left Sherri and rejoined Bradford. "You moved her car into the garage so Angie won't see it right?"

"Yeah. This is going to be fun buddy!" Bradford said. "Those last two tried so hard to scream through the tape and tried to get loose but couldn't. And I don't think they enjoyed the sex either. But strangling them was a blast. You know, at the beginning the one I strangled was trying hard to breathe so I let her neck go so she could catch her breath. Then I squeezed it again. The look in her eyes was invigorating! This was so much better than shooting your parents. There was not much fun in that. We going to bury them in the same place?"

"I don't see why not. I think I will try that this time. It really sounds fun, choking them and letting them catch their breath and choking them again. Maybe we should do it a bunch of times. Oh look, Angie's here." He pointed out a window. Angie pulled up and was getting out of her car. "Remember, act normal. And Sherri isn't here yet." Jason saw Sherri's glass and grabbed it and put it in the kitchen.

Angie found the house. The address was 1680 Old Pueblo Dr. It was just west of Silverbell Rd and between Grant Rd. and Speedway Blvd. It was on a small lot with a six or seven foot wall around it and looked relatively new. The whole house and the walls were stucco. There were a few Palo Verde trees. She parked in the driveway next to a white pick-up truck.

As Angie was walking to the door, she glanced at the Palo Verde trees and the branches reminded her of crooked witches' fingers. Somehow, she felt as if they were going to reach out and grab her. She was spooked. She thought, "Just like my dream. Why is this spooking me? What is wrong?" She was beginning to feel extremely uneasy, as if it was a warning, she was almost to the point of shaking. She noticed that her heart was pounding, she was breathing faster and she had a cold sweat. Then she noticed that she had butterflies in her stomach. And for some reason she felt that Sherri was confined and distressed, "no that cannot be right," she thought. She didn't understand the feelings. "Could this just be because I have never dated?" She reached to knock on the door and she could see her hand was now visibly shaking and her palms were wet. She thought, "If Sherri was not going to be here, I would just turn around and go home." She knocked on the door and Jason answered.

"Hello Angie, please come in. Sit down make yourself comfortable."

"Hello Jason." She looked around the room. "You have a beautiful house Jason. I love the Saltillo tile. It gives a warm feel to the room. Where is Sherri? Should she not be here already?"

"She was supposed to be here. She's probably just running late." Jason said. "And thank you for the complement on my house."

Just then Bradford walked in and said, "Hello Angelina, may I say you look beautiful today."

Angie held out her hand and said, "It is a pleasure to meet you Bradford."

Bradford took her hand lightly and kissed the back of it. "It is a pleasure to meet you as well." When he touched her hand, she felt the same inrush of dread as she did when she met Jason at El Corral although this was more intense. She had multiple images flash in her head which was different with Jason. She was certain they were dead girls, and their necks were horribly bruised as if they had been strangled. Again, she resisted pulling her hand back. "You are just as Sherri spoke. It is delightful to be with someone that knows how to be a gentleman."

"Thank you, Angie, I appreciate the complement." Bradford was remembering the things that Sherri had said to him when they first met.

Jason had gone to get a glass of cola with the sleep drug. He gave it to Angie. "You are not having any?" Angie asked.

"Yes, we already have some. I poured some for us while we were waiting." Jason reached for the cup he had used when he gave the spiked drink to Sherri. "Let's sit and talk while we wait for Sherri, shall we?"

They all sat down on the couch, Bradford sat on one side of her and Jason on the other. Angie was feeling extremely uneasy. She felt trapped sitting between the two guys but that was not all. She felt the kind of terror you feel when you watch a slasher movie. Her heart was pounding fast and hard. And a vision of the Palo Verde branches wrapping around her ankles and wrists flashed in her mind's eye. She was feeling as though she should not be there and she immediately stood up and said, "I would rather stand, if you do not mind. I have been sitting all day."

"Is there a problem Angie?" Bradford asked in a tone trying to be sincere.

"I would just rather stand if you do not mind." She was feeling more and more apprehensive every minute. She thought to herself, "Why do I feel this way. I am still shaking." Just then the cup fell out of her hand, crashed on the Saltillo tile and shattered. "Oh, I am so sorry," She put her hand over her mouth for a moment and blushed. "I do not know what is wrong with me today I feel so embarrassed. Let me clean this up for you. Do you have paper towels?" She stood there feeling a kind of embarrassment that she had never felt previously.

"There're in the kitchen." Jason said showing a slight bit of anger. "Dam it." He said quietly.

Angie went into the kitchen.

Bradford said, "What, we just get another glass. No big deal."

"No, I can't, I used the last of it in that cup." Jason said.

Angie returned with paper towels, the trash can and she found a small dustpan. She squatted down, carefully picked up the broken glass pieces and wiped up the mess. She put the wet paper towels and broken glass in the trash can. She returned it to the kitchen. Then she washed her hands and dried them on a towel hanging next to the sink.

"What are we going to do now?" Bradford asked.

Jason thought for a minute, "I need to find something to hit her on the head with to knock her out I guess." He looked around the living room then got up and walked away.

Angie came back and said, "I am very sorry, I do not know why I am so shaky. I guess it is just nervousness. I have never been set up to meet someone or been on a date at all for that matter." She was beginning to think this couldn't just be because of meeting someone like this. She never felt this way when she met someone new in the past. She happened to look across the room and saw Sherri's purse. Now she knew that something was definitely wrong. "Is that not Sherri's purse. Where is she? She would not go anywhere without it."

"Um, she musta left it here. I da'know." Bradford said.

"Where is Jason?" Angie glared at Bradford because he didn't answer in the manor he spoke initially. She was now tensing up and scanning the room. She knew something was wrong and she instinctively got into her stance.

"Hold her!" Jason screamed as he came running into the room with a hammer in his hand. Bradford tried to grab Angie but she was a moment ahead and had stepped back. She saw Jason with the hammer. She kicked Bradford in the chest using a side kick and he fell over the couch knocking it over. She turned and Jason was right there. She kicked Jason in the chest and he fell back against a cabinet, onto the floor, the doors broke and some things from on top fell off onto him. He didn't drop the hammer. She turned and Bradford had gotten up and rushed her. She used a forward roundhouse to his head and he fell and banged his head on a table. As she spun around Jason was getting up and he rushed towards her with the hammer and she grabbed his arm as he swung. She fell backwards using the momentum from Jason and rolled over and put her feet on his stomach with her knees bent and in one swift move threw him across the room and into another cabinet. The cabinet broke apart and fell over him. The cabinet knocked a small table over that had a lamp on it and the lamp shattered. She jumped up and saw that the two were unconscious.

"They have Sherri somewhere, where is she?" Angie said out loud. She ran to look at the bed rooms but they were empty. One room she thought was a bedroom was just an office. She passed it but something looked off in this room. She stepped back and stepped into the room and saw a pile of cloths that appeared to be Sherri's sitting on the desk chair. Then she saw a bookcase that had a piece of rope on it at the bottom. She reached and pulled it and a hidden door opened. She went in and there was Sherri tied up spread-eagle on one of two twin beds and she was naked with tape over her mouth. Angie was stunned for a moment and gasped.

Sherri saw Angie coming towards her and then Jason was coming in just behind her. She screamed "UUUUGGGMMM" it was muffled from the tape and her eyes were wide open.

Angie turned and saw Jason. She got into her stance he swung the hammer and she knocked his arm to her left, held onto his wrist and kicked him hard in the side of his ribs twice. He grimaced and stepped back grabbed his side and dropped the hammer. Angie got back into her stance as he looked back at her and rushed towards her and tried to punch her again.

She blocked his arm and kicked his leg out and he fell forward. He got up and his nose was bloody. He rubbed it and saw blood and screamed, "Shit!" He looked at Angie and lunged at her again and she did a 360 degree reverse roundhouse to his head and he fell like a bag of potatoes and then banged his head on the floor. Angie looked at Sherri and rushed to her and slowly pulled the tape off of her mouth trying not to hurt her.

"They were going to rape and strangle us and bury us in the desert." Sherri was talking through tears.

Angie was working to get the rope untied. Angie got Sherri's hands free and she screamed, "Angie!"

She turned around and saw Bradford coming in through the door. He looked crazy angry. Angie got into her stance again and as he came at her he threw a punch and she expertly blocked it and grabbed his wrist and rammed her forearm into his elbow.

Sherri saw a blur when Angie moved and thought she heard the cracking of his arm breaking as his forearm bent backwards. He screamed in pain. She continued with a knee to the stomach. He stumbled back into the wall then looked at her again. He lunged at her and she did another 360 degree reverse roundhouse. This hit him in the head and he went down banging his head hard on the floor.

Sherri was able to get the rope on her ankles untied. She screamed, "I'm going to call the police." and ran out to the kitchen where phone was and dialed 911.

When the 911 operator answered, "911 what is your emergency?"

Sherri said, "2 guys just tried to kill my friend and me and I think my friend knocked them out. 1680 Old Pueblo Dr."

The 911 operator asked, "What is your name ma'am?"

"Sherri."

"Sherri, please stay on the phone until the police arrive."

"They took off all of my cloths and I want to put them back on, I'm naked and freezing."

As Sherri was calling 911 Angie had a vision of a gun and scanned the room and felt as if it was hidden somewhere behind the wall. She could see Jason putting it through a hole in the wall and nailing the wood paneling back on. As she turned to leave the room, she saw a life size vision of Jason and Bradford forcing Jason's parents into a car and driving to the desert. Then they pulled them out and pushed them into an old shack. They each shot one parent in the head. She saw this as if it was playing out right in front of her. Tears formed in her eyes as she felt his parents fear. With each shot she jumped as if the guns went off in front of her. The vision ended and she rushed out of the room to get Sherri's cloths.

"Please stay on the phone until the police arrive, Ma'am."

"My friend is in a back room with both guys and I don't know if she is OK."

"What is your friends name Sherri?"

"Angie, Angie Tucci. The police are coming, I hear the sirens I am going to get dressed now." She hung up and raced back to the back bedroom to get her cloths.

Angie was waiting there. She had picked up Sherri's clothes and helped her dress. Sherri had a difficult time because she was shaking so much. They heard the police banging on the door then kick it in. Angie screamed, "Back here officers. We are in the back bedroom."

They heard one of the officers say, "What the hell happened here?" When they entered the living room was trashed. One couch was knocked over, some cabinets were knocked over and another was broken up into pieces and there was a table knocked over and a broken lamp. There were broken pieces of furniture everywhere. It almost looked as though a tornado went through the living room.

When they went to the back of the house Angie and Sherri were hugging. Angie said, "They are in that room over there. There are two of them."

Two officers ran into the room with their guns drawn and another walked up to Angie and Sherri. "It's over, you can relax now. Let's go to the living room."

They went to the living room and Angie and Sherri sat down on the couch that wasn't knocked over. One of the officers came to the living room and said one guy has a severely broken arm and they are both unconscious. They looked beaten pretty bad. He looked at Angie and realized who she was. "You were the girl that killed those burglars at your father's shop, aren't you." He said, "I was one of the officers that was there on the scene. What happened here?"

Angie said, "Yes sir that was me."

Sherri started speaking through her tears, "One of those guys was my boyfriend. I thought he was so nice and I was falling in love with him. Angie was going to meet the other for a blind date." She was trying to stop crying. "He gave me something to drink that knocked me out and when I woke up, I was naked lying on the bed in there with my wrists and ankles tied to the bedposts and tape over my mouth. He told me that they were going to rape us, strangle us and bury us in desert where no one will ever find us. I can't believe I was falling in love with him." Now she is crying hard.

Angie said, "Sir, for a while I had felt something off about this guy but thought it might be just because Sherri and I have a kind of special connection and I thought maybe I was just feeling protective. But I should have told her. I did not. They put something in the drinks they gave us. I accidently dropped mine so I did not drink it. The glass broke and I went into the kitchen to get paper towels to clean it up. That is when I heard them talking. I could not understand what they were saying but it put me on guard. Jason went and got a hammer to knock me out but I was ready and defended myself against both of them. They were not as threatening as the invaders at my father's shop were. I knew I could render them unconscious without killing them sir. When I found Sherri tied up naked, I thought the worst. I thought they had already done things to her. But it is fortunate for her that they did not get that far."

"You aren't hurt Angie?" the officer asked.

"No sir, I reacted quick enough to avoid injury."

Sherri was beginning to calm down. "Angie, you saved me. You said you would make sure no one ever did anything to me again and you did."

"Yes, I did promise you I would not let anyone do that to you again, and I never break a promise, and fortunately I was here. Sherri I should have trusted my instincts. I had a dreadful feeling something was off with Jason as early as our dinner at El Corral but I did not tell you. I am so very sorry Sherri." Angie was teary-eyed. "I feel as if I let you down. I have not had a situation such as this where I had feelings this pronounced previous to something happening and I did not trust them. I was almost feeling sick when I arrived today." Angie was just short of full-on crying.

"Angie, you saved me anyway. I believed Jason was my soul mate and I may not have wanted to listen if you told me. But after this I am going to have a difficult time trusting any guy. I finally got over the pain from Mike and then this happened. How could I be so blind?"

Angie had stopped crying. She sniffled, "Sherri, it is over. You likely know now that you can trust your deep feelings. You did feel something different about Jason, did you not? I feel that you did."

"Yes, I did.....um no, well yes, I did, maybe, but I didn't want to."

"We can discuss this at another time. Would you care for me to call your parents? I am sure they would come and take you home. We can come and get your car tomorrow."

"Angie, you are always so nice to everyone. Could you please call them? I would be grateful. I am still shaking. I'm freezing."

"That is because you are in shock. It is a normal response to a serious situation. Look, there is a blanket on that chair." Angie went over to the chair and grabbed it and put it around Sherri. "Is this better?"

"Yes, thank you Angie."

"I will go and call your parents Sherri." Angie went to the phone in the kitchen and called Sherri's parents. She asked if they could come and get Sherri and explained that there was an incident but she and Sherri were OK. They told Angie that they were on their way.

It took about 20 minutes for Sherri's parents to arrive. They were shocked to find police cars and news trucks all over. Her father parked and he and her mother got out and ran towards the house. Angie and Sherri were outside and hugging. Sherri saw them and let go of Angie and ran to them and they both put their arms around her.

"What happened here? There are so many police." Her father asked.

Sherri was having a difficult time trying to talk. By this time Angie had walked over to them.

"Hello Mr. and Mrs. Winston. It turns out that Jason was not who he appeared to be. He and his friend had planned to rape both of us and then strangle us and bury us in the desert."

Sherri broke in and said, "Angie saved us. Angie is a hero." She began crying again.

"I had a bad feeling about Jason but did not trust my intuition. I should have said something to Sherri when I met him but I thought that my feelings were just being protective of our friendship. I discussed this with my mother and she told me I would need to make the determination whether to trust my feelings or not. She said this is how I will learn how to use what I have been blessed with. Now I believe her."

"Father, Angie defended herself from these guys and knocked them out. Then she untied me and I ran and called the police. Afterwards she helped me get dressed. I saw her fight for the first time. I felt like I was in a Joe Singso movie. I saw it but still can't believe she took on two guys and won. She made it look like it was easy."

"Then what everyone had talked about last year and a few weeks ago is true?" Mr. Winston asked Angie.

Angie reluctantly replied feeling awkward, "I have been studying Martial Arts since I was 7 years old sir. And I have been fortunate to have been able to defend myself. If it was not for my training, I undoubtedly would not have survived the incident with Mike and would not have been here for this. I would rather not need to use it but I have been unlucky to have been in some situations that forced me to use it."

Mr. Winston told Angie, "Angie, I am very indebted to you for saving Sherri today and I am pleased to see you did not get hurt. I have also seen some very fine changes in how Sherri interacts with people and I have you to thank for that as well. Sherri told us that you helped her get past her problems from the rape. I want to thank you for that as well. We tried so many things. She was sad and depressed all of the time. Sherri is so fortunate to have you as a friend."

Mrs. Winston was teary-eyed at this point and agreed. "Angie, you are a very resourceful and polite lady. I always delight in seeing you. If your parents were here, I would thank them as well because they have molded you into a very special woman."

"Thank you for the complement, Ma'am." Angie was getting tears in her eyes again.

Then Sherri said, "Angie you are a hero. I know you don't believe it but you are."

"I just did what was necessary to survive. As I told you when we first met, I did not believe I was a hero then as well as I do not believe I am a hero now."

Mr. Winston said, "Angie, heroes do not usually believe that they are heroes and I believe it is for the exact reason you just said. You just did what you needed to do. I can understand that. But the truth is that you are a hero, you saved Sherri's life and your own."

One of the officers walked up and said that Jason and Bradford may be the ones responsible for the disappearances recently."

"Disappearances?" Mr. Winston asked.

"Maybe you do not pay attention to the news sir, but there are 4 girls our age that have disappeared over the past few months. The news said that it was thought that these girls ran away from home. But the police have been treating them as abductions. I know this because my father is friends with a few officers. And from what Sherri told me that Jason said, I believe these are the guys."

The Officer asked Angie and Sherri if they would give them a statement and answer some questions now. Sherri was calmed down enough that she thought she could do it now. Both Angie and Sherri went with the officer over to one of the police cars that was close to where they were standing. Angie made a point to ask if she could pull Sherri's car out of the garage so they could pick it up the next day. The officer told her it was OK. Sherri's parents waited at their car. While they were waiting officers walked out of the house with Jason and Bradford. Jason was handcuffed but Bradford was holding one arm and had an officer on each side of him guiding him to the police car. Mr. Winston wondered why.

News crews were all around the police and the front of the house. They did notice the Angie and Sherri standing off to the side. They were asking questions to people that were standing watching what was going on. There were questions about what happened and if they suspected that these two guys were responsible for the disappearances. Nobody there really knew what happened or saw much. Then Brian Atkins saw Angie and Sherri talking to one of the police officers so he immediately walked over. He had found out that there were two girls involved and since Angie was there, he figured one had to be her.

The officer asked them to please wait until he was finished with the interview and turned away. The news crew just stood there and waited. When the officer was finished with Angie and Sherri, he told Angie that she should move Sherri's car right away. She went and backed Sherri's car out of the garage and locked it. She went back into the house and, she grabbed Sherri's and her purses.

When the officer walked away and Angie returned, Brian Atkins walked right up to Angie and said, "Hello Angelina, could you tell us what happened here today?"

"Sir, I was here to meet one of the guys for a blind date and one thing led to another and I was attacked. I defended myself and found my friend tied up in a bedroom. I helped my friend and she called 911. That just about covers it."

"How did the guys get beaten and I understand one has a broken arm."

"Sir, as I said, I was attacked and I defended myself. You should be able to figure out from there. The bottom line is that we are both unharmed." Angie did not want to talk to any news people. Angie and Sherri turned and walked to Sherri's parents. Angie handed Sherri her purse and keys. Angie did not care much for TV reporters.

Brian Atkins wanted more but when he turned, he saw John Winston stand up from leaning on his car and he decided not to pursue. John Winston is a large muscular man and evidently Brian did not want a confrontation.

"I guess he did not want to deal with me." John said as Brian walked away. Sherri, why did they walk one of those guys out without handcuffs?"

"Father, he had a badly broken arm."

"How did that happen?" Mr. Winston asked.

"Angie broke it. And she did it so fast I'm not sure how, I just heard it crack."

Mr. Winston looked at Angie and said, "Really? How?"

Angie said, "I used a classic Aikido move and it is very powerful. Usually it incapacitates the attacker but it did not stop him. He came back at me so I used a 360 degree reverse roundhouse and that knocked him out."

"I thought that was just in movies, I never believed it actually worked like that. I am impressed. You are a special lady. When Sherri told me about the guys at your father's shop, I never really thought about it. You killed all 3 guys only using martial arts? I just thought you probably used something to hit them with."

"I only used my feet and my hands, sir. However, those guys had guns and knives. I knew I did not have a choice and I did what was necessary to survive. These guys today were not prepared for anyone to fight back. That was obvious because they did not have any back up plan. Evidently, they used the last of what they had to knock out the girls in my glass of cola. When I dropped my glass, it angered them. They had to look for something to use to knock me out and Jason grabbed a hammer. And by then I was already prepared to fight."

As they were talking, they heard a roaring engine and something skid to a stop. Angie turned and saw that it was her father in his pickup. He came running towards them. "Angie! Angie! Are you alright? Where is Sherri? Is she Ok?" He ran up and up and grabbed her. "Are you OK? Where's Sherri?"

"Father, I am fine and so is Sherri. She is right here." Angie just looked next to her.

"I'm here Mr. Tucci. Angie saved my life, sir. They were going to rape us then strangle us and bury us in the desert. We think they are the ones responsible for those missing girls. Mother and father, may I present Mr. Tucci, Angie's father. Mr. Tucci, these are my parents, John and Carol Winston."

"It is a pleasure meeting you." Carol Winston said as she held out her hand. "Although it would have been more pleasurable in a more appropriate circumstance."

Dominic took her hand lightly and said, "The pleasure is all mine ma'am." Then he reached out to shake John Winston's hand. He reached out with a firm shake and they each looked each other in the eyes.

"It is a pleasure meeting you as well, Mr. Tucci." John said.

"Please call me Dominic. Angie speaks highly of you. I am happy to finally meet the both of you." Dominic said.

John said, "Likewise. And I need to say you have a very special lady here. Angie saved Sherri's life and I am very grateful. And she evidently has rubbed off on Sherri. Sherri has been developing some very good manners and I find it pleasing how she has been interacting with others. I have Angie to thank for that, Dominic. Sherri has learned things that we have tried to teacher her but have not been effective."

Carol then said, "We would delight in thanking you and you wife as well as Angie at a more appropriate time Dominic."

"I do not know what to say. I am usually not speechless. Thank you." Dominic said. "Maybe this is not the most appropriate time but I would love to invite both of you and Sherri to dinner at our home sometime soon. I am confident that Lizzy, my wife, would delight in entertaining you."

Carol said, "This is a delightful surprise! We accept. Sherri speaks very highly of both of you. I am certain meeting your wife will be just as pleasurable. I would not have believed there were any real ladies in this day and age. But Angie is impeccable. I am certain your wife is as well Dominic."

"I will talk to Lizzy and she will call you and make plans. I look forward to seeing you again." Dominic said.

"Father, don't you need to close the shop?"

"When I received the call from the police that you were involved in another altercation I came right away. I asked Uncle Jack to close. We can go home now honey." He looked at Sherri's parents and said, "It was very nice to meet the both of you. I hope to see you soon. Good bye."

"It was nice to meet you as well Dominic." Carol said. "And I will look forward to hearing from Lizzy." Sherri got into her parents car and they went home.

Dominic told Angie he would see her soon. He got into his truck and left. Angie walked to the CUDA and drove home.

Johnny saw the report on TV and became beyond angry again. He kicked the TV and broke the tube. "Again? Why do they keep following her and do reports on her? That bitch! It should be me! Dam it. How does she always get the news to show her? She always acts like a hero or something." He was thinking that she somehow got the news to talk to her all of the time. He saw it as if she was bragging about her fighting where actually she did not want to talk to the news reporters.

He was so angry. Then he picked up the TV and threw it on the floor. He punched and kicked at the air. He had become completely obsessed. He had to find her and show her how she was shit. That was all he could think about.

Chapter 10

When Dominic and Angie got home Angie asked, "Father, how did you know Sherri and I were there?"

"I knew you were going to be introduced to someone today and Lieutenant Edwards called me and told me about this. He said that one of the officers radioed him and told him that the both of you were involved."

"I understand Father. I want to talk to you and mother about today. I want to describe what happened and I also have additional questions as well. And..." Angie was hesitant.

"And what honey? You know you do not need to be afraid to tell us anything.

"I need to talk to Lieutenant Edwards. I know something that will help him close a case. It has to do with the two guys today.

"I will go and get your mother and we can talk. Afterwards, when you feel up to it, we can go and see Lieutenant Edwards." He walked away. He came back with Lizzy right away and they all went into the Arizona room and sat down.

"Father, Mother, I want to tell you what happened today and I am also somewhat apprehensive. I arrived at Jason's house and as I was walking towards the house from my car, I began to feel very uneasy and worried. I began to shake. I also felt a terrible dread and I felt as though Sherri was trapped somewhere. And then something very peculiar happened. I saw Palo Verde tree branches and thought that they were witch's fingers and they were going to grab me. I also had a night-mare last night about Palo Verde trees coming alive and the branches grabbing me. I was spooked which again is unusual for me. When Jason invited me in, I saw that Sherri was not there and asked where she was. He said she had not arrived yet. Bradford, he was the guy I was going to meet, spoke very proper and also acted proper which surprised me. I did not expect that. Then they gave me a glass of cola to drink and I sat down on the couch. One sat on each side of me. This made me feel as if though I was trapped. I immediately stood and said that I wished to stand. I was so shaken at that point that the glass slipped out of my hand and broke when it hit the tile floor. I apologized and expressed my embarrassment. I then went into the kitchen and retrieved the paper towels; the garbage container and I also found a dust pan. I heard them talking in the other room and I could not understand what they were saying, but they sounded very angry. I cleaned up the broken glass and wiped up the cola. Then I put the paper towels, garbage and dust pan back in the kitchen and washed my hands. When I returned, I noticed that Sherri's purse was on a table across the room and I asked about that. Bradford said she must have left it there but he did not speak the same as previously. This caused me to be more alarmed. Sherri would not leave her purse anywhere and I noticed that Jason was not there. I felt at that moment that I was in great danger and got into my stance and I heard Jason scream, "Hold her!" and he was running back with a hammer. I kicked Bradford and turned and kicked Jason. Bradford fell over the couch and Jason fell into a cabinet and broke the doors. Bradford got up and I hit him with roundhouse and he went down and banged his head on a table. Jason still had the hammer and got back up and I used a judo move. I grabbed the wrist on the hand that he had the hammer in and rolled onto my back and put my feet on his stomach and threw him across the room. He collided with another cabinet and it broke apart and a small table with a glass lamp fell over and the lamp shattered. Both of them were unconscious. I then went to find Sherri. I found an office that appeared to have a poorly built partition and saw her cloths in a pile on the desk chair but she was not there. That is when I noticed a small rope sticking out from a bookcase at floor level and when I pulled it a secret door opened. Sherri was on a bed naked tied up spread-eagle with tape over her mouth. Before I could get over to her she tried to scream and her eyes got big. I turned to find Jason coming into the room."

"He tried to hit me with the hammer but I knocked his arm to the left and grabbed his wrist and kicked him in the side of his ribs twice. He grimaced and stepped back grabbed his side and dropped the hammer. I got back into my stance as he looked back at me and rushed towards me and tried to punch me again."

"I blocked his arm and kicked his leg out and he fell forward. He got up and his nose was bloody. He rubbed it and saw blood and screamed, "Shit!" He got up, looked at me and lunged at me again and I did a 360 degree reverse roundhouse to his head and he fell like a bag of potatoes banging his head on the floor.

I looked at Sherri and rushed to her and pulled the tape off of her mouth trying not to hurt her.

"This is when she told me that they were going to rape and strangle us and bury us in the desert." I was working to get the rope on her wrists untied. Just as I got Sherri's hands free and she screamed."

"I turned around and saw Bradford coming in through the door. He looked crazy angry. I got into my stance again and as he came at me and he threw a punch and I blocked it and grabbed his wrist and rammed my forearm into his elbow."

"He screamed in pain. He turned back and I rammed my knee into his stomach. He stumbled back into the wall then looked at me again. He lunged at me and I did another 360 degree reverse roundhouse. This hit him in the head and he went down banging his head hard on the floor."

"I rushed and helped Sherri get loose and she ran and called the police. As I was about to get Sherri's cloths, I felt something and turned to look but it was the wall. Then I had a very clear vision of something that Jason did. I went and grabbed Sherri's cloths and when I picked them up I saw Jason and Bradford doing something terrible. This is what I need to tell Lieutenant Edwards about. The vision was so clear it appeared that they were actually doing it right in front of me. Then when Sherri came back into the office, I helped her dress. That is when the police came and broke through the door. I called Sherri's parents and grabbed a blanket for her to wrap with and we went outside. Shortly after her parents came you came father."

"Why did they do that?" Lizzy asked. "I thought Jason was Sherri's boyfriend."

"We all thought that, mother. Sherri told me that after they tied her up Jason told her that all women are sluts and that they were going to rape us both then strangle us and bury us in the desert where no one would find us like all of the others."

"Thank God the both of you are alright! Angelina." Lizzy got up and hugged Angie.

"Mother, I do not understand, why do these things keep happening to me? Now Sherri was involved and she could have been killed as well. I could have lost my best friend." Angie was in tears. "I do not understand. This is the third time in just over a year's time already. What is wrong with me mother?"

"Oh Angie." Lizzy was hugging her tight. "There is not anything wrong with you. It is not you."

"I feel as if it is me, I feel as if I am attracting these people into my life. I do not want this. Why can they not just leave me alone?" She was still crying. Lizzy continued to hug her.

Dominic said, "Angie, I do not know what to say. I do not want this for you. But I will be here for you whenever you need to talk or need a shoulder to cry on. You know I love you."

Lizzy had let go and Angie sat down. "I know father. But I am just feeling overwhelmed. I feel as though too much is running through my head. And I did not appreciate the feelings I had before this today. I know this is what ultimately saved me but I do not appreciate feeling this way." Angie said. "My stomach was upset and I was shaking and I had a cold sweat."

"Angie, I wonder if talking to Aunt Maria might help. Although I am feeling that you have stronger intuition than she. However, she has found a method of managing this. I remember when I first married you father. She was still living with us and there were many times she felt as you do now."

"I was not aware she had trouble with these feelings. Everyone has said that she just has very strong intuition. But, but now I feel it is far more than intuition. I do not know why I never recognized this in the past. I now feel as if I always knew. This is so strange, just as I felt shortly after the incident with Mike during our talks, mother. I now feel as though I always had this ability. I believe I had not identified it. I feel so strange mother. I do not know how to feel. I believe there is some fear as well." Angie began shaking. "See, I am shaking, I feel fear now. Why do I feel this?" She asked this as if not expecting an answer. "Sometimes I wish that I could just be the same as normal people. But I do not know how. Why am I so different than everyone else? I do not know how I feel and I am afraid."

Angie had tears dripping down her face. Lizzy didn't know how to react to this. She was wondering if Angie was clairvoyant. She didn't know if this was good or bad. She just didn't know how to feel either. She looked at Dominic and she could see that he was feeling the same. They reached out and held hands for strength. Then they sat on each side of Angie and both put their arms around her and leaned into her.

"Thank you for being here with me. I feel lost now." Angie was still shaking. She was feeling small just as she did the first days back in school after the incident with Mike. She felt as if she was losing her confidence.

"You know we will always be here for you Angie, anytime." Lizzy said. "How would you feel if I called you Aunt Maria and asked if she would come here now to join in this discussion?"

"I do not know. Maybe. I just do not know mother." Angie said.

"How about I call her and ask. Would you be comfortable with this, honey?"

"Yes mother, could you call her? I think she is waiting."

"All right sweetheart." Lizzy stood up and went to call Maria. As she walked to the phone, she was wondering what Angie meant by, "I think she is waiting." Dominic stayed with Angie just holding her. She was still shaking but her tears had stopped.

Lizzy called Maria, "Hello Maria, Angie just had another fight with some guys and she is very upset."

"I know Lizzy, I saw it. She is all tied in knots is she not?" Maria asked then said, "I was expecting your call."

"Well, yes, she is. How did..."

Maria cut her off, "I am on my way Lizzy. I will help her understand. I will be there as soon as I can."

Lizzy hung up and felt baffled. She didn't understand how Maria knew. She walked back to the Arizona room with a shocked look on her face and told Angie, "Aunt Maria is coming now. I said that you were just in another fight and she said she knew. She said she was expecting my call. Angie, you said you thought she was waiting for me to call as I walked away. How did you know this? Maybe we do not understand her abilities either."

"I felt she knew and was going to come directly, mother. This scares me." Angie said.

The doorbell rang about ten minutes later. It was Maria. Dominic met her at the door and she had already felt his concern. "Hello big brother." She gave him a tight hug. "I knew this day was coming. Where is she?" Maria asked.

"Thank you for coming so quickly Maria. I can always count on you. She is in the Arizona room. Earlier she went through another incident with two boys and her friend," Maria cut him off.

"With Sherri, I felt it. I feel her horror and her fear Dom." Now Maria had tears in her eyes. They went into the Arizona room.

Angie looked up saw Maria and jumped up and ran to hug her. All she could get out was, "Aunt Maria."

Dominic told Lizzy what Maria had said to him. She was shocked. She wasn't aware how much Maria could feel or see. Dominic concurred. He knew her all of his life and didn't know this.

Maria took Angie's hands and sat down with her. "Angie, I know you are frightened. Frightened of what you just realized. I will help you embrace it and understand it. What you have realized is one of the greatest gifts from God. You need not fear it. It is a blessing. In time you will learn how to understand and identify what it gives you. Your father does not know this but I went through a period much the same as you are now and at about the same age. I was frightened as well and so much so that I never told your father. I finally went to seek out a medium and she helped me as I will help you now."

Dominic stood there in shock. He couldn't believe he didn't know this about his sister. How could he not know? He whispered to Lizzy, "I never knew this! I am shocked."

"You can never know everything about someone. Evidently, she was as confused and afraid as Angie or I believe she would have confided in you." Lizzy replied.

Maria sat with Angie and they talked for a while. Dominic and Lizzy left them alone. Maria explained that when she learned this about herself, she worried that people would find out and shun her. She explained that she was afraid to even tell Dominic. Maria told Angie that she is so fortunate to be able to be so open with her parents and how she should also consider that as a gift in itself. She told Angie that when she was at this place, she had no one. Both parents had passed away and she felt so alone. When Maria explained this, she got teary-eyed and Angie hugged her.

When they both sat back Angie had another jolt. She kind of jumped then looked stunned and stared into the distance as if looking at something.

"Angie, Angie?" Maria was concerned.

Angie shook her head a little and said, "What? Ah."

"What just happened Angie?" Maria was very concerned.

"It was just one of the strange visions I see at times."

"Strange visions? I don't understand."

Angie looked worried and hesitated looking at Maria's eyes. She never had any trouble looking at her eyes when she talked. "I have these instances that have the feeling of an electric shock, then I see a vision of a distressed and afraid young girl. I feel that she is about 10-12 years old. I do not know who she is and I thought it might be from something I saw before but I cannot think of anything.

"Angie, my gut feeling is that this is part of your ability. I have not felt anything as such so I do not know what to tell you other than you most likely will begin to see more of this until you can identify what it is. I will do what I can to help you if you have more of these.

"Getting back to the explanation of what I was faced with," Maria said, "I will tell you the story about finding the medium. I needed someone but did not know who or what I needed. I looked through a phone book at school and could not find anyone. I was distressed and thought "Now what" I was very anxious. I did not know what to do. I was very distressed and struggled to hold back tears. I picked up my books and left to go home. I was crying as I was walking and feeling sorry for myself. As I was walking down 1st Avenue something pulled me to turn down one street. I turned and walked down that street and found myself standing in front of a house with a sign that said "Readings." I thought that this was so strange. I walked up the steps and knocked on the door."

The medium opened the door. She said, "Come in please Maria. I've been expecting you."

I replied, "You were expecting me? How? I did not make an appointment; I did not call you." I was shocked.

The medium said, "I have felt your fear and I believe your ability guided you to me. You have a great gift and you need to embrace it and not fear it. Let's sit." I sat facing her. The medium reached out and said, "Hold my hands Maria. I believe this will calm you. Just relax my dear, what you have is the ability to see in the near future. What you see is what may happen if nothing is changed. You may feel something is not right or you may see things in your mind's eye. It can be different each time. These will most likely not be clear or easy to decipher but they will show you things that are coming. Some will be good and some will be bad, in time you will learn to identify good from bad. Sometimes you may be in a position to intervene in something bad but you need to remember that you may not be able to protect yourself from harm if you decide to intervene. There will be times that you may only want to warn someone or talk to the police but you need to only use vague references such as 'I have a strange feeling that something is going to happen." If you tell anyone that you see things and they usually come true you will open yourself to ridicule. People can be very cruel. You need to be careful as to what you say to others as you could end up alienating yourself.

Most people will not understand and most will call it crazy and distance themselves from you. You may also want to pray for direction because God has given this to you for a reason. Remember that God will guide you and give you strength. You may also find that this gift will guide you throughout your life. It will help you make decisions. Only you can decide what to do with this ability. It is not witchcraft or the devils work dear. It is a blessing. God chooses who will or will not have extra abilities and he will guide you in its use. But you need to ask for guidance. Ask God to show you the way and you will be guided. You would be surprised as to how many people have this same ability as it is more common than you believe. It is possible that you will be attracted to others with this ability. But again, you need to choose to learn to use this but you cannot dismiss it. It will always be there. This is all I have to say today, Maria. Come and see me again if you feel afraid."

I sat there for a few minutes. I said, "Ma'am, I feel much better now. But I am not certain why. What you said has made me feel more confident and knowing I can ask for direction in my prayers gives me hope. Thank you so much for this."

"That's it? And she knew why you were there and knew your name?

"Yes, that is how it happened. It is still a little frightening to me thinking about that now. So how do you feel Angie?"

"I feel better. I am not so frightened now. But the thought of having precognitive thoughts is terrifying. I was not prepared for this Aunt Maria. You know how I always desire to be prepared for everything. I feel disconcerted when I am not prepared. I had an extremely difficult time the first days returning to school after the incident with Mike because I was not prepared for everyone at school to be so kind and caring. But at least I had my friends there for support. And I cannot tell my friends about this. I do not want to lose them. I would feel terribly alone. But I do not want to lie to them either."

"Angie, you will not be lying to them. Lying would be telling them that you do not have this ability. You will only not be exposing them to something deep inside. It would not be unlike keeping to yourself about a deeply personal secret. And if you do not tell them they will not know any difference."

"I do not believe you need to be too concerned about the vision of the young girl, at least for now. This could be a vision of something long past and when and if you see anything additional, we can try to determine what it is."

"But I know that you have a friend that has this same ability and you share this with each other. I believe you already know who it is."

"Sherri. It is Sherri. I feel as if I always knew."

"Yes. Remember when you invited Sherri for lunch the first time?"

"Yes, what about that day?"

"That is when I knew she had this same ability. Although she had not identified it at that time, but she already fears it. I feel that you already questioned her about it just after the incident today."

Angie thought for a minute. "I said, "You know you can trust your feelings now." And Sherri said that she did not want to."

"When she does identify this, you will help her to understand just as I have helped you."

"I will? How are you so certain Aunt Maria?" Then before she could reply Angie said, "You do not need to answer. I now feel it as well. This feels so very odd."

Maria smiled, "You are already learning Angie. When you release your fear, many things become very clear and at times very intense."

"Now you sound as though you are, ah," Angie thought for a few seconds, "a spiritual guide."

"I am not a spiritual guide Angie, but I am always here and available to talk. You know how strong our connection is do you not?"

"Yes, I feel it. It is strong. Now I understand why." They both stood up. Angie hugged Maria very tight. "Thank you for talking with me tonight. Now I will be able to sleep tonight, well, if I can keep my thoughts from racing."

"I fully understand. We cannot just turn it off."

"You have racing thoughts just as I do?"

"I always have Angie. I thought you knew that."

"I did not. And I do not believe I have discussed this with you. I wonder how many other things we share. I love you so much. I am so fortunate to have a family I can talk to." Angie had tears in her eyes.

Maria looked at Angie, "Yes, we are very fortunate. I love you as well Angie. We can go find your parents, shall we?"

They walked together with their arms around each other and found Dominic and Lizzy sitting at the kitchen table talking. "How are you feeling Angie?" Lizzy asked.

"I am feeling much better mother. We had a very intimate discussion and I have learned quite a bit."

"Dom?" Maria said. "I believe it is time for me to explain myself. I kept this from you for a long time but there was a reason behind this. But the time has come. When you have some time, we need to discuss this just between us."

"I agree Maria. I am not angry; I was just stunned. It never occurred to me that there could be something that is so much a part of you that I did not know. Lizzy and I discussed this and I understand. No matter how well you know someone there are always things you do not know about them. I apologize."

"No apologies are necessary big brother." She usually called Dominic big brother when she felt as she had for the first years after their mother died. He always made her feel safe during that period. "We will go somewhere that we can speak freely without the possibility of being overheard. Some continue to say it is crazy to have this ability. Hence, I am still very cautious."

"I fully understand Maria." Dominic stood up and hugged her. "I love you so much Maria."

Then Dominic looked at Angie and asked, "Do you feel that you can talk to Lieutenant Edwards now? We can wait until tomorrow if you wish?"

I feel I can talk to him now. It is about what I saw in my head and I do not want him to think less of me."

"Angie, I do not think there is anything you could say to him that would surprise him at this point."

"Alright, but will you stay with me when I tell him father? I would feel much better if you would."

"Of course, I will. Anything you want. I will go and call him now." Dominic went to call Lieutenant Edwards.

"Hello Lieutenant, this is Dominic how are you sir?"

"Dominic, it is always nice to hear from you. How is Angie doing after this afternoon?"

"Well, she is mostly alright. She told me that she has some information for you regarding the two boys from today. She said it will help you close an unsolved case. I do not know what this is about but I should probably talk to you first so you have an idea about what she experienced today. Something not directly connected to the incident had her very worked up and I needed to bring Maria here to talk to her."

"OK, this sounds interesting. I don't know Maria so I am not certain what to expect. Do you want me to stop at your house? I could do that. Maybe whatever this is she would feel more comfortable."

"That is a great idea sir. When could you come?"

"I can be there in about 20 minutes if that is OK?"

"That would be fine. Thank you, Lieutenant."

Dominic walked back to the kitchen and said, "Angie, the Lieutenant will be coming here. He thought it might be easier on you this way. I trust this is alright with you."

Yes father. Maybe Aunt Maria could stay as well. I may need some support. I do not know how he will take learning about how I know this. But it is very important that I tell him."

"I will stay here for you Angie. Whatever you need." Maria said.

"Thank you, Aunt Maria."

About 20 minutes later the front door bells rang. Dominic went to answer. "Hello Lieutenant. Please come in."

"Dominic, you have a beautiful house."

"Thank you, sir, Angie is in the Arizona room." Dominic led him into the Arizona room. "Lieutenant, you know Lizzy and may I present my sister Maria."

Maria lifted her hand and Lieutenant Edwards took her hand and said, "I am very pleased to meet you ma'am. Lizzy, nice to see you again. Angie, how are you holding up?"

"I feel much better now sir. I am a bit apprehensive about what I have to tell you. Not so much the information sir, but how I obtained it."

"Well Angie, I don't know if there is much that you could surprise me with anymore. You are charming and probably the nicest and most resourceful young lady I have ever known and I have been surprised many times relating to things you have done."

"Thank you for the complement, sir. But I may shock you again tonight. Let us all sit. I believe it will be easier." Everyone sat down. "Lieutenant, I have information that I believe will finally close one of your cold cases."

"OK, I am listening Angie." the Lieutenant said.

This has to do with the guys that were arrested earlier, the ones that I ended up beating. I know you, I mean the police department, have a case open for Jason's parents' murders. You need to focus on Jason and Bradford. They got together and shot both of his parents out in the desert. The gun is hidden in their secret room. They murdered them for their money and the house sir. They planned this for some time beforehand."

"That is some news. We haven't been able to get a break on this since it happened. May I ask how you know this?"

"Yes sir. This is something you do not know about me yet. I only learned this about myself very recently so it is also new to me sir."

Maria was paying very close attention because she couldn't see or feel anything at this point. She could never determine why she could only see some things.

"Sir, I see things in my head sometimes. I also have some unreasonably strong feelings at times as well. I share this with someone else in my close family. Right after I knocked them out, I saw an extremely vivid vision that lasted for quite some time. I saw the two of them talking about the details of the murder before they shot them, then I saw them tell Jason's parents at gunpoint to get in their car and they told them where to drive. Then I saw the them pull Jason's parents out of the car and walk them over to a small old one room shack then each one shot one parent. Jason shot his father and Bradford shot Jason's mother. And Bradford made Jason's mother watch Jason shoot his father." Angie was crying at this point. I hate them for doing this because it caused me to see it. And I try not to hate anyone because I believe it is wrong to hate. It almost made me sick sir. I was only able to hide this from Sherri because she was so upset over what Jason put her through. Sir, Sherri also has this gift and I believe she may have seen at least part of this as well. She has not shared that she has this ability with me yet. I believe she is holding it in not believing what she is seeing."

The Lieutenant sat there and handed her his handkerchief to dry her eyes. "That is a very interesting story, Angie. We did not tell the media that this happened in the old shack and that we believed the two of them did it. That is amazing Angie. We never found the gun and they had an alibi that checked out. I need to get a team over to their house to look for the gun. Did you see anything about where the gun is hidden?"

"Sir, all I saw was them nailing on the wall in a corner just off of the floor in their secret room."

"I will send a team over there to look. If we don't find it, would you be willing to go with me to see of anything looks like you saw it?"

"Sir, I would be worried that people would learn about my ability. I do not know how I could handle that."

"I would make certain that does not happen. You would come with me alone and if anyone said anything we could say that you overheard them laughing and talking about it or something like that. And you would be just helping to locate the gun based on what you overheard. Would that be OK?"

Angie looked at Aunt Maria and she shook her head yes. "OK Lieutenant. I want these guys to pay. His parents were scared to death, so to speak, and it is sick to me that they made his mother watch him kill his father. I felt as though he did this for fun. I am completely repulsed by this. They do not feel anything about this, no emotion at all, almost as though they thought of them as things and not human. I have read about psychopaths but never thought I would meet one."

"Well Angie, believe me or not, I expected you to tell me something like this. I have always thought you seemed to always be ahead of everyone. Something like you know what is going to happen just ahead of time so it doesn't surprise me."

"Sir I feel somewhat better. I was very afraid that you would look at me as though I was crazy. You have been a good friend to my father and very respectful to me and I was worried that this would change everything."

"Angie, in my business I have seen and heard more strange things that you would probably imagine. So, you seeing things isn't much of a surprise. Although I would hope that if you see anything bad that you believe is about to happen or is happening you would come to me. I will keep this our secret and I will figure out a way to keep you safe. Hopefully you won't see anything like this again."

"Thank you, sir. I will keep that in mind. And thank you for understanding, sir."

Dominic and Lizzy were lying in bed talking about what they learned about Angie and Maria. Lizzy said, "I just remembered that Angie told me something after she met Sherri and Jason for dinner."

"What was that honey?"

"She told me that when Jason took her hand and kissed the back of it, she had a huge inrush of negative feelings and she thought she saw dead girls in her head. She knew about these guys already when they went to dinner! And she said it sounded as though he was covering something up in his speech. She already knew!"

"What did you say to her at that time?"

"I told her that possible she was feeling protective because of her connection to Sherri or possible it was a chemical Imbalance. I was completely wrong."

"You cannot blame yourself. You could not possibly have known that she that she can see things before they happen." Dominic turned and hugged her tight. "I did not know Maria had this same ability until today. And I still do not know how I feel about that."

"We have been faced with some overwhelming things today. I do not know how I feel either, Dom."

They kissed and laid back and fell asleep.

A team of police went to Jason's house the next morning. They searched the secret room and found a place in the wall that looked as though someone recently made a repair. They broke open the area and found the gun. It turned out they had not even cleaned it as it still had their finger prints on it. They test fired it and the ballistics matched the bullets taken from Jason's parents during the autopsies.

Jason and Bradford eventually made a deal to disclose the location of the bodies of the 4 girls they killed and buried in exchange for no death penalty. They admitted to killing Jason's parents as well. They were both sentenced to multiple life sentences in prison with no chance for parole.

Chapter 11

A few days later Sherri called Angie at work. "Hello Angie. I really need to talk to you but I am a little afraid to ask. There is something about me that scares me and I thought maybe you could help me understand."

"Hello Sherri, I have been expecting this call. We should meet somewhere quiet where we can talk without interruption. How about tonight after work and after your last class you meet me at my house and we could talk in the Arizona room. My mother and father will respect our privacy if I ask. This is a great room for things such as this because it is private and you feel safe surrounded by the mountains. Plus, we would be inside away from the weather. This is where I often talk to my mother about things that upset me."

"Alright, I will meet you after you get home from work. My last class today ends at noon."

"Alright Sherri. I will be looking forward to helping you." She hung up.

Sherri felt a little better. Then she realized that Angie said she was expecting this and will look forward to helping me. "I wonder what she meant by that?" She thought. "Maybe she knows. But she couldn't, could she?" Sherri thought about this all day but it didn't help.

Finally, the time came for her to leave for Angie's house. When she arrived, she felt somewhat relieved. She didn't understand why she would feel like this just from arriving there.

She rang the bell. Just as every time she rang the bell she thought, "Real bells!"

Angie opened the door. "Hello Sherri." She reached out and they hugged. Angie could feel her tension. "Come in Sherri. I can feel your apprehension." They walked into the Arizona room and sat down.

"Angie, I have something to tell you about that scares me. I am a little scared to say anything because I don't want you to think poorly of me. I talked to my mother about it and she suggested I talk to you. She said that since we have had some kind connection after what happened to you a year ago you would probably understand."

"Sherri, I am positive I know what you are about to tell me and I also have something to share with you as well. There is nothing you could say that would make me think poorly of you. You are my best friend and I do believe we have a connection but this is due to something else we share. Please go ahead."

"Ok." Sherri took a deep breath and let it out. "Remember when you were at you fathers shop late and those guys broke in?"

"Yes, how could I forget?"

A report broke into TV shows about it. I wasn't watching TV and had fallen asleep while studying. Gina called me and told me about it. She said something like, "there was another thing at Angie's fathers' shop, and the news is talking about it now." She told me about it and I said it involved Angie, didn't it? And she said, "Yes how do you know? Are you watching it now?" I told her, "No, I had fallen asleep." She told me that they didn't say if anything happened to you and I just blurted out that you were fine and I was certain. I told her that just before I fell asleep, I was thinking about what you did to Mike and then thought you will need to do it again. This scared me. I don't know how I knew this.

"This was what Gina was talking about that night at Tucson Burger was it not? I felt that you were very anxious when she brought it up. That was why I said what I did."

"Yes, I was anxious and I wanted to thank you for doing that for me. My mother suggested that I may be precognitive but that scares me. I don't know what to think." She looked as though she might start to cry.

Angie slid over and put her arms around her and said, "I knew this talk was coming Sherri. I know exactly how you feel. Let me tell you why and what happened after that day with Jason and Bradford. I believe this will help you."

"Ok." Sherri said feeling very vulnerable.

"I had just returned home afterwards and told my parents about what happened. I began to become very emotional and asked my mother why these things keep happening to me. I felt as though I was attracting fights and I do not want that. Then I began to tell her about all that I felt before that happened and I became almost hysterical. My mother asked me if she should call my Aunt Maria to ask her to come and talk to me thinking since she had such strong intuition she may be able to help me. I told her OK and that I thought she was waiting for the call. Then my Aunt told my mother she was waiting for the call."

"What I learned is that my Aunt Maria is precognitive and she had learned about this when she was about my age. She described what she did to get help and then told me the same as she was told. She also said that she knew you were also precognitive that day you had lunch with us before we went to the Nutcracker. She said that I have a friend that shares the same abilities as I do. I immediately said it was you and it then felt as though I always knew. You need not fear this Sherri, it is a gift from God and he will give us the strength to understand and use it. He will guide us and show us how to use it. And he will not give us anything we cannot deal with. We need to embrace this."

"Then afterwards I told my father I needed to talk to Lieutenant Edwards because I had information about a cold case. I was afraid the Lieutenant would look at me as if I was crazy because of how I learned the information. Lieutenant Edwards came here to hear what I had to say and he was not shocked when I told him that I saw this very vividly in my head. I think you know what this is about do you not?"

"It is about a gun, right? And, and, um, I see it now. Oh my God! They, they killed his parents! And they were nasty to them. I can't believe I just saw that. And they hid the gun in that room." Sherri began to cry.

Angie put her arms around her again. "This was very difficult to see. I saw this while you went to call the police but I did not know what to do about it. But I did tell Lieutenant Edwards and he promises to keep this our secret. He said he would figure out a way to sound reasonable. He told me if anyone asks him how I knew this he would tell them that I overheard them talking and laughing about it."

"I know this scares you and it scares me as well. But we also have each other we can use for support."

"Thank you, Angie. Hearing this makes me feel much better. I almost feel relieved. You know, sometimes I can't believe how good a friend you are Angie."

"The one thing we have as compared to my aunt is we have parents that are willing to listen and we have each other. My Aunt had no one. She was afraid to tell my father. In fact, he just learned about this."

"How did she cope then?"

"The story she told me is astounding. She said that she looked through a phone book at school because she felt desperate but found nothing. She said she was distressed and picked up her books and began to walk home. She told me she felt overwhelmed and afraid. Then as she walked home, she felt that she needed to walk down a side street and she stopped and turned and saw a house with a sign that said, "Readings." She went to the door and the lady opened it and told her that she had been waiting for her. She knew her name and why she was there. She said that they talked for a while and she felt better."

"She knew her name and why she was there? I think I may have run away. I can't imagine not having anyone to talk to about this. I still overhear people saying that they can't talk to their parents and that is so sad. We are fortunate to have parents that will listen."

"Yes, Sherri, we are very fortunate, and we have each other."

Angie and Sherri discuss this quite often and they both grow at using it. They begin to see things together at times. They each have times when they end up walking up to someone and tell them something that changes that person's life. Sometimes it keeps the person from doing something that they will regret and sometimes it helps a relationship.

There are times when Angie doesn't want to see things, such as when she is at work or when she is in crowded places. After some time, Angie realized that she can stop these visions by involving herself with something that will keep her mind completely occupied, something that requires concentration. These are the times that she thinks about and pictures project ideas in her head.

Sherri finds that when she draws, it blocks her visions. Probably because when she draws she concentrates on what she is drawing and it keeps her mind occupied. She bought a large drawing board about 2' x 3' and began drawing a color picture of Angie's CUDA. She wanted to do something to thank Angie for saving her life from Jason and Bradford. As she began, she decided to add Angie to the drawing. She needed a picture of Angie. She looked through her yearbook and found a candid picture of Angie and others in one from her classes. She used that.

Angie and Sherri decided to spend the following Saturday evening together. Sherri suggested she come and she could eat dinner with her and her parents. Angie accepted.

Angie drove and parked in Sherri's driveway. As she was getting out of the CUDA Sherri's father had come out to throw some garbage in the trash can and saw Angie arrive. He walked over and said hello as usual. He looked at Angie's CUDA as he never had been close to it in the past. "This is a very nice car, Angie. Could I see the engine? I never saw a HEMI in person.

"Absolutely, sir" Angie opened the hood.

I see it has air conditioning. I wasn't aware you could get air in a HEMI car."

"You cannot sir. I added this recently."

"You added it? How did you do that?"

"My father found a junkyard that had a wrecked 440 CUDA with air and bought all of the factory air conditioning parts. Then we transferred the parts to my CUDA. We had to modify the compressor bracket however."

"Wow! Everything looks as though it came from the factory. You did a nice job."

"Thank you, sir."

"Has Sherri told you about my muscle car?"

"No, she hasn't said anything. What do you have?"

"I have a 1969 GTO Judge."

"Really? Could I see it sir?"

"Follow me." He led Angie to the garage and opened the overhead door.

"This is sweet! Ram Air 4 and a 4 speed, I love the color."

"It's called Carousel Red. It also has the optional 4:33 Posi."

"This has to be fast. I see it has the hidden headlights as well. This has to be a rare car. I am surprised Sherri didn't mention it."

"She isn't into cars so she probably doesn't think about it. Let's go in. I'm sure dinner is ready."

"Thank you for showing me your car sir."

"You are welcome, Angie."

They went into the house. Mrs. Winston said, "Hello Angie. It is nice to see you. I see John showed you his GTO."

"It is nice to see you as well Mrs. Winston. And yes, he showed me his car. When he told me he had a GTO I asked if I could see it. He was gracious enough to show it to me Ma'am."

Just then Sherry came into the kitchen. "Hello Angie, you look nice. You didn't have to dress up."

"I know Sherri. I felt it necessary since you invited me for dinner with your parents." Angie had designer jeans, a very nice sweater and her favorite cowboy boots, and of course, she had her cross on.

"Angie, may I see your cross closer? It is beautiful." Mrs. Winston said.

"Of course, ma'am. I am the 5th generation of Tucci's to wear it." She walked over and showed it to Mrs. Winston. "It is a vine cross as referenced in John 15:1-8."

"I know those passages. That is wonderful!"

They all sat down.

Sherri said grace and Mrs. Winston began serving. She had prepared pot roast with potatoes, onions and green peppers. She also prepared peas and carrots and fresh baked rolls.

"Ma'am, this is wonderful! You are a wonderful cook." Angie commented.

"Thank you, Angie. Sherri told me that you had a very nice talk a few days ago."

"Yes Ma'am. It was an intimate talk. I believe I helped Sherri just as my Aunt Maria helped me."

"Your Aunt Maria has this ability as well?"

"Yes Ma'am. I recently learned this. It continues to be frightening but we have each other and Sherri has you and I have my parents and aunt for support. We are fortunate to have this support."

"It is good to hear that you have your parents as well. That is not very common now."

Mr. Winston did not comment. He knew about this because he and Mrs. Winston discussed this but he decided he didn't need to say anything. He figured it was already a difficult subject.

They finished dinner and Sherri and Angie went to Sherri's room.

They talked about their recent visions and then Angie got another shock. It was the same girl but now she is crying. "I keep seeing this same girl but now she is crying. I feel her fear, Sherri." Angie had tears in her eyes.

Sherri reached to hug Angie and she began seeing something. "I am seeing a dark room. It feels like there are lots of girls there but I don't see any. They are scared and they are being treated cruelly. I feel that some have been hurt but I don't know how."

"Do you see anything else? Where or when this is?"

"I lost it." Sherri said. "It's gone. I felt their fear and pain. They were hurt, I feel it in my stomach I think."

"Your stomach? What do you think happened?"

"I don't know. I can't tell. Maybe they were beaten? I don't know." She had tears in her eyes.

Angie hugged her. "I have been thinking that this is happening now or has not happened as of yet. I have been feeling as though it is not from the past. All we can do is wait until we see additional things. Then possibly we can determine what this is."

Chapter 12

"Hello Carol, this is Lizzy, Angie's mother."

"Hello Lizzy. It is a pleasure to finely talk to you. John and I have been looking forward to this for some time."

"We have been as well. We would delight in having your family over to our home for dinner. I thought possibly this Saturday night if you are free."

"We would love to Lizzy; Saturday would be fine."

"How about 6:30?"

"6:30 is good."

"Do you care for Italian?"

"We love Italian. We will be looking forward to it. Thank you, Lizzy"

"This can be casual. We will see you then."

Saturday came and Lizzy had been preparing food for Saturday night the past few days. Since she wanted dinner to be nice, she prepared baked Manicotti. (Mozzarella; Italian sausage; marinara sauce garnished with parsley and Parmesan cheese stuffed into pasta shells)

She also made lemon garlic green beans and zucchini fritters. Then she made cannoli for dessert. Carol, John and Sherri arrived to amazing aromas in the Tucci house. Dominic and Lizzy met the Winston's at the door and invited them in. **Then they** brought John and Carol around and showed them the house. Of course, Sherri had seen the house many times. John and Carol told them that they had a beautiful house. Carol loved the view from the Arizona room. Dominic and John sat in the Arizona room for a while as Lizzy, Carol, Angie and Sherri went to the kitchen to finish preparing dinner.

Carol was quite surprised from what Lizzy prepared. Lizzy explained, "I prepared Baked Manicotti with ricotta and mozzarella cheeses and chopped Italian sausage and stuffed the shells." She had them in the oven keeping warm. She removed the pan and placed them on a large serving plate and poured marinara sauce over them. Then she drizzled fresh grated Parmesan cheese over them and some parsley. She had finished the Zucchini Fritters just before the Winston's arrived. She transferred them to a serving plate. Carol helped with the final preparations of the Lemon garlic green beans. Lizzy took the salad she prepared out of the refrigerator and brought it to the table. Then she went to get the dressings. She had prepared vinegar and oil and creamy garlic dressings.

Angie and Sherri completed setting the table and Lizzy and Carol brought out the food.

Lizzy went to the Arizona room and announced that dinner was served and everyone went into the dining room and sat. Carol asked if she could say grace and Lizzy said, "Of course you may."

Carol waited for everyone to sit and began, "Lord, please bless this feast that we are about to partake. May it nourish out bodies. Thank you for this opportunity to dine with the Tucci's and thank you for watching over us all. Amen."

John said to Lizzy, "Lizzy this all smells and looks wonderful. You are an amazing cook."

Dominic opened a fresh bottle of chianti and walked around the table and poured for everyone.

"Thank you for the complement, John." Lizzy began by offering the main dish to Carol, John and Sherri. This was a family style meal. When everyone had been served, they began eating.

"Lizzy, these zucchini fritters are amazing. May I ask how you made these?"

"Of course, Carol. They are fairly easy. I grate zucchini then mix it with fresh grated parmesan, an egg and 5 tablespoons of flower, mix it well and form small patties. Then I fry them with olive oil until lightly browned."

"That is it? They are amazing!"

"Thank you, Carol."

They talked about many subjects. Dominic then asked, "What do you do for a living John?"

"I am a Structural Design Engineer at Hughes. I have been there for 12 years."

"Really? Do you know Enzo Bertini? He works on propulsion systems."

"I know of him. I have not worked with him. Why do you ask?"

"He is my brother in law, my sister Maria's husband."

Sherri asked Angie, "Your uncle Enzo works at Hughes? I didn't know that."

"I did not know your father worked for Hughes so it was not relevant to anything we have discussed."

Carol said to Lizzy, "Not to change the subject but I had wanted to make a point of thanking you and Dominic for Angie's influence on Sherri. Angie is such a polite young lady and Sherri has learned some wonderful things from her. Sherri has been learning how to be a lady from Angie and that is something we have not done well ourselves. I have seen many changes in how Sherri interacts with other people and I have been very pleased. And I wanted to thank you for what Angie did to save Sherri from those two monsters as well. We are so indebted to her for that."

Lizzy said with some surprise, "Thank you Carol. I have not yet heard anything such as this. I am very pleased that Sherri has picked up these mannerisms. We are very proud of Angie"

Dominic said, "Angie is our miracle. We have been blessed to have had Angie born. You see the doctors had informed us that they did not think it would be possible for Lizzy to conceive and one day we were surprised to find that Lizzy was pregnant. This was a miracle from my point of view." Dominic said.

"John said, "We have been blessed as well but in a different way. It turned out, that Carol could not conceive and when we found this out I was heartbroken. As far back as I can remember I wanted to marry and have a family. Then one of the nurses at the doctor's office gave us contact information for an adoption agency. We were not certain that we wanted to adopt but shortly after we contacted the agency, we were informed that there was a baby born to whom the mother died at childbirth and she had been a single mother. We went to see this baby and immediately fell in love with her. This was Sherri. I feel blessed as well Dominic. So, I can understand how you both feel."

"I never would have guessed that Sherri was adopted. She even resembles Carol." Dominic said.

"You are not the first that has stated that." Carol said.

Dominic said, "Does everyone have wine? Ah, I see everyone does. I wish to make a toast to all of us. May all of us continue to be blessed with fortune, with God's help." Everyone drank.

When everyone had finished and Lizzy and Angie had cleared the table, Lizzy brought out the cannoli. "You made these as well, Lizzy?"

"Yes Carol."

"You are amazing! It appears that you have endless talent's Lizzy."

"Your complement means quite a bit to me Carol, thank you. But I also need to thank Angie for her help. She mixed the filling and stuffed the shell pastries last night."

"Then Angie you are an amazing lady as well." Carol said.

They ate the cannoli and moved back to the Arizona Room.

Angie said, "Father, why do you not tell Mr. Winston about your gasser. I recently learned that he has a 1969 GTO Judge. He showed it to me last time I was at their house."

"A GTO Judge? Ram Air III? Auto or stick?"

"It is a Ram Air IV with a 4-speed rock crusher and the optional 4.33 Posi rear axle." John said.

"What color."

"Carousel Red."

"It sounds as though it is a beautiful car. How about the headlights? Are they hidden?"

"Yes, they are. It is a rare car. You have a gasser? Those are so raw. A shell with a big motor." John said.

"Yes, do you wish to see it? I store it here in one of the garages because we have become so busy at the shop I just do not have the space."

"Are you kidding? Of course, I would."

Dominic went and grabbed the keys and they went to the garage. As Dominic opened the door John saw it behind the pickup. "Wow! A 63 Nova! This is sweet." He began to look at it. "A 454? Really? How cool."

Dominic opened the door and sat in it, put the key in the ignition, flipped the switch for the fuel pump and fired it up. John had a big grin. Dominic only ran it for a few minutes as he did not want to bother his neighbors. He shut it down.

"Must be something to drive!" John said. As they walked past the pickup, he noticed the 427 insignia on the front fender. "They didn't make these with a 427, did they?"

"No, they did not. I found a 427 L71 and put it in last Thanksgiving week."

"L71? Isn't that the 3-2bbl Vette motor?"

"Yes." Dominic opened the hood.

"Wow! I'll bet this thing moves. You do amazing things Dominic. And Angie showed me her CUDA and told me she installed air on it. It looks like it came from the factory with air. She is doing amazing things as well."

"Yes, she does. We should get back to everyone. You should bring your GTO around sometime. I would love to see it." He closed the hood and shut and locked the garage door. They talked as they went back to the house.

"I wondered if you got lost." Carol said.

"No, I just saw a couple of amazing vehicles." John said.

Angie said, "Father, I didn't tell you about Paula's father."

"What about her father Angie?"

"I dropped her off at her house last Saturday night and found out her father has a 71 Plum Crazy Demon 340 somewhat modified."

"Really, that is a sweet car. Those 340's are fast."

Sherri went with Angie to her room and they talked about things the saw lately. Then Angie had another Jolt. Sherri did not feel anything this time. Angie still is only seeing the one distressed girl but just as last time she was crying. She didn't see anything else.

Lizzy and Carol went to the kitchen sat at the table and talked. Dominic and John remained in the Arizona room and talked. It got to be about 10:30 and John said it was becoming late and they went to get everyone.

They went to the door and said their goodbyes. Carol said, "Thank you so much for inviting us over Lizzy. Dinner was the best we have had in some time."

"Thank you, Carol. We enjoyed tonight very much. We should do this again soon."

"We would love that. Possibly next time we could do it at our house." Carol said.

Angie and Sherri hugged and said good bye. They walked to the car and went home.

Chapter 13

Angie and her friends met at Tucson Burger the following Friday night and while they are eating Gina said, "You know, we are all nineteen now. That means we can go to bars. Some of the girls at School have been telling me it is fun. They have dancing and karaoke."

"Do you think that's a good idea? You know because we never went to a bar before." Karen said.

"I would feel a little scared." Paula said.

"Me too." Janet said.

"I think it would be fun!" Denise said. "What do you think Angie?"

"Maybe. I just do not want to have any problems with any-one. That would be the last place I would want to have a confrontation. It just feels as though these things keep finding me. I would just worry somewhat." Angie said.

"Maybe it could be fun. We should try it. And since Gina brought it up it sounds like she wants to do karaoke. She can go first." Sherri said.

"That would be something to see." Paula said.

"You want to see me sing?" Gina said.

"Karaoke, I would like to see that. I know all of us sing sometimes." Paula said.

"Where would we go?" Denise asked.

Gina said, "There is a bar called "The Bum Steer." They say they have live bands and karaoke and the crowd is younger with a lot of the college crowd. It is on Stone. We could go tomorrow night."

They all agreed.

They met at the bar the next night and went in. They found a table big enough for all seven of them and sat down. They found this both exciting and a bit scary because it was their first time. They did not know what to expect.

There was a live band playing rock cover music and it was as loud as you would expect. The waitress came over and checked their ID's and took their order. Gina, Denise and Janet ordered beer and Angie, Sherri, Karen and Paula just ordered cola. Gina asked why they didn't order beer. They said they weren't sure if they wanted to drink yet.

After their drinks were served, they talked about what to do. Gina suggested they go and dance. Gina, Denise, Paula and Janet went to dance and Sherri, Karen and Angie stayed at the table. The dance floor was full of people dancing. Gina kept waving for everyone else to come and dance.

Then they played "I Saw her Standing There" Angie liked that so she got up to dance and then Sherri and Karen followed. Angie began to really get into it and danced a little wild. Gina thought it was cool and she started dancing like that as well.

During the night a couple of guys asked Angie to dance but she turned them down, very politely as usual. Gina and Paula danced with a few guys. Then as the night went on Denise drank a few glasses of beer she was dancing with anyone that asked her. It was obvious she was getting a little drunk.

Gina and Angie got Denise to sit down and they got her a cola. "I want another beer. C'mon, I'm not drunk."

"Denise, you are beginning to get drunk. It is very obvious." Gina said.

"What, me?"

Angie said, "Look all of the guys here are watching you waiting for a chance to get you to go with them."

"No, they're not."

Just then a guy came up, "Is she alright? I could give her a ride home if she isn't or help you get her to the car. I don't want to see her taken advantage of. I can't believe I am saying this cus I am a little shy around girls, I kind of like her and don't want to see anything happen to her. It looks like all the guys are staring at her. It makes me feel a little uncomfortable. Oh, I'm Ronny."

"Thank you, Ronny, that is gallant of you. But we can take her home. Thank you for the offer. Maybe we will see you here again." Angie looked at Denise, "We should go Denise, before you make a scene."

They paid they bill and left. They decided to stop at Tucson Burger to get something to eat. Denise was drunk. They had to help her into the restaurant and to a seat. They got some food and all sat. "This was a lot of fun tonight. I liked it." Karen said.

"I didn't think you were having fun. You sat for a while and it looked like you only danced because everyone else did." Janet said.

"Yeah, but she did dance. Maybe she is just a little shy." Gina said.

"I liked the music and watching the people dance." Sherri said.

"Maybe we should eat before we go next time. Maybe Denise won't get drunk then." Janet said.

Denise seemed as though she was drunker now than when they left the bar. "I think I am drunk. I feel funny." Denise said.

"Yes, you are. I hope this doesn't happen every time we go out." Gina said. "It messes it up for everyone else."

"I'm sorry, the room feels like its spinning."

"Denise, your eyes look weird." Karen said.

Denise was having a difficult time sitting up. Karen sat on one side and Janet on the other to keep her from falling. "We better get some food in her so she sobers up. We can't take her home like this." Janet said.

They got a hamburger for Denise and got her to eat it. After she ate, she began to look better. They all ate and talked. When Denise was able to sit up herself, they thought they could bring her home. Janet drove Denise's mother's car home and they got her into the house. Then everyone else squeezed into Angie's car and she dropped everyone off.

The next Friday night they went back to the same bar because they had karaoke on Friday's. This time they all ate before they went to the bar hoping Denise would not get drunk again. They found a table where they could all sit and then ordered. Everyone got a glass of beer this time. Angie and Sherri just sipped a little beer on and off while everyone else were drinking theirs. Gina, Denise and Janet ordered a second glass of beer. They kept telling Gina she needed to go sing because it was her idea. She finally gave in and went up. She asked the DJ to play "Piece of My Heart". She tried to sing with a gravelly voice. She did OK. She got clapping and a few whistles. The whistles were from guys that likely thought she was hot. Gina is a little wild looking with the look that Joan Jet took in the late 70's. She had black hair in a messy long Paige boy type cut and she dressed in washed out jeans with a chain belt, a Black Sabbath Tour 1973 t-shirt and a silver chain around her neck with a huge safety pin hanging from it. And she wore black work boots. She had a bad girl look.

Gina kept trying to get Angie to sing but she said no. She finally finished the glass of beer and gave in. They didn't know what they are about to see. Angie asked for "Angie Baby". The DJ put it on and Angie was ready. She began to get into it. She moved around just as she saw it performed on TV. She really got into it. Everyone thought she sang just as the recording.

The song was done and everyone in the bar screamed, whistled and clapped. So, Angie asked if he could do another. She asked for "You're So Vain." She really got into this one. She sang just like when she saw it performed on TV. Again, afterword's everyone screamed, whistled and clapped. She stepped down. Gina couldn't believe it. "Angie, it was like we were watching the actual people singing this in concert! You should be a singer!"

"Really? I do not think I was that good."

"Angie, you were amazing!" Sherri said. "I can't believe it!"

"That was great!" Paula said.

A few guys came up to her and told her she was amazing. They asked if she was going to sing again.

"I do not know. Maybe later." She couldn't believe she sang that well. She had another beer. Everyone kept asking her to sing again. After an hour of this she finally said she would sing another song. As she walked up everyone was cheering her on.

Angie asked for "The Night the Lights Went Out in Georgia." The song began and she sang just as well as earlier. By this time everyone was screaming just as though this was a rock concert. She must have been becoming somewhat used to extra attention now because it wasn't affecting her as negatively as in the past. Although she thought maybe it was an effect of the beer. She never drank anything alcoholic other than a champagne toast or a glass of wine so she didn't know how she would be affected by alcohol.

A couple of guys came up to Angie and asked, "Hey, do you sing in a band? You sound like it."

"No, I am an auto mechanic."

"No, you're not." They said not believing her.

"Yes, I am, and I am ASE certified as well. I work at Dom's Automotive and Performance Center on Stone. Maybe you have seen the advertisements. You should bring your car in if you need work or if you want performance modifications. Or you can see me run at the Tucson Dragway tomorrow." She thought she could do a little plug for the shop.

"You drag race too?"

"I run low 12's in my CUDA."

One of the guys said, "You're the girl that races that CUDA? Angie Tucci?" He turned to the guys, "I've seen her race, guys. She is almost unbeatable. I never saw anyone so fast out of the hole. The light turns green and she's gone!" He turned back to Angie. "I never saw you without your helmet. I can't believe it! You look like a model! Wow!"

Angie blushed again. "Thank you for the complement, sir."

"Sir? Just call me Rick. I'm Rick." He said to the guys he was with, "Remember I told you about the pink CUDA? This is her."

"She races? Really? Her?"

"My CUDA is parked outside if you don't believe me." She smiled at them and turned back to her friends.

They walked away and one said, "It has to be her, how many pink HEMI CUDA's could there be in Tucson?"

"You're becoming well known around here. You do amazing things Angie. Janet said. It seems you impress people everywhere."

"Yea, you're nice and sweet to everyone and they see it. Well, except when you fight for your life." Denise said.

"I am just being myself."

"I expect you are going to have lots of guys hitting on you here." Gina said smiling and giggling. "Let's go dance, c'mon." she went to the dance floor. They all followed. The disk jockey played music and every so often did karaoke.

They danced quite a bit. Angie danced with a couple of guys and a few guys complemented Angie. One asked her to go out but as usual she turned him down very politely. They left about 11:30 because Angie was going racing tomorrow.

Chapter 14

Angie is forced to fight Johnny
November 1975

"I got to find that bitch and show her." Johnny told Andy.

"She works at her dad's auto shop over on Stone. Bet you could find her there."

"I want to fight her when she is by herself. Too dangerous at her dad's shop. Who knows who might be there to help her. No, she needs to be by herself. I'll show her."

"Are you sure. With you fighting her who there could help. Maybe you shouldn't do this Johnny."

"What, you think I can't beat her?"

"I didn't say that. Just last time you did something like this you almost got arrested. That guy called called the police."

"Screw him. This is different. This is personal" Johnny said.

"You don't even know her. How can it be personal?"

"Because it should have been me that was on TV, not her. I'm the champion. She is stealing my fame, its personal."

Johnny was getting worked up even more. This was all he could think about. "I just need to find her somewhere. You gonna help me?"

"Yeah. OK." Andy said. "What does she look like?"

"Remember that girl that we saw going into that Dojo last week? The one with the long blonde hair?"

"Yeah, I remember her."

"That's her."

"She fought those guys and killed them? Are you sure it was her?"

"Yes. It was her. We gota find her."

They drove around looking. After driving for a while, they couldn"t find her. It was Saturday afternoon and they didn't know she was at work. So after about an hour and a half they gave up. Johnny dropped Andy at his house and then he went home.

He thought about showing Angie who's the champion all night. He obsessed about it so much he almost didn't sleep.

The next afternoon Johnny drove around downtown and happened to see her walking from in front of a store towards a parking lot with an older lady he figured must have been her mom. He turned into the parking lot that was right there and pulled into the first open space. Now he was getting excited. He was going to show her and no one could stop him. He was giddy. He got out and walked over to her.

Angie was with her mother walking through a parking lot back to her mother's car after some shopping. They were talk-ing about a gown that they saw in the store. "You would look beautiful in that gown."

"I think it would look better on you mother. I am not certain that I liked the color."

"Pastel blue? And with your beautiful long hair and blue eyes, I believe you would look stunning!"

"I do not know." They were interrupted by this big guy.

"I'm challenging you to a fight right now. I don't believe that bull from the news that you killed 3 armed guys."

"Sir, you have the right to believe what you want. There is nothing I can do about that. And no, I am not going to fight with you." Angie said as she and Lizzy turned from him trying to ignore him and walk away.

He stepped in front of them again and insisted, "Yes you are. You don't even fight in tournaments so how could you know how to engage someone."

"No, I do not fight in tournaments and that is my choice." She and Lizzy turned from him again. Angie was thinking, "What a jerk."

"You're going to fight right now so I can show you how you suck. I'm the champion." He said.

Angie stopped and turned to him and said, "Look, I am not going to fight. I only fight for self-defense, period. I am not going to engage you. We are out shopping and this is completely inappropriate behavior and not what the martial arts teaches us." They began to walk away again.

He stepped in front of Angie and said, "You're going to fight," and threw a light punch at her face.

She blocked it and said, "What is it that you do not understand? I am not going to fight you."

He tried a sucker punch and Angie blocked it hard. It was obvious she was angry now. "Mother will you please hold my purse?"

Lizzy said, "Do not do this Angie."

"It is obvious he will not stop mother. I will be fine. Maybe you should call Lieutenant Edwards, this may get ugly. I do not want to hurt him but I may have no choice."

Johnny overheard her say she didn't want to hurt him and chuckled.

Lizzy put the bags down and rushed to the phone booth at the side of the parking lot. She couldn't run because she was wearing heals. She dialed the police."

Angie got into her stance and was ready. "I do not want to hurt you."

He laughed, "Like you could do that."

Now people were beginning to gather to see what is going on. They saw a big guy and a beautiful girl with long blonde hair and it looked as if they were going to fight. "Poor girl," they thought.

He threw a straight punch at her face with his right fist. She immediately spun pushing it aside with her left arm and continued to spin and hit him extremely hard in the face with a "Rican" a punch shown to her by Hector's cousin Jose, using the back of her left fist with the momentum of her spinning and followed through with her right knee to his stomach. She did this so fast he didn't even get to pull his arm back.

He grabbed his face with one hand and his stomach with the other arm. His nose was bleeding, his eyes were watering and becoming black and blue and her knee to his stomach knocked the wind out of him. He started to groan and couldn't catch his breath for a minute.

He stepped back to recover and went with a straight kick with his right leg directly at her but she expertly pushed it aside with her left arm and followed through with her right elbow and hit him hard on the top of his upper leg right on the muscle. He screamed in pain and almost fell. With this move he went from smug to pissed off. He stumbled aside and re-gained his focus. He turned and stepped towards her and tried to punch but she just ducked away. This caused him to lose his balance because of his hurt leg. He almost fell. He then tried a reverse 360 degree round house but she was ready and she ducked and then kicked the back of his other knee and he fell forward hard on that knee. The fall tore his pants and scrapped his knee fairly bad. It was obvious his knee was bleeding.

He was now kneeling down and very angry. He struggled to keep from falling over. Then he pulled out a switch blade and clicked it open. Angie immediately saw it and before he could even begin to swing, she did a reverse 360 degree round-house full power to his wrist. The knife literally flew across the parking lot and his forearm smacked against a sign post and fractured. She continued spinning and did another not as hard to his shoulder and knocked him over. Now he was lying on the pavement holding his arm. He screamed, "You broke my arm you bitch!" It sounded as if he was crying.

Now this whole thing took less than a minute and a half and Angie never even broke a sweat. When Lizzy got back from phone booth it was over and Angie was leaning against her mother's car and she had already put their bags in. This guy was sitting up on the pavement and was holding his arm while leaning against another car.

Lizzy was shocked at what she saw. When he threw the first punch she expected the worst. But what Angie did shocked her. She thought Angie looked like a blur. She walked back to Angie and had a shocked look on her face. She couldn't think of anything to say.

Lieutenant Edwards arrived with another officer. They saw the guy sitting on the ground holding his arm and it was someone they knew of from another altercation recently. And Angie was leaning on her mother's car. He asked the other officer to talk to the crowd and find out what they saw. Then he walked up to Angie and asked, "Angie, what happened here?"

"Sir, my mother and I were walking to the car after doing some shopping and this guy walked up and started trouble. He said he was going to show me that I was shit and that he did not believe the news. I told him that he has the right to believe what he wants. I told him I was not going to fight many times and we tried to walk away. He kept getting in front of us. I was worried for my mother sir. I did not want him to do anything that would hurt her. And when he tried to punch me, I engaged him. It only took a minute or so and it was over. But when he pulled out a switchblade knife and clicked it open, I kicked it out of his hand and in the process, I believe I broke his arm.

Sir, this is not what martial arts is about. You are taught to use it only for self-defense. Evidently, he did not learn that."

"Where is the knife now?" he asked.

"It flew over that way sir" She pointed.

He walked over to look for the knife and found it. He walked back to Angie and Lizzy and told them they could go.

Angie and Lizzy drove away. Lizzy was still shocked. She saw Angie fight from the phone booth and she couldn't believe what she saw. She saw her take this guy out without much effort and she couldn't believe how fast she moved.

Then Lieutenant Edwards walked over to the guy. "What is your name?" the Lieutenant asked him.

"Johnny." He said.

"Well Johnny, you know she could easily have killed you? I have seen firsthand what she can do and I wouldn't engage her if I was holding a gun. Let this be a lesson to you. How is your arm?" the Lieutenant asked.

"It hurts. She broke my arm. I didn't know, I had no idea anyone could fight like that. I never saw anyone so fast. She did this before I could try to protect myself." Johnny said.

"Let's get you to the emergency room Johnny." The lieutenant and the other officer got Johnny into the squad car and drove to St. Mary's emergency.

The next day Johnny went to his Dojo and when he arrived his sensei wanted to talk to him.

"Johnny, I know what did. I know Angie sensei. You disgrace Dojo, I and students. I no want see you until you all healed. I want you apologize Angie. If no apologize no come back. Understand?"

Johnny looked at him with contempt. He didn't want to apologize. After all she beat him up he thought. He thought she should apologize. Johnny got up with his crutch and limped out without saying anything. He was angry. He already was thinking about how to get back at her. "It's her fault I got hurt and can't go to the Dojo." He thought. He also figured he is through with competition for this year now. He was talking to himself as he limped to his car.

As he drove home he was thinking, "If I want to get back to competition I have to apologize. I don't have to mean it though. He he. She won't know the difference.

About a week later while Angie was at work a guy came into the shop using a crutch and asked Uncle Jack, "Would it be possible to see Angie?"

Uncle Jack looked at him. He had obviously been beaten. He replied, "Let me check to see if she is free," and went into the shop to get her. "Angie, there is a big guy with 2 black eyes, tape on his nose, a cast on his arm and using a crutch up front to see you."

She said, "Are you serious? That describes the guy I had to fight in the parking lot last week." She took off her gloves and hat and walked up front already prepared to engage him.

The guys in the shop stopped and followed her to see what was going on.

He said, "I don't want to fight Angie. I came to apologize. I don't know what came over me that day. Maybe I didn't think a girl could fight, I don't know. My sensei kicked me out of his Dojo at least until my arm is healed. He told me I disgraced him and his dojo, I guess he knows your sensei." He walked up to her and bowed. "I bow down to you to show your superiority and I had no business engaging a fellow student. Please accept my apology."

Angie stood there trying to understand.

"Lieutenant Edwards took me to the emergency room and told me about you. I now fully believe what they said on TV about you. Lieutenant Edwards straightened me out and told me if there was a next time I would either end up in jail or possibly dead." He said. "I never saw anyone fight like you do, I was totally unprepared for anything like that."

"I accept your apology. You put me in a position I did not want to be in. I began fighting very aggressively when my life was threatened. Maybe you enter into tournaments but you do not know the feeling when your life is threatened. It changed how I react and fight. Now I just react. Besides you may not know that I have been training in 3 martial arts, Taekwondo; Aikido and Karate and have also learned some Judo as well. In tournaments you fight using rules. I only use this for self-defense and the only rule I have is to survive. I likely fight very differently than you have ever seen."

"You have taught me a valuable lesson. You should never believe you are better than anyone else and this is not something to show superiority. That's all I wanted to say to you Angie." He reached out to shake her hand and she shook. He turned and left. As he went to his car he thought, "I can't believe she believed that. She believed the whole thing. He snickered.

"That's the guy that wanted to fight you last week?" Uncle Jack asked.

"Yes sir, Uncle Jack."

"He is a big guy. You gave him the black eyes and it looked like a broken nose, broken arm and a limp?"

"Yes, sir, I did. Mother saw me fighting and it completely shocked her. I do not think about what to do when I fight, I just react."

"I believe you. Anyone would be crazy to go up against you." Uncle Jack said.

Angie went back to work.

Hector asked her, "That was the guy you fought with Angie? Wow! He is so big. I would think twice before I would fight him. It makes me proud to know you, Senorita Angie. You're one bad ass woman!"

"Thank you, Hector. And you know that move your cousin Jose showed me?"

"The Rican?"

"Yes Hector. I used it on this guy and that is how I broke his nose and gave him 2 back eyes."

"Shit, you must have really givin it to him. It's a good move but I never heard of anyone breaking a nose with it. I need to tell Jose about this."

The next day everyone was working and Angie was cleaning up the CUDA. A few guys walked into the shop. Hector said, "Jose! You brought a couple of the boys with you." He went over and they all hugged. "Hey guys." Hector said and shook their hands and talked a little. Then Hector pointed at Angie. She was wondering what he was saying.

They walked over to Angie and Jose said, "Angie, I want to shake the hand of the Legend," and reached out.

Angie stood up and said with an unbelieving smile, "Legend? What is this all about?"

Jose said, "You're a living legend Angie."

Angie smiled. "What are you talking about guys?"

Jose said, "You killed armed guys with your bare hands and feet. You stopped the 2 guys that were killing young girls, you're a legend, someone I feel proud to know."

"I don't know about a legend, but yes, I did those things. But I was put into those situations. It was not something I wanted to do."

"And Hector just told me about the guy that came in yesterday. I think I know who he is. He was always around bragging that he was this karate champion. And you took him out without any trouble. Hector said you didn't even sweat." Jose said.

"Well, it only took about one minute." Angie said.

"You did that in just one minute?" Jose crossed himself as he said. "Holy Mary, Mother of God!" He was shocked. "Just one minute? I was going to say I would like to see that but I don't think so now. You are something Angie."

Angie stepped over and gave him a hug. "I appreciate your complements, Jose."

He was shocked. He never expected a hug. "Angie, you are really something. Whoever you end up with will be one lucky guy."

Angie blushed and smiled. "Thank you for the complement, Jose." She turned back to what she was doing. Jose told Hector he just wanted to say that to her and left.

One of Jose's buddies said as they were walking out of the shop, "She's the one that killed those 3 guys? I knew them. I think we fought them once a while back, remember?"

Jose thought for a minute, "You mean those guys that wanted us to leave the park we hang out at?"

"Yah, those were the guys. I can't believe she took them out."

"Hector told me that she was pretty upset that she had to do that." Jose said.

"It's just hard to believe. She is so sweet to everyone and she is so hot! Hard to imagine her fighting like that."

Chapter 15

The next Friday Angie and her friends met at the bar for more karaoke. Gina loved it. Angie really enjoyed it but didn't want to admit it. She does have some shy periods sometimes. They got their usual table.

Rick saw them come in and sit down. He immediately walked up and said, "Hello Angie, Gina and friends. Great to see you again! Gonna sing again Angie? We really enjoyed last time." It seemed everyone already knew Angie and Gina. Angie for her singing and Gina due to her bad girl look. The guys thought she was hot and sexy.

"Hello Rick. It is nice to see you and your friends again as well. I do not know if I will sing tonight." Angie replied.

"Oh, c'mon, you got to. You're the best! Well, I hope you do." They went back to their table.

Gina said, "You're not going to sing? I thought you liked it last time."

"Well, I did. I do not know. Maybe later."

"If you sing Angie, I'll sing." Janet said. As soon as she said that she thought, "Why did I say that, I can't sing." And she blushed.

"Janet, you're going to sing? I want to see that." Karen said giggling. She never thought Janet would do that.

Janet leaned over to Karen, "I don't know why I said that. I can't sing. I'll be so embarrassed."

"You said you would sing. I hope Angie sings just so I can see you sing. Ha, Ha." Karen said.

"You're mean."

"Oh C'mon. Have a couple of beers and you won't care." Karen said.

"Thanks." Janet didn't want to sing but she wanted to hear Angie sing.

As the night went on Gina kept pushing Angie and finally Angie said, Alright." She stood and went up. She asked for "This Masquerade."

The song began. Angie took the mike. She began to get into it and moved around while singing moving her arm and hand in front of her.

When she finished the crowd roared! Clapping, whistling and screaming. Someone screamed, "Another, Another!"

Angie thought for a minute. She asked if they had At Seventeen. The music came in and she sang just as well as each time before. When she finished there was screaming, whistling and clapping again. She gave the disk jockey the mike back and went back to the able. "Janet, your turn." She said,

"I can't, I'm embarrassed."

"You said if I sang you would. Now you have to." Angie said.

As usual Gina spoke out, "You have to Janet, you promised. Angie would never break a promise."

"OK." She reluctantly got up and walked up to the stage. She asked timidly, "Do you have "Help Me?"

"Yes." He said and put it on.

Janet turned to the crowd. She was shaking. The music started and she began to sing at first a little quiet then someone screamed, "Oh C'mon." and she got louder. She actually sang quite well. Nothing like Angie but well enough for her to get whistling and clapping. She handed the mike back and quickly went back to the table and sat. She gulped down half of her beer. She was blushing and sweaty.

Angie got up and went over to her and hugged her. "You sang very well Janet! Maybe you should do it more. Everyone enjoyed it. I can say, the more you do it the easier it gets."

"Really, you think I sang Ok?"

Denise said, "Didn't you hear the whistling and clapping? You were great! I wish I could sing like that."

Gina said, "Maybe you should try then."

"I don't know." Denise said.

"Finish your beer and have another. Then you can do it." Gina said.

"Maybe. I da know."

More people sang. It was a busy night. After a while of pushing Denise decided to do it. She went up and asked for "Danny's Song." She began, "People smile and tell me I'm the lucky one, and we've just begun...." She got into it and sang fairly well. She got whistles, screams and clapping. Some of which was likely because she was a cute petite blonde. She wasn't bad. She went back to the table and sat.

"You were pretty good Denise! And you didn't want to sing!" Paula said.

"Now we gotta get Sherri, Karen and Paula up there! It's their turn. We did it, now they have to!" Denise said.

Paula said, "You guys sang all of the good songs. There isn't anything for us to sing now."

"Oh, c'mon, there's lots of songs." Gina said.

"I just thought of another one to sing." Angie said as she went to the stage.

"Hey, it's Angie again! Look!" Someone said loudly.

"What song Angie?" the disk jockey asked.

"White Rabbit" The song started. As usual Angie got into it. The crowd was screaming! Angie had a way to change the sound of her voice to try to mimic the original singer.

Gina had moved to the front of the crowd. She was whistling and screaming. Paula and Sherri joined her. Everyone was screaming and clapping.

When she finished Sherri got up on the stage. She took the mike from Angie. She asked for "You've got a Friend." The song began. She wasn't bad. There was whistling and screaming. This made her feel not so timid and she sang louder.

Gina, Angie and Paula stood in front and were screaming. The song ended and Sherri felt pretty good. To everyone's surprise Paula stepped onto the stage and took the mike from Sherri. She asked for "Son of a Preacher Man."

The music began and she sang. Fairly well. There was whistling and screaming. Not only from Gina and Angie but from the crowd as well. She finished and stepped down.

Gina stepped up on stage again. She asked for "Cherri Bomb." The song started and she sang. Just as before not necessarily very well but the guys loved it. She was dressed in her usual bad girl look and moved around kind of seductively and deliberate. The guys were all in front screaming. Gina loved the attention. Afterwards everyone went back to the table. They ordered another round of beer.

Sherri said, "Karen, you got to sing. The rest of us have."

"Paula said, "It was actually fun. I was really nervous at first but then I kinda got into it. It was fun! You gotta do it!"

A few others from the bar sang as they talked. They kept pushing Karen. "I don't know. What would I sing?"

Janet said, "How bout your favorite song?"

"What favorite song?"

"You know, the one you always sing when it comes on the radio, Rhiannon. Janet said.

"I couldn't do that."

"You know all of the words; you sing it all the time. C'mon."

Everyone was pushing her. "Well, Ok."

Gina screamed "Yea!"

When the current person finished Karen went up. She was visibly shaking. She almost dropped the mike. "Rhiannon." The disk Jockey played it. She began kind of quiet.

Someone in the crows screamed, "Louder, c'mon!"

She sang louder. She started to get into it. She did fairly well. The guys were whistling and screaming. She felt embarrassed but finished. She couldn't give the mike back fast enough and get off of the stage.

When she got back to the table everyone told her she did well. "See that wasn't so bad, was it?" Gina said.

"I guess not. I'm not doing it again though." Karen said.

Janet hugged her. "You were good. Wasn't it just a little fun?"

"I guess. No, I didn't like it. Everyone was staring at me. I felt like I was put on the spot. I didn't like that." Karen said.

They stayed for about another hour then they all went home.

Chapter 16

Maria talks to Dominic about her abilities

Dominic and Maria decided to meet at the shop after closing one Saturday late afternoon so they could talk. Dominic wanted to learn about Maria's abilities and hear her out. This was something he knew nothing about. Maria believed that she has owed him this explanation for some time now. However, she didn't feel right about it until she had the opportunity to talk with Angie first. They went into the office and closed the door even though no one else was there. Dominic wanted her to feel as if no one could hear.

"Dom, Big Brother," Maria began, "there is so much I want to tell you. I will just begin. Remember when mother got sick and we brought her to the emergency Room?"

"How could I forget?"

"Well, when the sister told us it was possible mother had cancer, I had already known it was pancreatic cancer. That is why I was so very upset and emotional. Just knowing this then realizing I knew this for certain and it just kind of came to me frightened me. This is the first time I consciously realized that I was different. And remember when you came home and talked to me about Lizzy? The second day when you were late and I asked if it was about the girl you met the day before. I think I said I just guessed."

"Yes, that is what you said. I remember clearly."

"I did not guess. I had seen the two of you together and felt the magnetism you each had. Then when you were getting ready to go to the party that Saturday and I caught you mumbling to yourself. A few moments before I had seen the two of you married."

"You knew all that? I remember you saying that I should know that I have to go to that party. You knew that we would marry already?"

"Yes, I knew. At that point I had already talked to the medium and it was she that helped me as I helped Angie. Do you remember how so often in the last year of high school and the beginning of college when I seemed to be upset quite a bit?"

"Yes, I remember that. And I tried to talk to you and help you but I felt as though I was failing."

"Big Brother, I was struggling with this ability and was afraid to say anything for fear you would treat me as if I was crazy."

"Oh, Maria, I wish I knew. I would never have thought that you were crazy. I thought you knew that. You could have told me anything and I would still love you just as much." Dominic had tears in his eyes now.

"I know that now Big brother. But at that time, I was struggling with all of the other female things along with this and I was a mess. Mother was not there so I had no one to help me understand about female things. Fortunately, I overheard some girls talking about having their first period or I would have thought I was going to die when I had mine. I trusted you with my life but I was so worried about seeing things before they happened, I was just terribly afraid."

"Not long before you met Lizzy, after classes one day at the U of A, I looked through a phone book trying to find someone to help me understand. I did not know what to look for and I found nothing. I felt completely lost. I picked up my books and started to walk home. I was trying to keep from crying and making a scene when I left. I cried as I was walking and then when I crossed one side street, something made me turn and walk down that street. I was feeling sorry for myself and was afraid. Then I stopped, thinking this was crazy. I turned to walk back and I happened to look at the house I was in front of. There was a sign that said "Readings." It was kind of a shock. I stood there for some time just looking at the house then I walked up to the door. I actually do not remember walking to the door but there I was. I reached up and knocked and the medium opened the door and said, "Hello Maria. I have been expecting you." I was speechless. I think I still had my hand up to knock. I remember saying, "You were expecting me? How? I did not make an appointment; I did not call you." I was shocked and shaking and still had tears on my cheeks. The medium said, "I have felt your fear and I believe your ability guided you to me. Please come in." I walked in not even realizing it. She continued, "You have a great gift and you need to embrace it and not fear it. Let's sit." I sat facing her. The medium reached out and said, "Hold my hands Maria. I believe this will help to calm you."

"I took her hands and immediately felt calmed. It was very strange. "Just relax my dear, what you have is the ability to see into the near future. What you see is what may happen if nothing is changed. You may feel something is not right or you may see things in your mind's eye. It can be different each time. These will most likely not be clear or easy to decipher but they will show you things that are coming. Some will be good and some will be bad, in time you will learn to identify good from bad. Sometimes you may be in a position to intervene in something bad but you need to remember that you may not be able to protect yourself from harm if you decide to intervene. There will be times that you may only want to warn someone or talk to the police but you need to only use vague references such as I have a strange feeling that something is going to happen. If you tell anyone that you feel things and they usually come true you will open yourself to ridicule. People can be very cruel. You need to be careful as to what you say to others as you could end up alienating yourself. Most people will not understand and many will call it crazy and distance themselves from you. You may also want to pray for direction because God has given this to you for a reason. Remember that God will guide you and give you strength. This gift will guide you throughout your life. It will help you make decisions. Only you can decide what to do with this ability. It is not witchcraft or the devils work dear. It is a blessing. God chooses who will or will not have extra abilities and he will guide you in its use. But you need to ask for guidance. Ask for God to show you the way and you will be guided. You would be surprised as to how many people have this same ability as it is more common than you believe. Although many choose not to use it. They bury it deep down. But that causes hardship for them. It is also possible that you will be attracted to others with this ability. But again, you need to choose to learn to use this but you cannot dismiss it. It will always be there. This is all I have to say today, Maria. Come and see me again if you feel afraid."

"I sat there for a few minutes. I said, "Ma'am, I feel much better now. But I am not certain why. What you said has given me confidence and knowing I can ask for direction in my prayers gives me hope. Thank you so much for this."

"Do you remember when I came home after school and told you I had had a flat tire at the U of A after classes one night?"

"I remember that, yes. You came home somewhat upset but I sensed there was something more but you did not want to talk about it."

"It was beginning to get dark. I was the only one in the parking lot and I had never changed a tire. I read the instructions that were in the trunk and thought it should not be too difficult as long as it did not get too dark. I got out the jack and set it up following the picture in the instructions. Then I tried to take the spare out and I could not lift it. It was too heavy. I kept trying and it was no use. I was upset and began to cry. I was leaning against the roof of the car crying and someone came up behind me and asked if I was Ok and if I needed help. He scared me and I jumped. He spoke with an Italian accent. He opened the car door and helped me sit on the front seat. I was scared to death. I had no idea who this was or what he would do. He was very polite and spoke well. He changed the tire and put everything back into the trunk. Then he asked me out to dinner. When I looked into his eyes I knew I had to go. Just as I knew you had to go to the party at Lizzy's house. I saw myself married with two baby girls. This man was Enzo. Enzo does know about this. I ended up telling him later on in our relationship. When I told him he looked at me with a strange look. At that time, I was afraid to tell him as well. I was afraid of losing him. But he understood, hugged me and told me that he loved me and he would stand by me regardless."

Other things have happened as well. Such as you and Lizzy buying the CUDA for Angie, I saw that long before her birthday. But unfortunately, I only see what comes to me and not everything comes to me. Such as the fights Angie has been in. I saw those afterwards."

"I still am afraid to let people know I have this ability. I am always worried that people will find out and shun me. That is why I warned Angie to keep it to herself and to also pass that on to Sherri." She paused for a minute or two feeling uncomfortable. "Big Brother, what are you thinking? I am somewhat worried."

Dominic sat for a minute or two trying to absorb everything Maria just said. He stood and went to Maria and gave her a tight hug. "Maria, you are still my sister and I will always love you. You have nothing to worry about. All I can comment on is I wish you could have told me about this when you first began to experience it. I could have at least tried to comfort you. I feel somewhat disappointed that you did not give me the opportunity. I understand your fear and why you did what you did. I still love you and will always support you through the good and bad. I do not believe I could have survived without you. Before I met Lizzy, I had no one but you. I would have done anything for you and still would."

They hugged for some time both with tears in their eyes.

"I believe we have a connection that very few if anyone has. I will always be here for you regardless of what you need Maria."

"I love you Dom. I could not have a more understanding brother. Dom, I had a dream last night that I wanted to tell you about before we leave. I almost forgot."

"What is it, Maria?"

"When I talked to Angie, she had told me she did not understand why she kept getting into situations where she had to fight for her life. This dream was reminiscent of the dream you had just before you met Lizzy that day. Remember when you told me that in your dream you were just there and you heard a voice?"

"Yes, Maria. I do not think I will ever forget that dream."

"Well, this dream was not unlike that dream. I was just there and I heard a voice, it sounded as if it was in my head, it was deep and calming and it said, "Maria, you have a strong connection to Angelina, you will explain to her why she continues to be put into these situations where she needs to fight for her life. Angelina has been chosen, because of her unique abilities and her pure heart, to end the reign of these persons that have been turned to sin. These persons, at the moment of their death, will ask for forgiveness and cleanse their soles. Some cannot be saved and she will stop their reign of terror. Angelina has saved herself and Sherri from two that could not be saved. They will no longer take innocent lives." I do not know how to talk to her about this Dom. I feel as if it is not the time now but I know I need to do this."

"That is what you heard? That frightens me. Does this mean she will be confronted again?"

"I do not know Dom."

"I agree that this is not the time. Maybe you should wait for a while. Angie has been very distraught from these situations and I believe she will not want to hear that there could be additional times where she will need to fight."

"I agree Dom."

"We should talk about this additionally before you tell her. Agreed?"

"I agree Dom."

They hugged for a while then decided they should each go home. Dominic knew Lizzy would be worried if this lasted too long and he felt the same for Enzo. They walked to the door and walked out. He made certain Maria waited until he locked the door before she walked to her car. He turned and walked her to her car, helped her in and said, "Maria, this was a nice talk. Please remember that I will always be here for you. I will see you soon. Drive safely Maria." He watched her drive away then got into the pick up and went home.

Chapter 17

Angie's Sensei talks to her
Mid November 1975

Angie had been going to the Dojo on Monday's and Wednesday's since she began at 7 years old. One Monday after Angie and the rest of the students finished the session, Angie's Sensei walked up to her, "Angie you stay after everyone go? I want talk about training, OK?"

"Yes, of course Sensei." When everyone left he locked the door and asked Angie to come to his office.

"Sit please." She sat down. "Angie, I like talk about training. It very good you advancing become 4th dan black belt. I proud but I worry you not have what need for protection. You put in bad place 3 time and you need special training. I not want see hurt you or death. I think you ready for different training. I had master teach different for fight real enemy. One day you meet enemy knows fight like you. That not good. I want teach you fight any and win. You special student and I not want see you hurt. You good person. I no want you face one to beat you or kill. You understand Angie?"

"Yes Sensei. I understand. I talked to my mother after last time. I fear fights are finding me. I do not want fights but I have had no choice. If you say I am ready for another kind of fighting then I will do as you suggest."

"You come different nights? I want train you alone. This not for regular student. This save life against anyone. You can come Tuesday Thursday now?"

"I can change things to come on Tuesdays and Thursdays. Do you want me to begin tomorrow?"

"Yes good. No can start too fast. OK Angie, I happy you get 4th dan black belt. I pleased at hard work. You very special student. Make I proud. Go home. We begin tomorrow. We work 4 hour start 6:00."

"Thank you, Sensei, sayonara." Angie picked up her purse and left.

Angie thought about what her Sensei said. She thought he was going to teach her something very different. Maybe this will help her if she is confronted again. When she got home, she walked in as usual and Lizzy said, "Hello honey how was your training tonight?"

"Mother I have some news to tell you and father. Is he here?"

"He is. I believe he is in the garage cleaning the truck. You can tell us your news there." She turned off the heat on the stove and oven and opened the oven door to the first catch to keep dinner from burning. They walked out to one of the garages. Dominic was there cleaning up the truck. He always keeps the truck clean because it represents the shop. "Dom, Angie has some news for us both."

"I am always up for news, as long as it is good." He said jokingly. He and Lizzy always make time for Angie regardless if she has good or bad news or whatever she needs to discuss. "Let us sit down over there by the table." They walked over and sat down.

"Mother, Father, tonight my Sensei awarded me 4th dan black belt. I am his first."

Lizzy reached over and hugged her. "That is wonderful Angie. You continue to astonish me, I could not be prouder!"

Dominic stood up and went to hug Angie as well. "Angie, I am speechless. You know that is not common for me." He had small tears coming from his eyes.

"I have more."

"More than that?" Lizzy asked

"After training tonight my Sensei wanted me to stay after everyone else left. Then he locked the door and took me into his office. He asked me to sit and then told me that he is concerned that I have been attacked 3 times already and said that he doesn't want me to need to fight against anyone and get hurt or worse. He said I was a good person. I did not know where he was going with this. He said I need to change to Tuesdays and Thursdays so he can teach me how to fight against anyone. He said one day I will come up against some-one that can fight equal to me. He said that is bad. He said he will teach me to fight anyone and win. What he said was, "*One day you meet enemy knows fight like you. That not good. I want teach you fight any and win. You special student and I not want see you hurt or death. You too good person. 3 time you fight bad people now. I no want you face one to beat you or kill. You understand Angie?*" It is difficult for me to speak as he does."

Dominic sat for a minute thinking, "He told you that? I do not want to see you hurt either." He remembered what Maria had just told him from her dream. "I do not know how I could survive another incident as you had that time with that Mike guy. If he believes he can teach you this I am all for it. You already scared Lieutenant Edwards and I would wish you would be able to scare anyone that you come up against."

Lizzy looked at Angie, "I would die if anything happened to you honey. I will support this any way I can. I do not want to see you fight again. But if you are put into that position again, I want you to be equipped with everything necessary to survive."

"Thank you for your support mother and father. I can always count on you. He has changed my training days to Tuesday's and Thursday's now. He said this is not for the regular students to see. Tomorrow night we begin. He also said we will work 4 hours each day. That means 6-10 PM."

"That is not a problem Angie. It will not interfere with work and you are not studying for school now." Dominic said.

"Let us go and have dinner. It was ready when you arrived home Angie." They all left the garage, Dominic shut off the lights and locked the door and they went into the house to eat.

The next day Angie worked as usual and told everyone that she moved up to 4th dan black belt. Everyone was happy for her and at lunch while everyone was in the break room Eric said, "Now that everyone is here, the boss man as well, I want to do a toast to Angie for her amazing achievement. Angie, you are one extraordinary woman in more ways than I could describe. I believe I speak for everyone here; we are proud to know you and be able to work alongside you." Then he got a mischievous smile, "And I am sure we all feel safer knowing you are her to save us if we are ever attacked." Everyone laughed a bit. "But seriously, we are very proud!" he raised his bottle of water and drank. Everyone else did the same.

"Thank you everyone." She had tears in her eyes because she knew it was genuine. "I also feel proud to be working with all of you as well. We could not have a better team here. I have a short story I believe led to the way we work together. And it all began with a young woman in 1953."

And Dominic and Uncle Jack looked as though they did not understand as well.

"Please just hear me out, if you will. There was a time when my father worked for my Uncle Jack's father at his gas station. And one day a young woman pulled off of the street with car trouble and my father went out to see what he could do to help. She was a beautiful, wealthy young woman in a new Cadillac Convertible."

Dominic now knew what she was going to say and he blushed.

"My father helped this woman and got her car repaired in minutes and that allowed her to make her appointment. The next day this woman came back to get her car serviced because my father had told her the day before that she needed a service. This woman could not believe that my father was a mechanic because he was a complete gentleman and spoke well and that impressed her. This woman is my mother. The point I want to make is that I believe the fact that my father is a gentleman, treats everyone with respect regardless of who they are or the circumstance, has built character and friendship here." Then she got a teasing smile, "And we certainly have some real characters here. Ha, Ha." Everyone laughed!

Angie left work in time to be at the Dojo by 6:00. Her Sensei took her into the room where everyone works out and practices. He took out something she hadn't seen and that was full body padding with a face shield. He helped her put it on. Then he went through some of the moves he would teach her first. He had her put on the padding because he wanted her to feel the force of these even though he pulled each one. Now that she understood how these differ from what she already knew he would discuss these with her.

"Angie, we work jumps and kicks from Taekwondo and Muay Thai. Also teach Shaolin Kung Fu. This need meditate to prepare. Can be very deadly. This not taught here and outlawed some places. When you learn you need careful. Very easy to kill. We work on speed. You fight so fast some not see. You learn disarm all weapon. Not matter type. When know you be one of 3. I one, brother and you."

"I did not know you had a brother. And he teaches here?"

"Yes, brother. We taught from same master. I already talk him and he agree you need know. Guy in parking lot go brother Dojo. After you fight guy in parking lot he call me. Guy scared of you. He say never saw fight like you. You fight like two young brother long time ago. Master did same for us. Different time then, fighting everywhere. This before come to US. US best country."

"I don't know what to say Sensei."

"No need say, just listen. Brother be here help with teach. He want meet you."

They heard knocking on the back door. "Ah, here now." He went to let him in.

"Angie, Sensei Akio." She bowed then he bowed. They both talked for a minute then turned to Angie. "Angie, I Sensei Kotomi. Brother, Sensei Akio."

Sensei Akio said, "Angie nice meet you. Kotomi say you impressive fighter. Johnny say he no defend against you. You too fast. He one of best students. I agree with Kotomi. We show what you learn."

Angie stood to the side and watched. The two Sensei's bowed and began. They used a toy gun, toy rifle, toy bowie knife. She found it interesting how easy they made it look to disarm and subdue someone. They demonstrated how to disarm someone that puts a gun in your back; how to disarm and subdue someone that holds a knife to your neck from behind; etc. Each time the aggressor ended on the mat on their back open to a finishing blow. Then they stopped and put on full body padding. Again, they bowed and began to fight. They used kicks she never saw, they used their elbows and knees in a way she never saw and their speed was unbelievable.

Then they took out Eskrima sticks and a Bo. A Bo is a staff about 6' long. The Eskrima sticks are about 26" long. They began with the Bo and they demonstrated how these can be used against an opponent with and without one. After this they showed her the Eskrima sticks. She really fancied these because they are light weight and can be used incredibly quickly.

They finished and Sensei Akio said, "You learn and you be unstoppable, nobody able to hurt."

They began with her warming her muscles then stretching. They began showing her proper movement and tone. They finished but 10:00. Angie left but was excited about learning this. She would return Thursday night.

Angie returned Thursday night and they began her with warm up exercises and stretching. They moved to a different form for her stance. They had showed her new positioning which is the basis of a few of the kicks she will learn. Sensei Akio demonstrated slowly the steps of the tornado kick. This is a more advanced kick with extreme power she will learn. He showed her this to plant the importance of the new stance. This kick has multiple parts and you spin multiple times and swing one leg before the final part of the kick. He explained that with an opponent that does not know Shaolin Kung Fu it may appear for the first few moments that you are just show-ing off but when they realize it is part of the kick it is too late.

They began showing her different moves with the arms based on the new stance and the increased power generated by these. Angie watched closely. She watched each of them and in turn tried each move herself. Each one she did slowly in order to try to mimic her Sensei's movements.

Sensei Akio was impressed at her concentration, balance and fluid movements. "Angie, I impressed. No see student focus on form like you. You do well."

"Thank you, Sensei Akio. I focus all of my efforts on learning regardless if it is martial Arts or anything else."

They continued.

Angie works out at home every night now except Tuesday's and Thursdays. In time she learns new routines to help her strength, form and stamina.

She with the help of Dominic set up two 100-pound punching bags from one of the garage beams about 6 feet apart. She will be using these to simulate fighting two opponents fighting together.

She also bought these things called gravidity boots that strap to her ankles so she can exercise upside down. She will use these to work on muscle groups while hanging upside down.

A couple of mornings each week before work she also goes running about one mile. She paced out a one mile route using her measured stride and mapped out running around the streets of the neighborhood.

Chapter 18

Beginning of December 1975

Angie was out on a Saturday evening with her friends. They had gone to the Tucson Burger to grab something to eat after shopping. They got their food and were sitting down eating when a group of guys came in. Right away Angie knew they were going to be a problem. She could see it as well as feel it. She looked at Sherri and knew she felt the same.

These guys were laughing and saying things they would like to do, "with the bitches over there." They were saying how they would have sex with them and what they would do. Sherri, Karen, Paula, Denise and Janet were all disgusted with what they were saying out loud.

Gina told them, "Just ignore them. Act like they aren't there."

Karen said, "They are so loud how can you do that? They're sick, there are little kids here."

Gina said, "I'm going to say something." And she got up.

Karen said, "Gina, No, don't"

Gina walked over to the guys and said, "Could you guys quiet down, there are little kids here. It isn't nice."

"This bitch has some balls, man." One guy said.

Another said, "Go sit down bitch. Unless you want to come with us. We'll show you a good time!"

"For you maybe. I doubt any girl could have a good time with idiots like you." And she turned to go sit down. One of them grabbed her arm.

"I think you are going to come with us. We need some fun. Ha, ha." Another one said.

"Let go of me asshole." Gina said. And tried to pull away.

At this point Angie got up and walked over to them. "Would you please let my friend go?"

"What are you going to do about it bitch?" The guy holding Gina's arm said. "Maybe we should take you too!"

As he reached out to grab her arm Angie grabbed his wrist and used a Nikyo wrist lock and immediately he let go of Gina and went down on his knees. Angie said sternly. "Are you finished? I can break your wrist if you wish" Angie said sternly.

He screamed, "Ahhhh."

"Am I going to get an answer?"

One of the other guys started to move towards Angie to help his friend. Gina said, "I don't think that is a good idea. If you try, someone we will need to call an ambulance for the both of you."

"What? You're crazy. My boy will take her out easy." Another guy said. The other guys stood there thinking they should do something.

Gina said, "Remember the news not too long ago about the 19 year old girl that killed three armed guys that broke into her father's shop?

One said, "Yea, I remember."

Gina smiled smugly and said, "Well, this is her."

"What? She was the one?" one guy said.

"Yes, she is the one. If you friend doesn't learn to stop, he's going to end up in the hospital."

"Holy shit! One guy said. "Joe, stop. She's the one that killed the three armed guys a few weeks ago."

The guy said, "Ok, Ok, Ok. I give up."

Angie let him go.

He stood up and looked at Angie. "You are her?" he looked in disbelief. "Ahh, I'm sorry. I didn't mean anything. Ah, I don't want to fight anymore. You win."

Angie didn't believe it. She remained ready.

He started to walk away and then turned and threw a sucker punch.

Angie just blocked it and twisted his arm back into the same position as before. This time she twisted a little harder. He screamed, "Alright! You win." She let him go again.

He was rubbing his wrist then tried to through another punch. She blocked it and broke his arm. She moved so fast nobody saw what she did. The guy screamed, "You broke my fucking arm you bitch!"

"You want me to break something else?" Angie said.

"No!" he said.

His friends stood there with their mouths open. They were shocked at how fast she moved and how she broke his arm and it didn't look as though she was even trying.

They said to the guy, "Joe lets go. We need to get you to the hospital. He looked at Angie and said, "Sorry we acted like assholes." They turned and left.

Angie then walked back to the table and sat down. Gina said, "I know what they said on the news but I never would have guessed it was like that. You made it look so easy and you were so fast. I didn't even see what you did. I can't believe it. You're bad ass Angie!"

Angie said, "I really didn't think he was going to try to fight. I thought he would just scream and that would be the end of it. I didn't want to hurt the guy but he wouldn't back off."

Gina said, "I guess he wasn't too smart."

Everyone laughed.

They finished their food and talked about what just happened. They were all shocked.

Denise said, "Like, when we met you, I never would have thought you could do anything like that. I thought of you as just another girl. You're not. I am speechless!"

Paula said, "I'd like to see that, Denise!" and laughed.

"You always say that, you and Gina. You make me feel stupid." She looked really hurt.

Karen looked at Denise, put her hand on her shoulder and said, "Denise, I think they do that because you are a good friend. They don't mean to hurt you." She looked at Paula and Gina and said sternly, "Do you?" Denise looked as if she was about to cry.

Gina and Paula looked embarrassed. Gina said, "Um, I'm sorry Denise, I don't mean to hurt you. I guess we haven't thought that this kind of teasing would hurt you."

Paula said, "Denise, you're my friend I'm sorry. I guess it has been easy for us to tease you and it isn't a nice thing to do to a friend. We don't think you are stupid."

"Really?" Denise asked.

"Yes really." Gina said. She got up and walked over to her, leaned over and hugged her from behind. "I hope you know we love you, just as we love everyone else here." Denise smiled.

Angie sat there looking at everyone. "You know, I do not think it was all that long ago that you would not have thought about this. My point being that you thought about what you said and apologized."

"You're right Angie." Gina said. "I guess we still have some learning to do."

"Paula said, "Yeah, we have you to thank for that Angie. I think if we didn't meet you that day, we would probably still be giving Sherri, Karen and Janet shit. I feel like a better person because we met you."

"I still do not know what I have done. But delighted that my influence has helped you." Angie said.

The store manager walked up to them and said to Angie, "Thank you. Those guys always come in here and cause trouble. Maybe what you did will keep them from doing it anymore."

"Ahh, ok, it appeared that he was going to injure my friend. If I improved the situation, you are welcome, Ma'am." Angie said.

"I overheard what you friend said. You're the girl from the news? That defended herself from the attackers?" the manager said.

"Yes, ma'am that was me."

"After seeing how you handled those guys, I can see how you could do that. Good for you. I am glad you are OK and I got to meet you."

"Thank you, Ma'am."

The store manager walked away. "Angie, you're becoming kind of a celebrity." Gina said.

"It is not something I did intentionally. I have been put into situations I would not have chosen to be in. I just defended myself. I do not know how that would make me a celebrity. I am just who I am.

"We know that. You just have done things that are unusual and everyone is seeing that. I don't think it's a bad thing." Gina said.

"I just do not desire the notoriety." Angie said.

"I can see that. I wouldn't like it either." Karen said.

They talked for a while more then went home.

Chapter 19

Angie and Sherri begin to see things other than the one girl. They begin to see things that haven't happened yet that other people are doing and because of what they see, at times they intervene.

Sherri sees a middle-aged man and has a vivid vision of him getting drunk, going home and beating his wife and young son. She feels that she can keep him from doing this if she talks to him. She walked up and asked him, "Excuse me sir? Do you really think that getting drunk and hitting your wife and son will solve your problems? Do you think losing your paycheck in a bet is worth destroying your family?"

"How do you know that? You can't. It is none of your business," and he turned and started to walk away.

"Sir, I know you care deeply for you wife and son and you don't want to hurt them. I know you aren't a bad man. If you just go home and tell your wife what you did and ask her for forgiveness, she may be angry for a while but you can work it out. Think about you son, how will he feel if you go and beat him? He knows you and your wife fight but I can see that if you let go of your fear you will fix your problems."

He turned and looked at Sherri. After a minute or two he began to cry. "I am such a mess. Why am I so stupid? I don't want to be like this she deserves better."

"She deserves your willingness to make amends. You will do well I see it."

"Who are you? How do you know this?"

"Sometimes I see things in my head. And I see you and your family happy. Isn't that all that matters?" She walked away.

A week later a woman with a young boy stop Sherri at a U of A parking lot and tell her, "My husband pointed you out to me. I want to thank you for what you said to him. I don't understand how and why you said what you did to my husband but it changed our lives. He stopped drinking and gambling and he promised never to do it again. The last week he spent with us at home. He hasn't done that for years."

"I am so happy that I was able to help, ma'am." Sherri said.

Angie was on her way to Martial Arts training and couldn't find a place to park close, so she had to park a couple of blocks away. Just before she got out of the CUDA, she had jolt and a vision where she saw a guy talking to someone that handed him a bag and it appeared that this guy handed the person some money. This was a quick vision. Then she saw a gun fight. She didn't know where or when this would happen but she thought she felt that the shooter from the vision was uncertain about what he was about to do. He didn't want to do it but he felt he had to do it. She didn't know what "it" was however but she felt it involved shooting someone.

As she walked to the Dojo, she saw this begin to play out right in front of her.

When the person turned to walk away, she walked up and said, "Excuse me, sir, will shooting someone solve your problems."

He was startled and argumentative and said, "It's none of your dam business."

Angie then asked him, "You know you girlfriend is pregnant? How is this going to affect her?"

"How do you know that?"

"Maybe I shouldn't tell you this but she is going to have twin girls." Angie said.

"Twin girls?" he replied smiling. Then he got an angry look again. "How could you know that? She's not pregnant, she would have told me."

"She just found out. She bought a test kit and it said positive. She couldn't have told you because you are not there." Angie replied.

"There's a payphone over there I am going to call her." He walked across the street to the phone and called her. Angie heard his excitement. He almost screamed, "Really? You just took a test? Oh my god, that's great! We should celebrate tonight."

He walked back to Angie and said, "You were right! I don't believe it! Wait, how could you know this, and twin girls? That would be impossible for you to know."

"Yes, twin girls. You will see soon. She will get an ultrasound and it will show twins." Angie said.

The guy just stood there dumbfounded. Then he said, "I'm going to be a father! Ah, I can't be doing these kinds of things now. Here take this, I don't want it now." And he held the bag out to Angie.

She replied, "No sir, I cannot take a gun from you. Bring it to the police station and give it to Lieutenant Edwards. Remember his name. Tell him a young girl convinced you not to commit a crime and bring the gun to him. Tell him you need some counseling sir. He will understand and help you. He is a good man and a friend.

"Uh, how do you know it's a gun? It's in a bag.

"That was in my vision, sir."

Ok. He won't arrest me, will he?"

"Did you do anything that would get you arrested, sir?"

"I just bought this gun."

"I believe if you tell him what I just said you will be fine, sir."

"Who are you?"

"Just a concerned caring person, sir. I need to go or I will be late." Angie turned and walked away.

He just stood there watching her walk away.

The next day after school Sherri stopped at the store to pick up some school supplies. As she was walking from her car towards the store, she saw a young woman crying while sitting in her car. As Sherri was walking past the car, she had a vision of her fighting with her new husband about kids. He told her he didn't want kids now; he didn't feel that they are ready since they have only been married a few months. She was upset because she just found out she was pregnant. She is afraid to tell him.

Sherri instantly felt her fear but she also feels her husband feeling bad for arguing. He really wants kids and didn't want to argue. So, she decided to talk to her. Sherri walked up to the car and taped on the window.

The woman opened the window and asked, "What do you want."

Sherri looked at her and said to her, "Hello ma'am, I feel your pain but your husband really does want kids and is sorry for arguing with you last night. I know you just found out you are pregnant but you need to tell him. He will be very happy."

The woman looked at her with shock, "how do you know I am pregnant? How do you know we argued? I don't under-stand."

Sherri told her, "Sometimes I see things, ma'am. I saw your argument in my head and I see your husband feeling very bad that he argued last night. He is at work now beating himself up for this. He is close to crying himself. He will be very happy when you tell him you are pregnant. I have seen it."

"Who are you? I-I don't' understand." The woman said.

"I can't bear to see you crying for something that will be a very happy time for you. Just please go home and tell him. I know he will be very happy." Sherri said.

The woman said, "Um, OK. If you say so. I hope you are right."

Sherri said, "Trust me ma'am. He will be very happy." She felt that she said enough. She said, "I have to go now." And she continued to the store. She couldn't believe she just did this but it made her feel good.

A few days later Sherri was walking to her car after school and a car stopped next to her. It was that young woman. She said, "I have been looking all over town for you. I still don't understand but you were right. I went home and told him I was pregnant and he was so happy it looked as if he was going to cry. Thank you so much."

Sherri said, "It was my pleasure. It felt strange when the vision came into my head and I needed to say something. I am happy for you Ma'am."

Chapter 20

February 1976

Angie and Sherri were at a store one Sunday afternoon and suddenly Angie had a jolt and looked funny and then got tears in her eyes. "What's wrong?" Sherri asked.

"I just felt them, all of them at once. So afraid, so scared." Angie said.

"Who's afraid and scared? What are you talking about?" Sherri asked. Then she saw something. "Oh my God Angie! They...they were kidnapped. They are in a warehouse somewhere. How do I know this?" Sherri was shaking.

Angie took her by the arm and guided her to a bench and they sat down. "They are here, in Tucson. I see it. There are a lot of them, maybe 20 possibly more." Angie said.

"I see it too. But I only see a door, nothing else. This could be anywhere. We need to tell the police." Sherri said.

"What are we going to tell them Sherri? We saw and felt a group of kids held up in a warehouse somewhere? They will think we are crazy. We need more than this if we are going to tell them." Angie said.

"You're right. It would sound crazy. But the feeling is so strong. I see lots of kids." Sherri said. "Maybe we should drive around. What do you think?

"We could drive around but I do not know where we would look. I only see the young ladies all cowering together but not the building." Angie said.

"I only saw the inside of a sliding door not the outside. I don't know what we would look for." Sherri said.

They left the store and started to drive. They didn't know where to go. They weren't sure where to find warehouses. After driving for a while Angie said, "This is useless. We do not know what we are looking for." They just went home.

Another whole week went by without even one vision. They had been having visions that were just quick flashes but haven't had anything at all for the last week. Angie and Sherri wondered why. They both went to visit Angie's Aunt Maria hoping she would be able to give them some insight.

"Hello Aunt Maria, we were hoping you could help us understand something." Angie said.

"Of course ladies, please come in and sit down." They all sat. "What is on your minds?"

"Mrs. Bertini, we have been seeing much more than just a distressed young girl lately. Quite a bit more. We have been seeing things every few days and now we have not seen anything for a week." Sherri said.

"We were hoping you could help us understand why we would be seeing pieces of the same thing very often then go for a week without seeing anything." Angie said.

"As I told the both of you previously your visions cannot be controlled and they can be the past or the future. I have not been able to learn how to determine past from future unless the vision shows something that gives you that information. And at times the visions can be very distressing. I have had visions that kept me from sleeping and caused me difficulty functioning. And there have been times I had not been able to determine what I was seeing. These can stop at any time and leave you upset and at a loss. I have learned to use these as a learning experience. You will find you require some closure for visions such as these. It is not unlike walking away from a movie without ever seeing the end. It can be difficult but I always ask for help to understand in my prayers."

Maria looked as though she was sad that she couldn't help them. "I do not know if I am able to help you additionally and that is saddening to me."

"Aunt Maria, I believe you have helped more than you believe. This ability is very new to us hearing what you have dealt with is helping us to learn. I appreciate your taking the time to discuss this."

"Angie, I am always here. And Sherri, I am here for you as well. Again, I am not certain I can help but I will listen."

Angie hugged her. "Thank you, Aunt Maria."

"Thank you, Mrs. Bertini." She also gave Maria a hug.

Chapter 21

March 1976

Angie went to work the next couple of weeks and went racing on Sundays with her father and Uncle Jack. Sherri went to U of A. Angie and her friends met on Saturday nights and it began to be a weekly thing sometimes meeting on Friday nights as well. The whole memory of the visions was fading from their daily thoughts. They still thought about the visions but other things covered the memories most of the time.

Angie met her friends at Tucson Burger on a Saturday in the evening. They decided to sit outside because the temperature was in the upper 70's and the wind from the afternoon had died down. The sun was setting and the sunset had the usual vibrant colors which is typical for Tucson.

Sherri, Karen and Janet arrived first. Sherri picked them up because she was still the only one with her own car, of course besides Angie. They parked and walked to one of the outside tables and sat. They saw Denise driving her mom's car and Paula and Gina were with her. She parked and they walked over and sat town. At the same time Angie arrived in her CUDA. She walked over and sat down as well. As they were saying hi to each other Gina said, "Let's go get something to eat right away. I am starving." They all got up and went in to order food.

When they got their food, they went back outside to eat. Gina complained about how hard her Pharmacy class is. "I'm having a hard time with the math in my pharmacy class. I need to pass this and I don't know if I will. I'm really worried about it."

"What is so hard?" Paula asked.

"It's all about proportions and figuring out how to mix different medications. It isn't like math in high school it is hard and I don't understand it."

"I would be delighted to help you, Gina." Angie said.

"Really? I figured you wouldn't have time."

"I will make time Gina. You are my friend. I will always make time for any of you. I do not want you to fail." Angie said.

"That's so great! Thanks Angie." Gina said.

"You are welcome."

They talked about her classes then the subject changed. Janet said, "I've been getting a lot of guys flirting with me at work. I get weirded out from this. It's sick sometimes because they are married."

"What, you don't like guys?" Gina said as she laughed.

"Ha ha. These are old disgusting guys. Some are as old as my dad. Yuck, it makes me cringe just thinking about it. And their wives are there shopping. That makes it even worse."

"Really, you get guys like that wanting to go out?" Paula asked. "I would cringe too. I get a lot of old guys flirting with me at the law office but I don't think they mean anything. I just smile and ignore them."

"Many of the guys from the track come into the shop and ask me out. I always turn them down politely. I am not interested at this time." Angie said.

"Not interested? Why?" Gina asked.

"I want to become established first. And I do not have much time for anything such as that. I enjoy racing quite a bit and I do not think I could stop martial arts. I began investing with the tutelage of my grandfather recently and I want to develop my abilities in that area. I am spending time learning about how to run the shop. And I always have ideas for projects running through my mind and at some point, I want to begin working on some of these. I also want to become financially stable first."

"Why can't you go out and do all of that at the same time?" Gina asked.

"I have a plan worked out for my life and I do not want to be distracted. I always want to be prepared and I am not prepared for a personal relationship at this time. Furthermore, I still have issues with guys as a result of the guys that attacked me and those creeps Jason and Bradford. I still have nightmares from that. I do not think I could trust any guy at this time."

"I guess. You don't think if the right guy walked into your life you might want to change you plans?" Gina actually looked concerned.

"I know my mother and father meeting was their destiny and possibly if I had the same type of experience, it would be possible. It was a different time then." Angie said. "I plan to marry and have a family but not at this time. I need to build trust and I want to be prepared financially."

"Isn't that something you do whenever you meet someone new, build trust? I think it is part of any new relationship." Gina said.

"I completely understand Angie." Sherri said. "After Jason and Bradford, it feels like it will be difficult for me to trust any guy."

If that's how you feel. I just hope one day I will meet the right guy. It has been kind of a dream for me." Gina said. "But he has to be fun. I don't want someone that is boring."

"I feel like it will come when it comes. I'm not looking for a guy but if the right one asks me out, I'll go." Paula said.

"I feel like that too Paula. I have guys talking to me at the doctor's office all the time. But I don't really like any of them like that." Denise said. "I dream of getting married to a rich guy and living in a big house with kids."

"Even if he is really old or ugly? Yuck." Karen said.

"I don't want someone old or ugly. I don't want a guy for his money. But I can dream, can't I? Wouldn't you want someone rich? So you don't need to struggle to pay bills?"

"Of course you can dream Denise." Janet said. "Who doesn't dream of the perfect guy? I don't know if I believe there is really someone like that."

"I believe my mother and father fit that description perfectly. Although I believe that is an exception not the norm." Angie said.

"Yea, from what I know about your parents they seem to be perfect." Karen said.

"They have disagreements as everyone does but they always talk through it and never just walk away. They don't raise their voices either. They talk to each other all the time as well. I believe that is the key. I would love to eventually find someone that has those qualities." Angie said.

"So you do think about guys." Gina said.

"Of course I do Gina. And likely more than you may believe."

"Oh, I'm just teasing you a little. I have seen you looking at guys just like all of us." Gina said.

Angie smiled showing she understood.

"What did you mean when you said that you parents meeting was their destiny, Angie? I don't understand." Denise asked.

"My parents meeting is a story that is not unlike a fairytale. It explains the uncommon dynamics of how I grew up with rich and poor families." Angie said.

Sherri said, "You said you would tell us about it sometime. Could you tell us about it now?"

"Yea, now I would like to hear about it too." Janet said.

"Me too." Paula said.

"I would like to hear about this too. I always wondered about how you had rich and poor families. I mean if you are OK with telling us." Gina said.

Everyone was looking at Angie wondering about what she was going to say. "This story usually makes me teary-eyed even when I just think about it. But if you want to hear about it, I will tell you." Angie said.

They all looked at her and said they would like to hear about it.

"OK. To fully understand I need to start at the beginning when tragedy hit my father and aunt's family. This part is sad.

"I still want to hear it." Denise said.

My father and Aunt Maria suffered terrible tragedies. They lived in a big house in the foothills. My grandfather was an attorney at that big law firm downtown. Both my father and aunt have revealed to me that their life was very good and my grandparents were very caring and loving to them. One day my grandfather was killed in an automobile accident and because of that my grandmother needed to sell their house and buy a much lessor house in order to survive. She never had worked so she ended up with a job as a clerk at Seinfeld's department store. They barely survived. Even though, she kept teaching my aunt and father how to be a Lady and a Gentleman. My father has said that his mother always told them that one day they would live in the same manner as they did before their father died so they needed to know how to act and present themselves properly."

"Three years later my father came home from school and my aunt was crying about my grandmother because she was very sick. Shortly thereafter she died from pancreatic cancer."

"My grandmother died at St. Mary's hospital and the sisters told them they would be placed in foster care because they were minors. They were and still are very close and my father said he thought it would kill him to be separated from my aunt. My father told me that my aunt just cried and couldn't stop because of this."

"Oh my god! They would have still been in high school! What did they do?" Gina asked.

"My father went to talk to the only person he remembered that my grandfather worked with and was able to get guardianship granted for my aunt. By then he had just turned 18. He graduated high school and got a job from my Uncle Jacks father at his gas station. He worked and supported them both. Then he helped my aunt get grants to go to the U of A."

"He did all that? When he was only 18? Wow! That's unbelievable!" Denice said.

"I couldn't imagine how they felt. If both of my parents died while I was in high school, I think I would have died." Janet said.

"From what my father told me he struggled to pay for everything. He worked long hours and helped my aunt as much as he could. He never thought about himself much. Then one day he woke after having a strange dream. He told me he dreamt that a voice in his dream told him he had supported my aunt and himself selflessly and he would be rewarded when he least expected. This made him think about how his life had been and how alone he had felt all of this time. He felt very down. That day while he was at work a beautiful young woman in an Eldorado Convertible broke down in front of the gas station and he went to help. She was very upset because she was going to meet her mother and sister for lunch and the car broke down. My father got her car repaired quickly, evidently it had a minor problem and she thanked him and she went on her way. He had told her that she should get her car serviced soon and he would be happy to do it.

"He could not get the vision of her out of his head that day. The next day she came back for the service and during that time she invited him to join her for coffee after he was finished with work. He went and she kept complementing him on his manors and told him it was unusual for an auto mechanic to have good manners and to always be a gentleman. He said that he told her the story about his parents dying and why he had good manners but was an auto mechanic and broke down and cried. She sympathized with him. Then she invited him to a party her parents were having the following Saturday. He went and they began dating and were married six months later."

Everyone sat there teary eyed looking at Angie. "That's amazing, Angie. Now I understand why you grew up like you did. You dad, um, father is an amazing person. How he took care of your aunt when he was 18. I don't know what to say. Karen said.

"I am amazed too. Now I understand why you speak and act like you do." Paula said. "That is an amazing story!"

After a few minutes of all of them sitting there quietly Janet changed the subject, "I started to save for a car. It's so hard to get to work. My mom usually takes me now. It's such a pain to need to get driven around all the time."

"Really? I feel the same way." Karen said. "I just started saving for a car too. My mom drives me all the time. I want to be able to leave when I want and I can't do that now."

"I guess I am lucky then." Denise said.

"Why do you think you are lucky Denise?" Gina asked.

"The doctor I work for is a few blocks away and I usually walk." Denise replied.

"You wouldn't want your own car?" Gina asked.

"Well, yea, but I don't have the money for one. My mom does let me use her car a lot." Denise said.

"I usually use the bus to get to school. I still gotta walk a lot. I think I need to wait to even think about a car until I start working. Nursing pays pretty good, I think. I've been thinking about getting a part time job now but I don't know if I could work while I am in school. I am having a hard time with all of the studying now without working." Gina said.

"I have my mother's old car. It would be nice to have a newer car but just like Gina, I can't buy a newer car until I start working." Sherri said.

"I can see all of your points. And only a few years ago I would have been in the same position as all of you. I do feel somewhat uncomfortable because I am in a position where I have an almost new car, a well-paying job and I live in a big house already. And all of you are struggling." Angie said.

"Angie, don't feel bad. You are fortunate to be in the position I think all of us would like to be. But you also grew up with some difficulties all of us probably couldn't really understand. I mean you were poor but brought up in a wealthy atmosphere. I would think this alone would be difficult. Then you had to go to Amphitheater high school and deal with teasing because of how you talk and act. I think I would rather be where I am saving for a car." Karen said.

"Thank you, Karen. Sometimes I do not think about the position where I was before I moved. It was difficult. I did not have all of you and when I look back, I do not know how I managed without friends. Now that I think about it, it was less than 2 years ago when my family and I moved. And to think two years ago I was going to Amphitheater. Many things have changed since then." Angie said.

Gina said, "I still don't know how you did it without friends. And even though you had wealthy grandparents, from what you told us all of us were better off than you. Don't feel uncomfortable Angie. I think it is great how your life changed. And moving from that little house to the one you live in now had to take getting used to."

"Yah, you didn't have it easy growing up. As hard as you work you deserve to be where you are." Janet said. She got up and walked over to Angie and put her arms around her and hugged her from behind. "I think all of us have something special between us. In this short time, I feel like you and everyone else are my sisters. I love you all. A lot has changed for all of us. Just a little over a year ago Karen, Sherri and I were depressed because of what Mike did and we only had each other. No one would talk to us. We had three people we considered enemies, Gina; Paula and Denise, and now they are very close friends. And you somehow made this all happen."

"I still do not know what I did. But I am very grateful to have all of you as my friends." Angie said.

Sherri said, "I think we all had this in us deep down somewhere but Angie brought it out of us. I can't even think how I would feel without you guys. And Angie, I don't care if you have money and we don't. What matters is our friendship. Right?" She looked around the table and everyone smiled and shook their heads yes.

Paula said, "I agree. But, Sherri, Karen and Janet, I want to say that I still feel bad about what we did to you. Still some nights when I am lying in bed, I get tears in my eyes. Like now." Her eyes were tearing. She reached for a napkin. As she blotted her eyes, she saw that everyone was a little terry eyed.

"I'm sure I speak for the three of us, we know you have changed along with us. You guys have turned out to be like sisters to us." Janet said. "It is almost hard to believe it wasn't that long ago. But now I can't imagine you guys acting like that."

Angie said, "Would all of you want to go to my house? We could go into the Arizona room. It feels as though you are outside. I am certain it would not be a problem with my parents. It would be much nicer than sitting here with the chilly breeze."

Everyone said OK. Denise wanted to know where it was since she has never been there. "Just follow me. It is not far. And if we get separated just take River Road to 1st Ave, then turn left. Keep on 1st Ave and pass Orange Grove then Ina. Keep driving and my house is the third house on the left side.

It is not difficult to find. If we get separated, I will leave my car in the driveway so you can see it."

"Ok, it doesn't sound hard. We will follow you." Denise said.

They all got into their cars and followed Angie. They didn't have any problems finding Angie's house. When they all got out of their cars Gina said, "Wow, your house is nice Angie. I was never in a house this big."

Denise, Paula and Gina had not seen her house yet. They all walked to the door. Angie opened it and they went in. "Wow, this is beautiful! I can't believe it." Paula said.

Angie told them to wait there so she could tell her mother they were there. She came back with her mother. "Hello ladies, it is very nice to see each of you again." Lizzy said.

Almost in unison they said, "It is nice to see you too, Mrs. Tucci."

"Please come in." Lizzy led them to the Arizona Room. "Sit down and make yourself comfortable ladies. I will bring some refreshments for you."

They all sat down. "Angie your house is beautiful! I can't believe it, and the view, I almost don't know what to say." Paula said.

Lizzy returned with the serving cart with a large pitcher of iced tea, a container of ice and crystal tumblers for everyone. "Thank you, mother. This is very nice of you." Angie said.

"If you would care for anything please ask." Lizzy turned and left the room.

Gina said, "Angie, you mother is so elegant. I almost feel like I'm in an old movie."

"Thank you for the complement, Gina. Help yourselves everyone." Angie offered drinks.

Denise said, "I could just sit here and look at the mountains forever. I never knew a house could be like this."

"If you like, I will take everyone on a tour. You could see the house and I can show you our pool."

"You have a pool?" Karen asked.

"Paula said, "I thought you guys visited Angie when she was laid up."

"We did but we only saw the entry way and her room." Karen said.

"Oh, I guess that makes sense." Paula said.

Angie took them around the house. When she showed them her room Gina saw Angie's displayed car models and said, "These cars are cool. You collect these?"

"I built them from model kits Gina. I built the first one when I was 13."

"You built them? Really? You are amazing!" Gina said.

Angie smiled and continued and showed them the kitchen, "Mother I am giving them a tour."

"You are a fine host, Angie." Lizzy said.

"Thank you, mother." Angie showed them the rest of the house then she brought them outside. "This is our pool area."

"I love this." Janet said. "You could have a fun party here."

"Like, this is a dream." Denise said. "Angie, after you told us about where you lived before and how you were teased, you deserve this. I am so happy for you!"

"You are very sweet Denise. We can go back to the Arizona room. It is a little chilly." By this time, it was dark and the temperature was dropping.

They went back into the Arizona room and sat and talked. After a while Angie suggested they see if there was a movie on TV and turned the TV on. It wasn't quite late enough. The news was still on. "There should be a movie after the news. I'll turn down the volume and we can wait and see what the movie will be."

Denise changed the subject. "Angie, Paula told me you saw her dad's devil car."

"Demon." Paula said.

"OK, Demon. I never thought about it but my dad has a Mustang. I think it is called a Boss 302. At least I think that's what it says on the big black stripe on the side. It's kind of loud and it bumps around like your car Angie."

Janet then said, "My dad has a car in the garage he got when my grandfather died. He doesn't drive it though. It's some kind of Camaro. He says it is rare whatever that means."

"Do you remember anything else about it Janet? Depending on what it is it could be a very special Camaro. Did he say it has a big block in it?" Angie asked.

Janet thought for a minute. "I think so. He said they didn't make many and there is something he says is all aluminum but I can't think of anything else."

"Could it be a ZL1" Angie asked.

"That's it. That's what he said." Janet said. "What does that mean?"

"It means it is one of 69 cars built. It has an all-aluminum 427 big block engine that they say makes well over 500 horse power. This is a very special car. And he doesn't drive it?"

"No. He starts and runs it sometimes but I never saw him drive it."

"I would very much love to see this car. This is something equal to my Cuda having a HEMI."

"I don't understand what HEMI really is so I don't really understand why his car is special." Janet said.

They were all talking when out of nowhere Angie started crying, sat down and said, "Oh my God!" The tears were flowing down her face. All of the others were shocked and asked what was wrong. Angie couldn't answer yet.

Then Sherri said, "That's sick! Why would anyone do that?" Then she realized she said this out loud.

Everyone was shocked. "What is going on?" Denise said out loud.

Angie, through her tears said, "You know how I see things sometimes?"

They all almost said yes in unison.

"This is so terrible. I do not know how to describe it. I am seeing young lady being raped! And slapped! I do not want to see this. Oh God!" Angie said. "And I am feeling their terror!" She cried harder.

Sherri said, "I am seeing the same thing but I don't feel it like Angie." Sherri was crying now.

The other girls tried to console them. They knew that they both had some visions but they never knew that they were this powerful. They were kind of shocked. Gina said, "What can we do, tell us. We want to help."

"Angie said, "I do not know. There are so many. They are chained up. Some are crying for their mothers." She was shaking now.

Janet went to hug Angie but she pushed her away and said, "Get away I want my mommy." Janet was shocked! Was Angie repeating what one of the kids said?

Sherri was sitting on the couch and started kicking and swinging her arms as if she was trying to fight someone off. And she looked as though she was seeing what one of the kids saw. "Sherri, Sherri you are here with friends" Paula said sternly. "You aren't really there, you are here with us, Sherri." Finely Sherri started to calm down. Then she stopped crying.

"It was so terrible. I was there with them. I saw a few guys there. I don't want to know." She reached out for Janet and hugged her.

Angie was calming down somewhat. She was just crying as though she just saw someone killed. She reached out and Karen was there and she hugged her. "It was terrible. I do not ever want to see anything such as that again. How could anyone do that to a little kid, my God! They are doing it now, right now."

Denise said, "Like, how do you know that it is happening now Angie?"

"I saw a clock and a calendar on the wall over an old wood bench. The time was the same and the calendar had the day's X'ed off up to today. The bench is covered with lots of junk that is all dusty. It is a dirty messy place. It looks as though it had been vacant and unused for a long time. The walls are metal with peeling paint and rust. The lights are old factory lights that look like bells and there are not many. There are a myriad of dark areas which make the place look eerie, almost as if it is foggy." Angie said. "Oh, and there were 6 or 7 guys sitting at a table playing cards."

Sherri said, "She's right. It is here in Tucson. I saw something familiar but I can't place it. I didn't see enough but I know it is something I have seen before. I got a flash of an old dilapidated brick building but it was just an instant. But somehow it is familiar."

"Like, you can see all that? That's scary." Denise blurted out. "Shouldn't we go to the police? We need to tell them?"

Gina looked at her and said, "What would we tell them Denise? That Angie and Sherri saw this in their heads? They would think we were crazy. We don't know where they are either."

Denise said, "I feel so helpless. Like, we have to do something." She was very upset as well.

Angie and Sherri were finely calmed down and stopped crying. "I felt as if I was standing there watching but I could not do anything. I mean I really felt as if I was right there, in the room as if I could reach out and touch things but I could not. It felt as though if one looked my direction, they would have seen me." Angie said.

Sherri was very distraught. "I was there looking through the eyes of one kid, somehow, I know her name is Amy. I saw the guy that was trying to grab me, um her. His face was right there staring at me, well I mean the little kid. I would recognize him anywhere. He is Mexican with a big mustache and he has a scar from above his right forehead down across the right cheek."

"Angie and Sherri, how do you deal with this? I don't know if I could." Gina said.

"We do not have a choice. It is not something we asked for. The visions just come. Somehow my Aunt Maria handles it well. I did not know she had this ability until after the thing with Jason and Bradford. When I got home afterwards, I was almost hysterical. I felt as though there was something wrong with me because I felt as though I was attracting fights. My Mother assured me that it was not true. She called my Aunt Maria thinking I may want to talk to her about it since we all thought she just had strong intuition. When my mother came back from calling her, she had a strange look. She said that my aunt told her that she had been waiting for her call and she already knew what happened. It turns out that she suffered from this same kind of thing when she was going to U of A, and right about my age. She told me she did not tell anyone, even my father. I never would have guessed before that day but when she told me I felt as though I always knew. This has all been quite traumatic for me. And I know it has been for Sherri as well. We talk about this quite often.

Sherri said, "What Angie said is all true. It is so hard. I learned about it just after Jason and Bradford. I know I knew about it before then but I put it out of my head. Now when I think about it, I knew about Jason and what he was doing but I didn't want to believe it. I was thinking my imagination was just running away. But now it is so vivid and clear. And it seems that every time I see something it gets more vivid. I don't like it and I don't want it but there isn't anything I can do."

Janet looked at them for a minute and said, "You guys told us about this but I thought it was just like a little premonition or something. You know like feeling that something is going to happen. I never even considered it was like this. I am so glad you both told this to us today. I think all of us kind of understand what you see."

Denise said, "Yea, like, I know all of us will be here for you. I don't know if we can help but we will be here to support both of you. And Angie, I can't believe we just met you just over a year ago. I feel like we are so close now."

Gina, Karen and Janet all agreed, "We feel the same." They all got together and did a group hug. It was a very emotional hug.

Angie and Sherri finally calmed down. They spent some time talking about this then decided to see what was on television. They found a movie to watch. It was one of those old B rated horror movies, the kind that really aren't scary.

They all laughed together and after the movie everyone went home.

Chapter 22

Then on June 3, 1976 Angie and Sherri were shopping and Angie's visions came back. Fortunately, they were in Angie's car just getting out so they sat back in. Sherri began to see them as well. "Oh my God! The kids are sitting in a corner with their arms around their legs pulled to their chest. Some are crying hard. Someone is telling them if they don't do what they say they won't get food. I feel that a couple were raped by many guys." She was now crying.

"My God! They don't care if they hurt them. They had one kid tied down while they take turns on her." Angie was crying as well. Then her body jerked.

Sherri said, "oh no! What?"

"I am seeing through one of the guy's eyes. He is sitting drinking with other guys laughing and talking about selling the kids. "We're gonna make lots of money this time, Ha Ha. This was the perfect place. Nobody knows we're here. This abandoned building was a good idea." Angie said in a deep voice. She was upset that the guy's words came out of her mouth. "This is frightening! I spoke his words." Angie was shaking. "There are tall and scruffy weeds growing covering part of the front." Then she lost the vision. "I just want to go home Sherri. I do not want to shop anymore."

"That is fine with me. I don't want to shop either."

Angie started the CUDA and drove Sherri home then went home herself.

The next day Sherri was walking to her first class and she had a vivid vision of two of the kids in the back of an old van. Their mouths were taped closed with duct tape and they were chained to the van. They had been beaten. They had bruises all over and their faces were swollen. They were crying as the van was driving through the desert somewhere. The van stopped and the doors opened. There were two guys each grabbed one kid, unlocked the chains and dragged them out of the van. They dragged them over to a low rocky area that dropped off about 10 feet. Each one pulled out a bowie knife and reached and slashed the throat of the kid that they were holding and pushed them over the edge. The two kids' bodies bounced off of rocks as they fell. They landed on the bottom limp.

Sherri sat down on a bench to try to compose herself. She was shocked and horrified. She felt sick and was shaking. She pulled out a tissue to blot her eyes and cheeks. She thought to herself that she needs to compose herself before she goes to class. She cannot be crying. She didn't want anyone to ask questions. After a couple of minutes or so she took a deep breath and went to class.

Angie just got to the shop, walked in and went to the bathroom. As she was there, she had a vision of a metal building that was dull brown with a metal roof that was rusty. There were a few windows but they were boarded up. There was also a large double sliding door in the middle of the building and chain link fencing on each side. She knew this was the place but she could not see anything to identify where it was. She could not see anything around it as each side faded away to black. This frustrated her. Little did she know that this place was only about 4 blocks from the shop just off of Stone Ave.

That night Angie woke and looked at her clock. It was 3:00 AM. She had just had a disturbing dream. She had been fighting a guy from her Dojo and she knew she would need to kill him. It was very strange. She lay there wondering why she dreamt about fighting with this guy and why would she need to kill him. After a few minutes she closed her eyes. She was back in the dream and now she was standing in front of the abandoned building in the middle of the street looking at it. The building came alive. The upstairs windows that were boarded up turned into giant eyes and opened. The roof that covered the entry way turned into a mouth. As she stared at it, it began to laugh. It was a deep loud sinister laugh that shook the street. As it laughed the whole building began to move as if it were a giant head and alive. The raised concrete area in front of the doors turned into a giant double chin. Somehow, she knew the building knew she was looking for the kids. Then it spoke. "You will never find them in time. Ha, Ha, Ha, Ha!" Then she woke and sat up. She realized her heart was beating hard. She said to herself that it was just a dream, laid down. She tossed and turned then finally fell back to sleep.

Angie and Sherri continued to see more bits of the kids and abductors. At one point Sherri saw an address number. It was strange because Sherri saw it through the eyes of one of the kids. Angie, "I see 540 through a kid's eyes. Oh no! The girl is Amy, she is getting beaten." Sherri's eyes are tearing. "She got away for a short time. Enough time to run in front of the building but someone grabbed her. They are beating her and saying next time they will kill her. My god." Sherri was crying now. "I saw the address number 540 but I don't know the street." She and Angie looked at a map and decided that there were too many streets that could have the address 540. They still didn't have enough to go to the police. But the more they talked about it the more they believed they have seen the building where they were holding the kids. They just don't have enough information to find it.

Sherri was with her mother at the grocery store and when they turned down one isle Sherri looked at the person walking towards them. He was holding some things to buy and he glanced at her. He was Mexican with a big mustache and he had a scar from above his right forehead down across the right cheek. He was the guy she saw when she saw through the girl's eyes the other day. She didn't think she would ever forget how he looked.

Sherri's mother was looking at her and could see she immediately was terrified. She turned and saw the guy but didn't know why Sherri reacted like this. After the guy passed them and they were at the other end of the isle she said, "Sherri, what is wrong?"

Sherri was upset to the point that she almost couldn't speak. Tears were dripping down her cheeks. "Mother, that was one the guys." She was so upset she couldn't continue.

"One of what guys?"

"One of the guys that," her jaw was quivering and her speech was shaky, "I saw fighting with one of the girls."

"One of what girls?" Her mother was showing concern now.

"One of the girls Angie and I have been seeing. I haven't told you much about this. I don't want to talk here. He might hear."

"Who might hear?"

"The guy we just saw."

Sherri's mother didn't ask anymore until they got home. Then Sherri told her what she knew. Now her mother understood why Sherri was so upset.

Over the next few days, they had additional visions of the group of guys that kidnaped the kids and sometimes having sex with some of them. Sherri told Angie about seeing the guy with the scar and how it affected her. Angie was sympathetic.

The kids were malnourished and some have been beaten. They were kept locked up in chains in a room in the back of an abandoned building.

Angie had been able to cover up the visions when she was at work. She would cough or go to the bathroom. Sherri has had difficulty at school because she can't just run out of classes and go to the bathroom. She did the best that she could to not be obvious.

Angie and Sherri got together and they discussed their visions and finally thought they may be able to find the building. There are subtle clues in everything they had seen. They have been writing down each thing they see and they have been discussing these and looking on a map. Sherri said, "Angie, I keep thinking about when Amy ran outside and I saw the address. I just realized that when they grabbed her and pulled her back, I saw the building with the Tucson Warehouse and Transfer Company sign on the top and it was not far in the distance and it looked like it is on the same street. We need to find out where that building is. I remember seeing this building but I can't remember where it is."

They decided that they needed to drive around and try to find the Tucson Warehouse and Transfer Company building. They also decided to take Sherri's car because it isn't as obvious as a pink CUDA. Sherri still drove her mom's old 1965 Plymouth Valiant which wouldn't look out of place in a neighborhood that would have an abandoned building and warehouse.

On Saturday, June 5, 1976, Angie told Dominic that she had something to do with Sherri right after work Sherri would be picking her up. When Saturday came Angie washed up, changed her cloths and met Sherri in front of the shop. They left to drive around. They thought that when they find the Tucson Warehouse and Transfer Company building, they would be close to the abandoned warehouse and building that they continued to see in their visions.

Sherri turned south onto Stone from the shop. They drove past the rail road tracks and began looking. Many warehouse type buildings were around there. They turned on and drove on some streets and then on others. They drove around for maybe an hour when they decided this had to be the wrong area. They made their way to 6th Avenue and turned north. "I know I have driven past that building many times. I just cannot remember where it is. I never paid attention." Angie was becoming frustrated because she knew it must be somewhere around this area. She was certain.

They came to 6th Street and stopped for the light. It turned green and Sherri drove. Just as they crossed the intersection Angie said, "There it is!" with some excitement. "It is to the left."

Sherri turned left on 5th street and drove towards Stone. She drove slowly and they were both looking around. As she crossed Ferro Avenue Angie said as she was looking to the left, "There it is. I just saw a piece of the Tucson Warehouse and Transfer Company sign! Turn left at the next street." It was 7th Avenue. As Sherri was turning, she slammed on the brakes and stopped.

"They're here. I feel it." Sherri said.

"I feel it as well. Drive a little more." Angie said sounding a little indignant. Sherri drove slowly. When they passed the second building from the corner Angie watched it as Sherri passed it. "This is the house, Sherri. I recognize it from my dream."

"Your dream? What dream? You never said anything about a dream."

"Maybe I did not tell you. It was more of a nightmare." Sherri was still driving. "First, I was fighting a guy from my Dojo and

I was feeling that I would need to kill him and I woke. When I fell asleep again, I was standing in the street in front of that building and the windows on the top turned into eyes. And the roof over the doors turned into a mouth. Then the concrete landing in front of the doors turned into a double chin. It said in a deep tone, "you are too late" and laughed Ha, Ha, Ha and the ground shook. I woke spooked and sweaty. That is the house."

Sherri turned left again on 6th Street then left again onto Ferro Avenue. She was still driving very slowly. When they got almost to 5th street, they saw a metal warehouse type building that was dull gray. Sherri shivered. "Angie, this is where they are. I feel it."

"I do as well. They are here. They are using the building in front as well." Angie said.

Sherri continued to drive and turned onto 5th street again and stopped.

"Why did you stop?"

"Aren't you scared Angie?"

"Of course I am, but I am more afraid of what these kids are going through. Besides we are just driving past and just looking."

"I guess that's OK."

"If we just drive past how would anyone know we were looking for this place?

"I guess you are right." Sherri turned left onto 7th Ave. and drove slowly. They looked closer at the building. It was a dilapidated building that looked as if it used to be a house or maybe a duplex. It was built from light colored bricks and had two front doors, well used to have doors but they were covered with plywood. There were large cracks in the bricks and looked as though it could easily break apart and fall. There was an upstairs but the windows were covered with plywood as well. There was an address sign but it had fallen down and was laying on the concrete next to one of the doors. It said 540. "It doesn't look like anyone has been in this building for years."

"They are in there or the warehouse behind it. I know they are. I feel that as well. This is so odd. It is just a few blocks from the shop."

"I think you are right. Seeing it makes me shiver. And the big doors on the side of the metal building look like the doors I saw in the vision but I think I saw the inside of them." She continued driving to the end of the block. "Do you think we can tell the police about this?"

"Well, we have not seen anything that looks suspicious so what would we say. We have to see something first then we can tell the police."

"How are we going to see something?" Sherri asked.

"We can look in the side windows or anywhere else we could see inside." Angie said.

"You mean get out of the car and sneak around? I couldn't do that. Besides it is light out and everyone could see us."

"We can come back after it gets dark and I will go and look around. You can watch in case anything happens."

"What do you mean in case anything happens?"

"Well, I do not know, anything. If I am reasonably careful no one should know that I am even there."

"I don't know if this is a good idea. If this is the place what if someone comes out and sees us?"

"No one will see us. We have to do this for the kids. I feel that something is about to happen. It feels bad. We need to do it tonight." Angie said.

"If you say so. I am just scared."

"It will be Ok Sherri, you will see."

"I wish I had the confidence you do."

"We can go somewhere we can sit down and wait, OK? How about Tucson Burger. We can wait there until it gets dark. It is just after 7:00 and it will be dark soon." Angie said. "There is one on 1ˢᵗ and Grant."

They drove to Tucson Burger but neither were hungry. This whole thing killed their appetites. They each got a drink although neither actually drank much, they just sipped a little.

Angie and Sherri drove back after it was dark. Angie said, "Pull up to the corner, I will get out there." Sherri stopped and Angie got out. She bent over and looked in the window and said, "I am going to look around. If I am not back in two minutes go to the police."

"How will I know if something happens? I can't see much."

"Pull up so you can see in between the buildings and wait there. I just want to look into a few windows. If you do not see me something happened. Then go to the police and make certain you ask for Lieutenant Edwards." She turned and walked away.

Sherri was afraid. Her hands were sweating and she was shaking a little. She didn't have a good feeling about this.

Angie walked back through the overgrown weeds in between the buildings and she peeked into each window. Then she felt a gun pushed into the middle of her back. She immediately used one of the moves she recently learned. She spun and grabbed the barrel of the gun with her right hand, stepped aside out from the front of the barrel. Then she grabbed the back of the gun with her other hand, twisted it up and pulled it away. This always breaks the finger that is on the trigger. She tossed the gun down. He screamed, "Ahhh!" when his finger broke. Then he tried to punch her and she blocked and grabbed his wrist and rammed her left arm into his elbow breaking it. She used the V between her thumb and fore finger and hit him in the neck knocking him down onto his back. When he was on the ground, she cocked her right arm and fist back and punched him full force on the throat three times crushing his larynx. She left him to die. This only took seconds.

She stood again and continued looking. Then another guy with a shot gun came up behind her. "Walk to the door or I will shoot." He kind of pushed her with the barrel. "Open and walk through the door."

As soon as she was inside, she used another new move. She spun and grabbed the barrel of the shot gun, pushed it away and kicked the side of his ribs with her foot. This cracked his ribs and then she licked his knee and broke it. He fell onto the floor on his back. As he fell, she pulled the shot gun from him. She took the shot gun, swung it and hit him in the face and head repeatedly with the butt until he wasn't moving. She tossed the shot gun down. Again, this only took seconds. She turned and continued to explore the place.

While this was happening, Sherri thought she saw Angie do something to someone and it looked as though she was squatting, then she stood again. She was becoming worried. Then she could see Angie again but then she saw someone with a shot gun. She immediately started her car and drove to the nearest police station. She ran in frantically. "My friend and I were looking at an old abandoned building and someone came up behind her with a shot gun and put it to her back. My friend is Angie Tucci and she said I should make sure you radio Lieutenant Edwards. We are positive this is where the guys are that have been abducting young girls."

"Calm down Ma'am. I will call someone to talk to you." The officer at the window said.

"You have to call Lieutenant Edwards. She will kill everyone there. We need to get back before this happens. This is an emergency!" Sherri was trying to get this officer to understand that this was not a good situation. Please radio Lieutenant Edwards. He knows about my friend and me. She is the one that killed the three guys that broke in to her father's shop a while back."

"Angie Tucci?"

"Yes."

The officer got on the police radio and called Lieutenant Edwards.

"Lieutenant there is a young girl here that is frantic and saying some girl is going to kill everybody at an abandoned building."

"What are their names?"

"What is you name Ma'am?"

"Sherri and my friend is Angie Tucci."

Lieutenant Edwards heard her and immediately said, "Oh shit! Ask her the address." He knew that if this was the place where they were holding the abducted girls there would be just bodies if they didn't get there fast enough.

Sherri blurted out, "740 7th Avenue."

Lieutenant Edwards screamed, "We need every available car there and probably every ambulance. Now!"

The officer put out a call for every available car and stated the address. Then the officer called for an ambulance.

While she was doing that Sherri ran to her car and drove back to the building. As she was driving, she heard sirens from all directions.

Angie explored the warehouse and found a plywood door with a simple latch made from a lock hasp with a screw through it to lock it. She slowly opened it. Inside were the kids. They were all sitting on the floor cowered at the back of the room. She stepped inside and whispered, "I will be back when it is safe. I will get you out of here." She backed out and carefully closed the door.

The kids began whispering to each other, "Was that an Angel?" Since they were in a dark room the outside light only showed her shape and it appeared that she was glowing. They were all in aww. They continued to sit still.

Angie looked around and then heard some muffled laughing and screaming. The laughing sounded was obviously a guy and the screaming sounded like a little kid. She was both worried for the kid and angry about what they were doing. She followed the laughing and screaming and found a door to a room and carefully cracked it open. She saw this big fat guy on top of a young girl maybe 10 or 12 years old raping her. She immediately swung the door open, rushed in and kicked the guy in his side. It was hard enough to knock him off of the bed onto the floor. The guy got up and rubbed his side and said, "Who the hell are you?"

Angie said, "I am your worst nightmare!"

Once he was standing, he went to grab her and she kicked him in the chest and it knocked him back. She did not see that when he grabbed at her he had grabbed her cross. He let go and it fell on the bed but Angie did not see that. He was a big guy with a big belly and went to punch her she grabbed his arm and by this time she is going all out. She broke his arm then kicked him in the ribs a few times, then broke his knee. He fell over onto his side. He was a little delirious. He tried to stand but couldn't because of the broken knee. Then he began to scream for help. She did a kick to his jaw which severely broke it and his screaming stopped. Angie jumped up and came down with her right foot in his neck. This crushed his larynx. He instantly could not breathe. All that could be heard was gurgling. She just left him there. She turned to the girl, "Stay here. You will be safe for now. I will be back with help."

The girl sat up and she saw a gold cross and chain on the edge of the bed.

She wiped the tears from her face. Her cloths were partially torn but she was able to pull them on. Then she put the cross in one of the pockets and sat on the bed. She hurt all over and she was bleeding from the rape. Her face was black and blue, her arms are bruised from beatings. She knew the cross was from the girl that stopped the guy raping her.

Angie got a few feet from the door and was met by two guys. She kicked the first in the chest and he fell back onto the floor. The other went and grabbed her around the arms. She immediately pushed back, reached behind and wrapped her arm around his neck and then bent forward and flipped the guy over and on to his back. Then before he could move, she jumped and cocked her leg came down on his neck multiple times crushing his throat. The other guy said, "Angie? What the hell are you doing here?"

"Pablo?" Angie was shocked because he is one of the guys that trains at her Dojo. "I did not expect to see anyone I know here."

I got 6 years of training." He tried to engage her. She did not allow him to kick. She stopped his kick using a Maui Thai move. She engaged him. He tried to kick her again and she used the same Maui Thai move and stopped his leg and she moved in and hit him hard in his stomach with her knee then she kicked him in the ribs multiple times using the shin of her leg. He stepped back wheezing obviously from cracked ribs. He looked angry. "You're gonna die! Our sensei treats you like you are special, you're not." He tried to kick her with a straight kick but it was slow due to the cracked ribs. She caught his leg under her arm and came down with her elbow 4 or 5 times on top of his leg. This damaged the muscle. Then she kicked him in the groin multiple times. She dropped his leg and he stumbled back holding his groin and kind of hopping on one leg. He looked scared. Then he pulled out a gun.

As soon as Angie saw it, she did a full power reverse 360 degree roundhouse which hit him in the side of the head and he went down and his head slammed and bounced off of the floor and hit the floor again with a loud bang. The gun fell out of his hand and he laid there limp. She looked at him and whispered, "So much for your 6 years of training."

She turned and took a few steps and heard someone say "stop right there." He was pointing a shotgun at her and he was only a few feet away. Without thinking she stepped forward and grabbed the barrel and pulled it aside and held it then kicked him 3 of 4 times in the ribs as she pulled the gun away. He was now bent over slightly laboring to breathe. She spun around with the shotgun and hit him in the side of the head with the side of the butt of the shotgun so hard the wood stock cracked. She tossed the gun aside as he fell on his face. She immediately jumped on his back, grabbed his head and pulled it back hard and quick which broke his neck.

She walked around a large wooden crate and the lights came on. There were six guys there. Without the slightest hesitation she ran and engaged the first with a side kick to the throat and he went down choking. She ran towards the next guy jumped and kicked in the chest and he fell backwards into a window breaking the glass. A piece stabbed the back of his neck. She continued with her elbow down on his chest and you could see the glass come out the front of his neck.

Two others came at her and she did what looked resembled a cartwheel and kicked them both in the face, one right after the other and they fell back. She jumped back up. Another came at her and tried to kick her and she stopped it with the same Maui Thai move using her foot then she stepped in and hit him in the jaw with a forward roundhouse and broke his jaw. The other two got up and came back at her again and she kicked one guy in the side of the knee and broke it and he fell. For the other she spun around and hit him with a Rican and broke his nose. She continued the spin and hit him in the stomach with her knee. As he bent over, she grabbed his head and slammed his face into her knee. He stood and backed up, his nose was broken and dripping blood, his mouth is bleeding. Angie did a straight kick to the chest and he hit the wall. He was barely able to stand and she did a forward roundhouse to his head and he went down face first. He didn't move. Then the guy whose knee she broke grabbed a pipe that was laying on the floor and started crawling towards her. She just did a reverse 360 degree roundhouse to his shoulder. His body flipped over on to his back and she grabbed the pipe and thrust it through his chest and he went limp.

There wasn't anyone else at the moment. But as she turned to go back to the kids and another jumped out from behind some crates and he engaged her. This guy knew some martial arts. She blocked and kicked him, he backed off. He tried a round house and she just ducked. He tried to kick again and she stopped it with the Maui Thai move then stepped in and spun and broke his jaw with her elbow then continued with her knee to his ribs. He stepped back. His jaw is crooked and his ribs are cracked. She did some oblique kicks to his leg and he almost fell. Then she stepped back and took a running start, jumped and kicked him in the chest and he fell back onto a pile of broken wood and a piece of wood came through his chest.

She turned and there was another. Just then Lt Edwards came through the door with his gun drawn. He saw her punch the guy then kick him then she grabbed his head pulled hard and fast breaking his neck. She threw him to the side as if he was a piece of trash. He fell dead. She turned just as someone with a gun from behind a cabinet shot Lieutenant Edwards and hit him in his side. He fell down.

"Lieutenant!" Angie screamed.

He wasn't dead, just hurt. He waved her on.

She turned and kicked the guy's wrist so hard that the cabinet fell over. This broke his wrist and the gun flew out of his hand.

Then she got into her stance and kicked and punched him over and over so fast he was not able to put his other arm up to block. She continued punching him kicking as he was stepping backwards. Finally, she stopped for a second. The guy was barely standing. He was breathing hard and bloody. She said, "This is for Lieutenant Edwards, asshole. She spun and did a 360-degree roundhouse. She hit this guy so hard that he flew to the side. His head slammed into a wood beam and sounded as though it was hit with a sledge hammer and he bounced back onto a pile of broken wood on the floor dead. By this point she was breathing hard and covered with sweat. She ran back to Lieutenant Edwards and ripped a piece of shirt from the closest guy, wadded it up and told him to hold it tight against the wound to stop the bleeding.

When she stood someone from behind her put a piece of rope around her neck and tried to choke her. She tried to hit him with her elbow a few times but could not contact. Then she stepped to the right to face the wall and ran up the wall using his body as a brace and flipped over the guy with the momentum and landed behind him which freed her from the rope.

Lieutenant Edwards was shocked to see this move.

She cocked her right arm back and swung and hit him in the head with her fist. Then she did the same with her left arm an instant later. Then she cocked her right arm back and screamed, "AAAHHHH" as she punched him with all of her strength in the neck. As she was doing this he screamed. He fell back choking. By the time other police arrived he had choked to death.

They heard sirens and soon there were police everywhere. Paramedics came in she helped Lieutenant Edwards onto a gurney. This was the first time Lieutenant Edwards was able to ask anything of Angie and he struggled, "Did you leave anybody for us?"

"Just the young ladies sir. And some have been beaten and raped and require medical care. There is a girl that was being raped when I arrived. I am positive she needs medical care. There are 25-30 kids in a room in back. I can show the officers where it is."

Lieutenant Edwards said to one of the officers, "Angie will show you where all of the kids are." Then he reached for his radio and called for more ambulances.

The officer followed Angie. She pulled open the plywood door and he saw all of the girls. They looked relieved when they saw Angie and the officer. One said loud, "There's the Angel!"

Angie left them and went to the room where the girl that was being raped when she arrived. She opened the door and said, "It is safe now. The police are here and ambulances are coming." She took her hand and walked with her slowly to the gurney that Lieutenant Edwards was on. Angie could see that the girl was in pain and was crying. Tears were dripping off of her face. There were many officers bringing the other girls to the door. Angie tried to leave the girl with the officers but she would not let go of her hand.

Lieutenant Edwards said, "Angie, I can't believe what I just saw. They didn't have a chance. You are so fast I think I would have needed to film this and play it back in slow motion just to see what you actually did. Nobody got a chance to hit you. And you fought so many guys at the same time." He tried to move and grimaced hard. "You have changed your fighting. It's like you are a different person."

Angie said, "Sir I have had some special training in the last few months. This is why I fought differently. My Sensei said he needed to teach me different techniques because sooner or later I will come up against someone who can fight like me and that would not be a good thing."

Sargent Hernandez walked up to talk to Lieutenant Edwards looking shocked, "What happened to all of these guys here?" He looked around the place and there were dead guys all over that appear beaten to death.

"Angie did this Sargent."

"What? C'mon. You expect me to believe that Angie did this herself?"

"Yes Sargent. Remember when I told you she looks like Joe Singso with her head?"

"That's unbelievable! I still think she doesn't look like she could fight anyone."

"One day you will see. Will you deal with the news people please? I am not in the condition to talk to them and I do not want to be on TV like this."

"Yes sir, I will talk to them." Sargent Hernandez replied. He looked at Angie and saw that she was soaked with sweat.

"Angie," Lieutenant Edwards continued, "you should have at least told me what was going on here. You should not have done this by yourself."

"Sir, I was not planning on doing this at all. I just wanted to verify this was the correct place before I told you. And one of them came up behind me and put his gun against my back. This is where it began. I took him out in seconds. Then another came and put a shot gun in my back. Then everything began happening. I did not think you would believe me if I told you I saw this in my head."

"You mean like with those two guys that killed those girls?"

"Yes sir. Just as what I saw those two guys do and where they hid the gun. We, Sherri, my Aunt Maria and I have been seeing visions of things here, in our minds eye."

"Your Aunt Maria too? Lieutenant Edwards said not expecting an answer.

The news people were all over trying to get information from anyone that would talk to them. The police would not let them inside and that was where Angie, the girl and Lieutenant Edwards were.

A paramedic walked up and wanted to clean up and check the girl but she hugged Angie with both arms and would not let go.

Angie continued, "This, however, was more vivid. This was so vivid that we saw some things through the kid's eyes and through one of the guy's eyes. We could not verify where this was happening from the things we saw. The only thing that we saw that was definite was the address number but that could have been anywhere in the city. We drove around and when we came upon this building, Sherri and I felt as though it was correct. But I did not want to send you to the wrong place. We were fairly certain this was it but I wanted to verify first. I just intended to look into the windows to verify. I did not expect anyone to come up behind me. Much of what we see is vague which makes it is difficult to know for sure." Angie turned and pealed the girls hand off of her waist and took it in hers. The girl just had tears running down black and blue and swollen cheeks and had her head down. Her long blonde hair was tangled and dirty. Angie walked along with the girl and the paramedic to the ambulance. The paramedic helped the girl into the ambulance but she wouldn't let go of Angie's hand. She wanted Angie to go with. She began to cry again. Angie got into the ambulance with her. They also put Lieutenant Edwards in the ambulance and Angie rode to the hospital with both of them. When they got to St. Mary's Emergency Lieutenant Edwards told them to let Angie go with the girl.

As usual, the media was all over asking questions. This was a big thing so it was a news story cut into whatever show was on.

Johnny was watching and when he found out that Angie was involved, he went insanely crazy. He kicked his chairs and his table; he threw things around. He was so angry he felt like tearing something apart. "Dam her! Again? That bitch always gets on TV! It should be me dam it!" He was so angry he felt he could tear her apart if she were there now. He called his friend Andy and Andy reminded him she killed his brother at her dad's shop. Andy wanted her dead as well.

At this same time Dominic and Lizzy were relaxing watching TV and saw the news break. Their eyes were wide open when they saw someone getting into an ambulance with a young girl and a police officer on a gurney that looked as if it was Angie. "What! Is that Angie!" Dominic said. They listened to the reporter saying that an unknown young woman fought at least 10 maybe more guys freeing at least twenty five young girls from a prostitution/slavery ring. Had they seen Angie get into the ambulance in the background?

Just them the phone rang and Lizzy got up to answer. "Hello?"

"Lizzy, this is Maria. Angie was just involved with something involving young girls that had been abducted. I am watching it on the news now. I saw her fighting with multiple guys then turned on the TV and saw the news. She is OK but very upset. I feel her crying about one of the young girls. That is all I know."

"We just saw it in TV. We thought it looked as though Angie was getting into an ambulance."

They recently had a new thing added to their phone line called Call Waiting. This allowed them to put the current call on hold and answer another. The phone beeped. "Can you hold on Maria? I have another call."

"Alright."

"Hello?"

It was Lilly, her sister. "Lizzy we were watching TV and the news came on it looked as though Angie was getting into an ambulance. They did not say who it was but judging by them stating a young woman fought at least to men we figured it had to be her." Lilly was frantic. "I hope she is OK. I'm worried because she got into an ambulance."

"We were watching the same thing, Lilly. Can you hold, I have Maria on the other line."

"OK."

"Hello, Maria?"

"I am here."

"Lilly is on the other line. Could I ask you to call my mother please Maria? I may be awhile with Lilly."

"Oh course. I will call her now, bye."

"Hello Lilly?"

"I am still here."

"Maria called shortly before you did. Remember I was telling you about how Maria, Angie and her friend Sherri see things?"

"Yes."

"She called to tell me that it was Angie and she is alright except she is very upset about a young girl. I am guessing it was the one also getting into the ambulance."

"How did she know? Oh wait, you just said she saw or sensed it, right?"

"Yes Lilly." They talked for a while then hung up. No sooner than she hung up the phone rang again. It was her mother.

"Hello Elisabeth, I just got off the phone with Maria. I think I understand a little now what she, Angelina and Sherri can do. Although somehow it doesn't seem real."

"Hello mother. I agree. I don't understand it." They talked for another ten minutes or so and hung up. She turned to go back to sit with Dominic.

"Have they said anything else?"

"No, just that there were thirty one young girls and fifteen guys. They said all of the guys were dead! They also said Lieutenant Edwards was shot! But is not life threatening."

"Did they say anything about where everyone was taken?"

"They said due to the volume of injuries they were taken to various area hospitals. That's all. Hopefully Angie will call and let us know how she is."

"I hope so. I'm worried Dominic. How did she get involved in this? I know she; Maria and Sherri were seeing things. But how did she end up needing to fight? She said she would tell Lieutenant Edwards if she saw anything."

"I do not know honey. I do not know."

Angie stood there while they cleaned the girl up and bandaged her. They also gave her ice packs for her face. The girl wasn't talking and they asked Angie questions. She said that she could not answer. She told them she just rescued her and did not know her. They put in an IV of ringers; gave her some pain medication and connected her to a heart monitor. Angie waited at the side of the bed. The girl fell asleep. Angie had tears running down her face. She was feeling bad because she didn't get there before that guy raped her.

Angie waited there for a few hours in Acute Care watching the girl from the bedside, tears running down her face. She felt terrible. This girl was bruised all over her face. They had beaten her. Angie thought, "I wonder if she was the girl that ran and got caught." She kept wishing she could have stopped the man before he raped her. Tears continued dripping from her face. Her eye liner had run down her cheeks and she looked terrible. A nurse came up to her and gave her a cloth to wipe her face with. She pointed out a bathroom where Angie could go to clean up. Afterwards Angie came right back to watch over the girl. She reached and picked up the girl's hand and held it in both of hers.

The girl's parents had been notified and they had come. The girl's mother asked the nurse, "Who is the woman standing at the curtain watching our daughter?"

The nurse told them, "One of the officers told me she was the one that saved your daughter and all of the others. According to him she fought and killed 15 guys with her bare hands and saved almost 30 other kids as well."

The mother was shocked, "15 guys? Really? That is un-believable. Do you know her name?"

"I was told it is Angelina."

"Thank you." The mother said.

They walked to the bed and Angie turned and saw them. They saw that she was crying and holding their daughter's hand. The mother said, "They told us you saved our baby. I don't know how to thank you." She reached out to hug Angie.

Angie put the girl's hand down and said through her tears, "I am so so sorry I did not arrive in time to stop the man from raping her and beating her." And she cried harder.

"Honey, you saved her, that's all that matters. You are a hero. They say you saved thirty more kids and you fought fifteen guys doing it. You are more than a hero."

"I do not feel as if I am a hero. Some of the other kids were raped as well. I did not act soon enough. I did not see them soon enough. I feel as though it is my fault." And she cried more.

"What do you mean by you did not see them soon enough?"

"Sometimes I see things in my head and that was how I found them. I should have seen them sooner."

"Are you saying you are psychic?"

"More or less Ma'am. I feel as though it is my fault for not seeing this sooner."

"Don't feel bad dear, you saved all of them." She and her husband went around to the other side of the bed.

The mother took the girl's other hand and she opened her eyes and looked at her mother.

"Mom? Is that really you?" the girl asked.

"Yes sweetheart, I am here with your father."

"It's really you? I'm not dreaming?"

"Yes, it is really me." She had tears in her eyes.

"Where is the girl that saved me? I have something for her." The girl said sounding strained, weak and raspy, her throat was sore from screaming and she was groggy from the pain medication.

This was the first time Angie heard her speak.

Her mother was surprised. "She is right here Amy. She has been watching over you since they brought you here. Her name is Angelina.

She looked to the other side of the bed and said, "I'm Amy, you saved me. I have something for you." She desperately wanted to give Angie the cross. She knew it belonged to her. "Mom, can you go in the bag with my cloths and get what's in my pants pocket?"

Angie was surprised. She thought, 'What could she possibly have for me?'

Amy's mother looked in the bag and pulled out a gold cross on a chain that looked antique. She looked at it strangely and brought it to Amy. She took it in her hand and reached for Angie's hand with her other hand. She put it into Angie's hand and pushed Angie's fingers closed. "This got pulled off of you when you fought the guy."

Angie opened her fingers and immediately felt her neck. She hadn't noticed it was gone. She looked completely shocked then she smiled and said, "Thank you Amy. I did not know I lost this. Thank you so much." More tears rolled down her cheeks.

Amy's mother looked at Angie and said, "There must be some history behind that cross. It looks like you have a deep attachment. I see it in your expression."

"Yes Ma'am. I am the fifth generation of Tucci's to wear this cross. It is very dear to me. I would have been heartbroken if it had been lost."

"Tucci? Angelina Tucci? Why do I know that name?" Amy's father asked. He looked as though he was thinking very hard. "You're the girl that fought and killed the three guys that broke into your dad's shop and attacked you, Angelina Tucci. You're her? I would have expected a tom girl type. But you are beautiful. You did that?"

"And she fought fifteen guys today saving all of the kids." Amy's mother said.

"How did you do that? I am shocked." Amy's father asked.

"Sir I am a 4th degree black belt in Taekwondo, Aikido and Karate and I have recently been learning Muay Thai and Shaolin Kung Fu. I have been studying since I was 7 years old."

"The news said that. They didn't show any pictures of you so I just expected someone big. I seem to remember there was something else," he thought for a minute. "Yes, you stopped those guys that murdered those girls and buried them in the desert too. And now that I'm thinking about it, wasn't there something maybe about year ago? You fought that jock from school that tried to kill you! You are a hero, more than once."

"Yes, that was me sir. People have told me a few times in the past that I was a hero. I did not feel as though I was a hero then as well as now, sir."

"You're my hero Angelina" Amy said. "You saved all of us. We should all call you Saving Angelina cus you save everyone."

"I do not know what to say Amy. But thank you. It makes me feel happy that you are doing well and you are speaking again. When we arrived here you would not say anything. You are a very strong young lady. I believe my friend saw what they did to you through your eyes. Now that you parents are here, I will leave you. I could not leave you alone until they arrived."

The phone rang again. "Hello?"

"Hello Lizzy, this is Carol. Carol Winston."

"Carol, how are you? Well, that likely is not a proper question right now. Have you heard from Sherri?"

"That is why I called. I just talked to Sherri. She said they are both fine but Angie is very upset about what happened to the girls. Particularly the one that she got onto the ambulance with. Evidently this girl wouldn't speak to anyone or let go of Angie. Sherri said Angie rode to the hospital with her. She said she needed to bring Angie to her car when they leave the hospital but she was not certain when that would be."

"Thank you so much for calling Carol. I have been worried about this whole thing. How is Sherri doing?"

"She sounded fine. She said that she was just very tired. But she was worried about Angie because she is so upset. Maybe it is due to what happened and likely that she is tired as well."

"Thank you again Carol. We will talk soon, alright? Thank you so much for calling."

"You are welcome, Lizzy. Bye."

Angie was about to leave when Sherri walked up. She had just called her mother to tell her what happened.

"Sherri, could you please come here?"

"Ok." She walked up to the bed.

"Sherri, I wish to present Amy. Amy this is my friend Sherri. She saw some things that I did not and together we found you. I believe she saw through your eyes. She saw what they did to you."

"I am so sorry for what happened to you Amy. I cried after I saw. You fought off one of those guys, you are a very brave young lady."

"You are also psychic?" Amy's mother asked.

"Yes ma'am."

"Thank you, Sherri." Amy's mother walked to Sherri and hugged her. She was teary-eyed again.

And thank you for helping to find me. I think all of the other kids would feel the same. You are a hero too." Amy said.

"Me, a hero? I just helped. Angie saved you."

Amy's mother said, "Sherri, you are as much a hero as Angelina. The two of you worked together and without you Angelina may not have found them at all."

"I don't feel like a hero. I just did what I had to do," She stopped and looked like she was thinking. "um, ah," She thought for an additional minute and looked at Angie, "now I sound like you Angie. Now I understand how you feel."

Angie said, "Maybe your father was correct when he said heroes do not usually feel as though they are heroes because they feel as though they just did what they had to do. I did what I had to do to stop those guys from continuing to hurt these young ladies. Maybe that does make me a hero." Angie looked at Amy's parents, "We will leave now that you both are here. It was nice to meet you, and thank you again for returning my cross, Amy. In a way you are a hero to me. And I hope you heal fast."

Amy reached out and grabbed Angie's hand and squeezed. It hurt her hand but she wanted to touch her again because she kind of felt that Angie was a dream and feeling the warmth of her hand would make her real. "Bye Angelina and Sherri."

Angie and Sherri left. "Sherri, I wish to visit Lieutenant Edwards."

"Okay. What happened to all of the other kids? Are they here?"

"I was told they were brought elsewhere because they did not have the space for all of them but I was not told where."

They walked to the Lieutenant's room. The door was open so they knocked on it as they walked in. "Hello Lieutenant. How are you feeling sir?"

"It's nice to see the two of you. I am fine, thank you. How is the girl doing?"

"She is doing quite well for someone that young having just been raped and beaten. Her name is Amy. She is a very sweet girl. We just met her parents as well. I did not know that I lost my cross fighting the guy that was raping her. I would have been very upset if I would have known that. She picked it up and gave it back to me sir."

"That was nice of her. Do you know you may have saved her life? We believe those dead kids that were found in Cochise County were the work of those guys. We believe that the ones that fought hard were killed and you told me that Sherri saw her fight through her eyes. They may have killed her after they were finished. So, the two of you may both be heroes for more than you think."

"Thank you, sir. We just did what we needed to do so we don't feel as if we are heroes. I just wanted to check up on you. How long do they expect you to be here?"

"They said I will be released tomorrow."

"I wanted to send you flowers sir. Now I will not be able to have them brought here."

"Angelina, you are an amazing woman. I am proud to know you. And Sherri, I am beginning to see that you are just as amazing too. But you don't need to buy me flowers."

"I do not need to buy them; I truly want to sir. I wanted to cheer you up."

"Angie, just seeing you cheers me up. Thank you for checking up on me. I look forward to seeing the both of you again. Hopefully it will be in a better situation. Thank you for the thought though."

"Thank you, sir." Angie said.

"Thank you, sir." Sherri said.

As they walked out of the room Sherri told Angie that she called home. Sherri took Angie to the shop to get her car and then went home. Angie went home as well.

The following Friday night Angie got together with her friends and they went to the Bum Steer. She wasn't really in a party mood. She was still upset that she didn't find all of the girls before some of them were raped. Gina and Sherri were able to talk her into coming out with them.

They sat at the usual table and ordered. Paula sat next to Angie. Angie just ordered cola. "Angie, you're not going to have beer?" Paula asked.

"I am not in the mood for beer, I am sorry."

"You don't need to be sorry Angie. C'mon you did such a good thing saving all of those kids. You can't be happy at least for that?" Paula was worried that maybe there was something wrong with Angie. It was almost a week and she was still depressed and she didn't understand why. She put her arm around Angie and hugged her. "Angie, I wish there was something we could do to make you feel better."

"I will be alright. I believe it will just take some time. That is all. I do not want to make you feel down. I am sorry."

"Angie, don't feel sorry. We wanted you to come tonight so we could maybe cheer you up some." She thought for a minute. "Hey, remember when we were at Tucson Burger and you told us that joke right when Denise was sipping her cola? Remember she laughed and some went up her nose and we all laughed so hard?" This was all she could think of. She really wanted to see Angie at least smile.

"That was funny" Angie said. She looked like she smiled a little.

"Hey Gina? Remember when Angie told that joke and Denise's cola went up her nose?"

Gina turned and laughed. "That was so funny!"

Denise overheard and laughed. "But it actually hurt. But I couldn't stop laughing."

Sherri, Karen and Janet overheard and laughed too. Angie did smile. It was the first smile they all saw all night. Angie just sat at the table. She didn't dance or sing karaoke either. All of her friends were worried about her. A few of the guys that always talked to her tried but she really didn't want to talk either.

They ended up leaving earlier than they usually did.

Chapter 23

They released the Lieutenant the next day but he could not return to work for a while. A week later while he was still off on medical leave, he received a phone call from Mrs. Carver from Department of Health. He was relaxing at home when the phone rang. "Hello, Lieutenant Edwards, how can I help you?"

"Hello Lieutenant, this is Mrs. Carver from Department of Health. I wanted to give you an update on the kids. All but one has been released from the hospital. The one, Amy, they say will be released tomorrow. We have found and contacted all of the parents and we have arranged for them to come to pick up each girl on the afternoon of June 25 but the girls have a request."

"What would that be ma'am?"

"They want to know if there was a way for them to thank Angelina and Sherri for saving them. Some of them said they wanted to see them so they can see that they are real. Some still think Angelina is an angel and not a real person. Do you think that would be possible?"

"I think I could set something up. Angelina's father is a good friend. I can call him and see what we could do. Did you know that Angelina works as a mechanic for her father in his auto repair shop?"

"Really a mechanic? Her? Really? I didn't know that."

"Yes, she has many talents. How about this, I think I could set up a time where the kids could go to Angelina's father's shop and surprise her. Do you think they would like that?"

"I think they would love it! They all say that when they first saw Angelina, they thought she was an angel. They didn't believe someone would come to save them. And a few still don't think she is a real person."

"Great! I'll call Dominic now. When do you think is a good time and day?"

"The parents are coming on Friday so maybe they could come as well. So Maybe Friday about 2 PM?"

"OK Ma'am. I'll call Dominic and I will get back with you."

"Thank you, Lieutenant. Talk to you soon."

As soon as he hung up, he dialed Dominic at the shop. "Hello, Dom's Automotive and Performance Center, this is Dominic. How can I help you?"

"Dominic, how are you?"

"I am doing well, how are you Lieutenant, Angie told me you were shot?"

"I am much better. I'm still very sore though. Dominic, I have a favor to ask."

"A favor? Anything lieutenant. How can I help?"

"I just got off of a call from Department of Health and they were wondering if there was a way that all of those kids that Angie and Sherri saved could come and thank them in person. I suggested they come to the shop and do it there. Would this be possible?"

"Of course, sir. I believe Angie would love that. She is still upset that she did not find them sooner. She feels as though she should have known before the girl was raped. We have been telling her it is not any fault of hers but it does not seem to be helping. This might just be what it takes to bring up her spirits, sir. Do you want to do it a surprise?"

"That is exactly what I was thinking Dominic. Department of Health suggested Friday afternoon about 2PM. They said that the little girl, Amy that Angie was so worried about, would be there as well along with all of the parents."

"I think that would be great, sir. Go ahead and set it up. I will not say anything about it. And I will have Lizzy talk to Sherri. I will be looking forward to see Angie's response."

"Ok Dominic. I will set it up. Nice talking with you."

It is good to hear from you as well sir and I am glad you are doing better." He hung up.

He thought that he should pick up some water for this to give to everyone. He was thinking this was going to really bring up Angie's spirits.

That night when they laid in bed Dominic turned to Lizzy and said, "I talked to Lieutenant Edwards today."

"How is he feeling?"

"He said much better. He called to ask a favor."

"What would that be Dom?"

He wanted to know if all of the girls that Angie and Sherri saved could come and thank them in person."

"How wonderful! That may be just what Angie needs to finally get over this. O talked to Maria today. She said that she feels strongly that this is from Angie's maternal instinct. She said it is her internal drive to protect the young and since this is the girl that would not let go of her she developed this bond."

"He is going to set it up for Friday afternoon at 2 and they will all come to the shop and surprise her. I was thinking that possibly we could get Sherri there."

"Dominic, Angie will be so surprised!"

"I thought you may want to be there to see as well."

"I would love to see her reaction. How about Sherri?

"I was hoping you could call her and see if she could be there as well. But I wish to keep it a surprise for Angie. Maybe she would be able to come to the shop shortly before and wait in my office.

"I will call her tomorrow. And I will bake cupcakes for everyone at the shop and then have lunch with everyone. I'll just say that I baked cupcakes and wanted to bring them for everyone. That can be my excuse to be there."

The next day Lizzy called Sherri and Sherri answered. She explained what was going to happen and Sherri thought it was a wonderful idea and also thought that it would bring Angie out of her funk, as she called it. Sherri said that she could come after her last class which would get her there on time.

The next morning Dominic talked to Jack about it and he would look for Sherri on Friday and get her into the office so Angie doesn't see her.

Friday came and everyone was working as usual. Lizzy arrived about thirty minutes prior to lunch and brought chocolate decorated cupcakes. She, Dominic and Jack sat with everyone to eat and then she served the cupcakes. Angie asked, "Mother? What is the occasion for the cupcakes?"

"I just felt like making them and thought everyone would enjoy them. That is all."

"Mother, you are very thoughtful."

All of the guys also thanked her. After lunch everyone went back to work.

Sometime after lunch Sherri came and Jack brought her to the office to stay out of sight until the kids showed up. She just studied while she waited.

Then later in the afternoon a school bus pulled up in front of the overhead door. Angie saw this and she asked if anyone knew what this was about. None of the guys knew. They were all looking wondering what was going on. Then the bus door opened and a huge bunch of young girls came out and into the shop followed by quite a few adults. Dominic, Lizzy, Uncle Jack came out to see. The girls all went up to Angie and were very excited. Angie didn't know who they were until she saw Amy. The first thing she thought was, "These cannot be all of those young ladies, could they?"

Mrs. Carver walked up and asked, "Are you Angelina?"

"Yes ma'am."

Dominic went to the office and got Sherri. She walked out to everyone.

"I am Mrs. Carver from the Department of Health. These are all of the girls you saved. They wanted to come and thank you and Sherri in person. You may like to know that they thought you were an angel when they first saw you."

Angie was speechless. She had tears in her eyes as she squatted down.

Each one wanted to hug her and say thank you. Then Amy came to Angie and said, "Angelina, you are my savior, like a guardian angel. You rescued all of us." Everyone, this is Saving Angelina! I gave her that name while I was at the hospital." She turned to Angie again, "The police told me that those guys probably would have killed me like some others because I fought so hard. You saved my life." She reached out and hugged Angie again. "And my mom and dad told me that you stayed with me from the time they brought me in the ambulance until my parents came." Amy had tears in her eyes. "You didn't know me and you stayed with me."

"I don't know what to say Amy. I had to stay with you until you parents came. I could not leave you alone after what they did to you. And you returned my cross. I would have felt dead if I had lost it so you saved me as well."

"Wow. When you fought that guy and I saw the cross I just knew it had to be yours so I grabbed it right away and put it in my pants pocket hoping I would see you again. I wanted to give it back to you."

"You are a very sweet and brave little lady Amy." Amy gave her a tight hug again. Then Angie turned and saw Sherri.

"How...?" Angie turned to the girls and said, "Everyone, this is Sherri. She helped me find all of you. Without her help I would not have found you."

They all crowded around Sherri and she squatted down for all of them to hug her.

All of the parents gathered around to thank Angie and Sherri as well. One mother had tears in her eyes and said, "I can see why they thought you were an angel; you look like an angel. And you brought our daughter back to us. We thought we would never see her again. She was gone for over 3 weeks. They said that if they don't find them in the first 48-72 hours most likely the case will turn into a search for the body." She cried hard.

Angie reached out and hugged her. Then the mother turned to Sherri and hugged her.

Throughout this whole time Dominic and Lizzy were watching and they had tears in their eyes. They knew what Angie did was dangerous and she might have been hurt or worse, but they were very moved from seeing the girls and the parents thanking Angie. They thought what she did was a good thing. Lizzy said to Dominic, "Dom, is there anything Angie cannot do?"

"I do not know sweetheart. All I can say is we could not be any more fortunate."

"These kids were all kidnaped for a sex ring?" Jack asked.

"Yes Jack. And Angie and Sherri saved them all."

"I can't believe anyone could do something like that to kids. And Angie fought and killed fifteen guys? That is un-believable!"

"And Lieutenant Edwards said that the guy that shot him she beat the most. And just before she killed him, he said he heard her say, 'This is for Lieutenant Edwards.' Then she kicked him once more and that killed him. Then he told me that when Angie helped him to stop the bleeding from the gunshot the last guy put a rope around her neck and started to choke her. She did something I would not believe if the Lieutenant didn't tell me."

"What did she do?"

"He said she ran up the wall and flipped over this guy to free herself from the rope."

"What! She ran up the wall?"

"That is what he said. He said he still cannot believe it and she did it right in front of him."

"This whole thing is unbelievable. I watched the whole news report and I still am having a difficult time believing it." Jack said.

Just then, someone came up behind them from the front of the shop. "Excuse me sir, would it be OK if I went there and interviewed everyone? No one has been able to talk to Angelina, Sherri or the kids."

Dominic turned to see who it was. It was Brian Atkins from KDLT News. He was surprised that he was asking. Usually, they just go in. He looked at Lizzy and Jack and they both thought it would be fine. "Yes, you may sir." Dominic said.

"Thank you, sir. You are Dominic? Am I correct? The owner of this establishment?"

"Yes sir, I am."

"You have an amazing daughter!" He waved to the camera crew to come in.

As they were walking into the shop Mrs. Carver met Brian Atkins before he got to the kids. "What do you plan on doing here? You're not going to do some kind of smear thing are you? Because if you are I can't let you near any of the kids."

"No Ma'am, I just would like to do a follow up and possibly talk to Angelina, Sherri and maybe a couple of kids and parents. I want to show what she did and what the reactions are. We rarely show anything about good people."

"Ok just wait here a minute and let me ask if there is anyone that would not want to be on TV." Mrs. Carver walked back and told everyone that the news was there and wanted to talk to Angelina, Sherri and maybe ask a few parents and kids how they feel about what Angelina did. Is there anyone that would not want to be part of this?" Everyone said it would be fine. Angie stood there feeling kind of shocked that they would want to talk to her. She and Sherri stood there looking at each other.

Mrs. Carver waved to Brian to come. There were only 4 people. Brian Atkins, the camera man, a guy with a mic on a boom and another helping with cables.

Brian stood in front of everyone and was signaled they were live. "Hello, this is Brian Atkins for KDLT news. We are here at Dom's Automotive and Performance Center to see the result of amazing thing. These are all of the kids that Angelina Tucci and her friend Sherri Winston saved from child trafficking. Angelina would you please come here as say a few words?"

Angie felt as if she was put on the spot. She walked over to Brian. She didn't know what to say.

Brian asked her, "Angelina, how do you feel now that you saved all of these children? Do you feel like a hero?"

"I am elated that they are with their families again. However, I do not feel that I am a hero. I just did what I had to. I was thrust into an unreasonable situation and just reacted. That is all."

"That's all? I understand you fought with fifteen suspects and overcame all of them. I think that is amazing. And you saved thirty one young girls."

"It was a difficult situation, but I managed. I cannot really say much more because when I am faced with defending my life I just react. All that is going through my mind is to survive."

"I understand you have been studying Martial arts for over twelve years. What level have you reached?"

"Yes sir, that is correct. I have recently achieved 4th Dan Black Belt sir. I have worked very hard to achieve this sir."

"I am sure your parents are proud Angelina."

"Sherri, how do you feel now that you helped save thirty one girls from trafficking?"

Sherri didn't know what to say. "I guess it feels good. I don't know what else to say"

"You are a hero just as much as Angelina."

"I don't feel as though I am a hero. Once I learned about what was happening, I couldn't turn away. I did what I had to do to save them."

"Thank you, Sherri." He turned to the kids, "Would any of you girls like to say anything?"

Right away Amy raised her hand and said, "I do, I do!"

Can you come over here please?" Amy came over. She still had bruises and swelling all over her face and her speech was still strained and gravelly. Brian was shocked when he saw her. "What is your name?"

"My name is Amy and Angelina saved me from a big guy that was hurting me. She is my hero and I am very grateful. I call her Saving Angelina because she saved all of us."

"Saving Angelina? That sounds fitting. May I ask how old you are Amy?"

"I am 12 years old."

Another one of the girls asked if she could say something. "Can you come over her?"

"Hi, I am Gabriela. When Angelina found us, we were all locked in room. She is so beautiful that we all thought she was an angel. We thought she was sent to help us die. She said she would be back to get us and she came back. She is my hero too. And I am so happy to be going home. I didn't think I would ever see my mom and dad again."

"That is very nice to hear Gabriela. Is there anyone else that would like to say something?" None of the other girls wanted to. Brian looked towards the parents. "Would any of you like to say anything?"

Amy's mother said she would. "I would."

"Please come here ma'am." She walked over.

She came over and said trying to hold back tears, "I am Amy's mother and I feel indebted to Angelina for bringing my daughter back to us. We believed we would never see her again. I believe she is angelic. I understand why they thought she was an angel. She looks like an angel. I don't know what else to say."

"Thank you, ma'am." He turned to the camera, "As you can see this has been a very emotional moment for all here. This is Brian Atkins KDLT news." The camera man motioned that the camera was off. He looked at Angelina, "Angelina, you did a good thing. We could use more young people like you."

"Thank you, sir." She was blushing.

By this time Dominic, Lizzy and Jack had walked over to everyone. Amy's mother looked at Lizzy and said, "You must be Angelina's mother. You look like an angel too."

Lizzy was a little stunned. No one ever told her she looked like an angel. "Yes, I am Elizabeth, Angelina's mother. ma'am."

"You have a wonderful caring daughter. Do you know that Angelina stayed and watched over our Amy until my husband and I arrived? She told us she couldn't let Amy be alone after what had happened to her."

"Really? I did not know that." Lizzy said as she turned towards Angie. "Angie, you did not tell me that. I am so proud."

In the background Eric; Scott; Johnny; Miguel and Hector were watching. They were talking between themselves. They couldn't believe what Angie had done. They felt overwhelmed from seeing all of the girls.

Chapter 24

Across the city Johnny was watching TV and saw the report with all of the girls and their parents. This made his anger escalate, so much so that he kicked the screen in on his TV again. He had a real anger problem. "Again? Why does that bitch keep getting on TV? It should be me, dam it! And they call her an angel?" He punched the wall and put a hole in it.

Since he lived in the guest house above the attached garage on his mother's house his mother heard this and came running. She pounded on the door. "Johnny, Johnny! Are you alright? What was that noise?"

Johnny opened the door just enough to see his mother. "Nothing. I just knocked my TV over and the screen broke."

"I keep telling you to practice your karate outside. Now you broke your TV again."

"Yea, I got to go." And he closed the door. "Where am I going to get another TV? She made me break that too. I'll get her back." Johnny couldn't think about anything else. He was seriously obsessed and fuming.

Chapter 25

A week later was July 4th and as usual the whole family got together to celebrate. This year they celebrated at Angie's house and had a pool party. This year Lizzy also invited John, Carol and Sherri Winston. Dominic and Angie had been outside greeting everyone when the Winston's arrived. "Look father they drove the GTO!"

Dominic walked over and greeted them. "You drove the GTO! This is nice, very nice." Since it is a Ram Air IV it had a definite lope. Just then Enzo, Maria, Bella and Rosa arrived and Enzo drove the new Impala SS. "It almost looks like we have our own car show." Dominic said. Now there was a 1969 GTO Judge, a 1967 Impala SS, a 1969 428 Catalina Wagon, Angie's CUDA and they had the garage open and you could see the Nova and the 427 powered truck.

Joseph and Kristina along with Lilly, Carl, Shelly and Edward had already arrived and were in the house. Dominic greeted John and Carol then introduced them to Enzo and Maria. Enzo said, "John, hello, nice to see you. I never expected to see you here. I did not know you knew the Tucci's."

"Nice to see you as well Enzo. This is my wife, Carol. We are Sherri's parents."

"Really? Sherri is such a sweet lady." They went and each hugged. "This is my wife, Maria. She is Dominic's sister. And this is Bella and Rosa."

Bella and Rosa held out their hands. John took each and lightly kissed the back of each. "It is a pleasure to meet you both." Then he did the same to Maria, "The pleasure is all mine ma'am. As he took her hand."

"Such a gentleman John. And Carol," She went and they hugged, "I can see where Sherri received her beauty." She didn't know Sherri was adapted. "I feel something." She looked at Carol then at Sherri.

"Ma'am, I was adopted right after I was born." Sherri said.

"Oh, now I understand. But it is amazing the resemblance."

"Thank you, Maria. We did not notice until Sherri was maybe 3 or 4 years old." Carol said.

"Well, you have been blessed Carol. Sherri is a special lady. Come let us go inside. I will introduce you to everyone else. Ladies, come along." Maria said as they went into the house.

Dominic and Angie remained with John and Enzo to talk cars. They checked out each other's cars, chatted and then went inside.

It wasn't long before everyone wanted to go into the pool so everyone changed and went outside. It was a clear day with a light breeze. It reached 103 degrees so everyone really enjoyed the pool.

A little later Dominic began grilling hamburgers and Italian sausages. The food was set up on the patio. Everyone brought dishes as usual. They had potato salad; a Jell-O mold; fruit and cut vegetables with dip; chips with homemade salsa. Lizzy called everyone to eat. They each got a plate of food and sat down. Grandfather Joseph said, "I wish to say grace if I may." Everyone bowed their heads. "Thank you, lord, for bringing us together to celebrate this holiday. Thank you for all of the people that fought to keep this nation together long ago. Thank you for keeping us safe and healthy, and thank you for watching over Angelina while she freed those young girls so that they may live full lives. Thank you for this feast and may it nourish our bodies and I give you great thanks for everything you do for everyone. Amen."

Angie was the spotlight the whole day. She was asked about her fight with all of the guys that kidnapped the girls.

Shelly told Angie, "Cuz, I cannot believe how you look. You have an amazing body now, well-toned without showing your muscles. After all we have heard about you fighting, I expected you to look like a body builder. But all I see is that your ABS are defined. I am jealous."

Bella, Rosa and Edward had joined the conversation.

"Thank you, Shelly. It is all of the working out I have been doing learning extreme defense. There is much more physical exercise. See, if I tense my muscles, they all they are quite defined." She tensed her arm and torso muscles and she appeared as though she was a body builder.

"I cannot believe that." Shelly said.

"What is extreme defense Angelina?" Edward asked.

"Edward, I have been learning some moves, because of the situations I have been in, that generally are not taught. I have also been learning Muay Thai and Shaolin Kung Fu. I am told that these forms are the most effective stand up and striking martial arts."

"Wow! Did you use that on those guys you fought while saving all of those girls?"

"Yes Edward. Along with much of everything else I have learned."

Rosa asked, "Angelina, do you think you could show us some basic self-defense?"

Bella said, "There has to be something simple that could help any of us if we were to get attacked is there not?"

"Of course I could. There are many basic moves that you could easily learn. I did not know any of you were interested."

"I do not know if any of us will need to use this but it would be nice to know what to do it the situation were to arise." Shelly said.

"I could show each of you a move now if you wish."

"That would be so cool cuz!" Shelly said.

"Alright." Angie pulled Edward towards her and put her arm around his neck from behind. "If someone did this, what would you do?"

Edward pulled at her arm and said, "I don't know. What could you do?"

"There are many things, Edward. Here, stand behind me and put your arm around my neck." He did that. "The simplest thing would be to grab a finger" she grabbed one of Edwards fingers from the hand on the arm around her neck, "And pull like this," She showed him without hurting but he could feel how it would hurt, "then pull back as hard as you can. You will most likely break the finger and if you attacker is not high on a stimulant they will instantly let go. If it was a bully, it is likely they will not bully you again."

Angie went behind him and put her arm around his neck again and asked him to try it. He reached and grabbed her finger and pretended to pull.

"Wow! That is easy!" Edward said.

"This is how many things in Martial Arts are. You use simple things to neutralize your opponent. But it takes practice." She had each of them try. This excited all of them.

Edward ran over to his mother, "Mother, Angelina just taught us how to defend ourselves if someone put their arm around our necks."

"Really? You're not going to kill anyone are you?" Lilly teased.

"No mother, this will not kill anybody. It will just make them let go. I cannot believe how easy it is."

"Really?" Lilly called Carl. "Carl, Angelina taught the kids how to defend themselves. Do you want Edward to show you?"

He was talking to Dominic, Joseph, Enzo and Jack. "Come here Edward."

Edward walked over. "Father, stand behind me and put your arm around my neck." He did that.

"Do you believe you can get out of this?"

Edward reached and grabbed one of his fingers and pulled a little hard. "Ahh! That hurt!" he pulled his arm away.

"See father, and I did not pull hard. Angelina said if you pull hard, you will break the person's finger and they will let go. See you let go." Edward said smiling. He never thought he could defend himself. Now he did not feel so small.

Angie, Bella, Rosa and Shelly watched. Shelly thought it was funny when her father screamed. "I cannot believe it. My father did not expect that. I guess no one that did that to you would expect that. Thank you, Angelina."

"You are very welcome, Shelly. Maybe each time we get together I can show all of you something else. And soon you will be able to perform basic self-defense."

They were getting hot so they went back in the pool.

This year Maria baked a cannoli cake and Lilly brought an assortment of homemade cookies. Lizzy said it was time for desert. Sherri went up to Lizzy with a question. She didn't want anyone to hear. She whispered, "Mrs. Tucci, before you serve desert could I have a minute or two. I have something I drew for Angie to thank her for saving my life."

Lizzy said, "Sherri you are sweet. You may."

"I need to run to the car to get it. It will only take a minute." She got the keys from her father and went to the car and took out the color drawing she did for Angie. She had wrapped it so no one would see it before she gave it to Angie. She went back into the house and out to the pool area. She gave the keys back to her father. She walked in front of the tables. "Everybody, can you gather around please." Everyone gathered. "I have a gift I made for Angelina for saving my life from those two guys. Angelina, this is for you." She handed it to Angie.

Everyone started saying, open it, open it." She tore off the paper. She couldn't believe it. It was a color drawing of her standing next to her car. She held it up for everyone to see. She got tears in her eyes and got a little choked up. It took a minute for her to be able to speak.

"I don't know what to say Sherri, it is beautiful! I cannot believe you drew this!" She now had tears dripping from her cheeks. Everyone also thought it was beautiful. She went to Sherri and gave her a hug. "I don't know what to say. This touches my heart. Thank you." She took it inside so nothing would get spilled on it or it wouldn't get splashed on.

Grandmother Kristina walked up to Sherri and said, "That has to be the most thoughtful gift ever given to Angelina, Sherri. You are a wonderful friend."

"Thank you, Ma'am. It was the least I could do. If it wasn't for Angelina I would not be here now."

Lizzy said, "Please everyone, come and have desert." Maria had cut the cake and put pieces on small plates.

Cannoli cake was new to most but they all loved it. Lilly and Kristina said to Maria that they were amazed with the cake. Maria was still getting used to how differently Kristina and Lilly had been treating her since Angie's 18th birthday. Her complements meant quite a bit to Maria as Kristina had treated her callously all of the years she had known her. Maria went up to Kristina and hugged her. "Thank you for the complement, Kristina. This means quite a bit to me."

The party continued well after dark. They were able to see some of the fireworks from the house. They sat together and watched. This is one of the benefits of living in parts of the Foothills. There is a very good view of most of the city.

Chapter 26

As time went on Angie continued learning more from her two Sensei's. She became even faster and more lethal than she had been when she fought the guys that abducted the young ladies. She was beginning to resemble the fighters in the Japanese martial arts movies that move so fast it appears that trick photography was used. And she was becoming very deadly. Part of this training was to teach her when she should use this as using it on a typical opponent could easily kill or severely hurt them. And they did not want her going around and killing people because of a fight. These were last resort tactics for use when she had no choice, where her life was in danger.

Angie continued to do her workouts after work most days in the garage. She had a routine worked out where she worked on all of her muscle groups each time. She had two large 100 pound punching bags hung in the garage about six feet apart. She worked out using these as if they were two different people. She also had things called gravity boots to strap to her ankles so she could hang on a beam upside down to do sit-ups. Her muscles are toned throughout her body now. When she tensed up they were very visible. Otherwise, she just appeared very fit.

On Tuesday's and Thursday's, she worked with her Sensei's perfecting using her Eskrima sticks and the Bo along with all of the new fighting techniques. They practiced disarming attackers with knives; hand guns; rifles; pipes and most anything they could think an attacker could use. She was becoming expert at these moves even surprising her Sensei's. They worked with her doing different scenarios and then moved to both of them attacking her at the same time. She defended herself and proved her ability to immobilize anyone attacking her. She was jumping and was also able to flip over backwards to get away from attacks with the Bo.

Then one night Sensei Kotomi had a piece of rope and flung it around her neck to simulate choking her. They had not taught her anything about getting out of this yet but he wanted to see her reaction. She tried to hit him with her left and right elbows but couldn't contact him. After three or four tries she pulled him a little closer to the wall and ran up the wall and flipped over him getting out of the hold and she cocked her right fist back with her arm straight and swung and hit him in the side of the head, then she did the same with her left. (They were all wearing padding)

Kotomi turned and bowed and said, "Good Angie! I no need teach. You make solution. I impressed."

Akio also bowed. "I proud Angie. I impressed you do yourself."

"Thank you, Sensei Kotomi and Sensei Akio. My confidence has grown from your teachings. Thank you." Angie said. At this point she was covered with sweat and did some stretches and drank some water. She was also catching her breath. Sensei Kotomi, I was just thinking about when I began here. I was 7 years old and did not want to be here. You made it fun for me then. I would never have believed at that time I would be at this point. I have you to thank for that, sir. And Sensei Akio, I owe you thanks for what I have learned from you as well. I want you both to know that I look up to you both as great instructors."

"Angie, no need thanks. Just keep working. Sign good student is continue to learn. You do well."

"Thank you, sir. I will clean up now and go. I will see you both on Thursday."

Chapter 27

Angie was able to go back to her normal life. She had been worried that possibly there would be people that would challenge her to fights because of all of the news reports. But no one did. She resumed her normal life of working Monday through Saturday; training on Tuesday and Thursday nights; going out with her friends and racing on Sunday's. She helped Gina with her Pharmacy math and Gina passed this course.

And as usual, Angie's mind was always thinking of things she could do to improve the shop or car projects she could begin. She began sketching out ideas and then showed her father and Uncle Jack. Usually they would look and listen then think these were just abstract ideas. They never thought she was serious with these ideas.

Then she began showing them her sketches of car bodies she said she might want to attempt to make. Dominic and Jack looked at these and thought they actually looked like real exotic cars. She had sketched some dashboards and interiors as well as suspensions. They thought her ideas could be viable but they would take an enormous time to complete. But they just thought these were thoughts and dreams. Because of this they didn't think about it much.

Angie said that she would like to learn to fabricate so she could actually build something. She continued to look for and buy any books she could find on fabrication and she also found a good book on constructing things from fiberglass. This book touched on making molds and how to lay up fiberglass. I did not go into as much detail about making molds as she had hoped. She figured she would need to just try making molds of things and then try to pull fiberglass parts from them.

She went to the junk yard and found a Barracuda front bumper to use to practice. She figured it was not too large and if she was successful she could use it on her CUDA. She did not have much success at first. She tried to make a mold from the bumper but due to the complex curves she broke it trying to remove it. She decided she needed to make a multi-piece mold. But the book she had did not say much and only had a few pictures of multi-piece molds. She thought about it for a while and came up with a solution. She used heavy cardboard and cut it to fit the contours of the bumper in a few places and then covered the cardboard with duct tape. She attached these to the bumper with duct tape on one side and then used modeling clay to fill the imperfections on the side where she would lay up the fiberglass. Then she used the mold release wax and painted on the PVA. She continued with laying up fiberglass. Then she removed the cardboard and used mold release wax and PVA on the other places and on the flanges left from the cardboard. She laid up more fiberglass. When it was set up she drilled a few holes in the flanges and removed the mold. Then she put all of the pieces together. Now she had a mold she could take apart and hopefully use to make a fiberglass bumper.

She cleaned the surfaces up on the mold and used mold release wax and PVA on the inside them laid up multiple layers of fiberglass. When it set up she trimmed the edges with a saber saw and pulled the mold apart. The bumper came out nice. She took this to her father and Jack to show them. They were shocked as it appeared to look like a part out of a catalog.

Now all she had to do is drill the bumper bolt holes and get it painted Panther Pink.

Dominic and Jack couldn't believe she did it. They thought maybe she would be able build what she had showed them. Maybe her ideas weren't so bad after all.

Angie kept coming up with ideas and more sketches. One day she was showing Eric these and he asked her if she would like to become a master fabricator. She thought about it and told him she would love that. But they would need quite a bit of equipment to set up a fabrication shop. So for now, she just thought about it as a dream for another time.

But time was passing quickly and Labor Day was coming fast. She loved this holiday because the AHRA Winter Nationals are on this weekend. This was one of her favorite racing weekends. However, she and Dominic don't race. They spend the time watching and walking through the pit. She was looking forward to talking to some of the big-name competitors and maybe she could talk to Shirley Moldowney. She hoped this year she could meet her and maybe get a picture with her. It was still a few weeks away. She was hopeful nothing would happen before then. She went on with her life.

AVENGING ANGELINA
An Angelina Tucci Novel

Chapter 1 (Preview)

Aug, 1976

It was the end of the week and they needed to deposit the week's proceeds in the bank. Usually Dominic does this but because Angie has been learning about running the shop she wanted to make the deposit. This had been a busy week with a few big jobs completed so they had an unusually large amount to deposit.

Angie took the checks and cash and placed all of it in the bank pouch along with the deposit slip. Then she put it in her purse and left for the bank. She got to the bank, parked and went in. She got in line for one of the tellers and patiently waited.

As she waited two guys with guns and ski masks came running into the bank. They screamed for everyone to not move. Angie scanned the lobby and watched these guys. One screamed for everyone to move towards the back of the bank. One stayed at the door watching. The other continued to tell everyone to walk to the back. Angie was moving slowly and ended up following the last of the people. The guy was behind her aiming a gun. Angie waited until they were out of the first guy's sight and she spun, grabbed the gun and pushed it away from everyone and herself. Then she grabbed the rear and twisted it up and pulled it from his hand. The guy groaned because this broke his finger. She tossed the gun aside. This took seconds. She turned and faced the guy and hit him with a palm heal punch and broke his nose. He grabbed his nose and she did a reverse 360 degree round house to the side of his head and his head slammed against the wall, which was brick and fell. He did not move.

When everyone heard something happening they turned to look and he was laying on the floor already. All they heard was a grunt and his head hitting the wall. Angie picked up the gun and handed it to one of the tellers and told them all to go into the back room out of sight and stay there. Everyone went fast.

Angie grabbed the guy's legs and dragged him into an office and put him behind the desk. She left the office and stepped around the corner and waited. Within a few minutes the other guy came looking for his partner. He had his gun in front of him and was walking slowly cautiously calling his partner, "Where the hell are you? This isn't what we planned, where are you?"

He was walking slowly and the bank guard ran out of the back room pointing his gun and the robber shot him. Angie saw this and immediate came out from around the corner and kicked the gun out of his hand. He was shocked at the move as he did not see her. She got into her stance and he threw a punch and she expertly blocked it and broke his arm with the usual Aikido move. He screamed and she followed with a few kicks to his side which likely fractured ribs. He grabbed his side from the pain and bent over some. She then kicked out one of his knees and he fell hard. As he tried to get up Angie said sternly, "Get up and they will take you out in a body bag." He stayed down.

Angie turned to check on the guard and he was just hit in the side of his abdomen. She looked and grabbed a sweater that was on a chair, wadded it up and had the guard hold it on to help stop the bleeding. One of the people screamed, "He's getting up!"

Angie turned to look and the guy pulled himself up and went for his gun that was on the floor across the room. She jumped up and ran at the guy and jumped and kicked him in the head and he flew back and his head crashed against a post and he fell back limp.

Sargent Hernandez came running around the corner just as Angie had jumped. He saw her mid-air then hitting the guy in the head with her foot.

When she landed, Angie saw Sargent Hernandez and screamed, "Call an ambulance, the guard was hit."

Sargent Hernandez called for an ambulance. Angie said, "The other one is laying in the office over there." She pointed at the office and another officer ran to check. Both guys were out cold and one had a broken arm and knee.

Sargent Hernandez was shocked. He had never believed Lieutenant Edwards when he told him about Angie. Now he saw it firsthand. Angie, "I just saw what you did and I can't believe it. What happened here?"

"These two guys tried to rob the bank and ushered everyone to the back. I didn't know what they were going to do so I engaged the first one and dragged him into the office out of sight and when the second one came looking for him, the guard jumped out and got shot by the second guy. I came out and ended it sir. I kicked his gun out of his hand and he tried to punch me and I broke his arm. Then I kicked his side a few times which likely broke his ribs. Then he did not back down so I broke his knee. As I went to help the guard and someone screamed the guy started to get up and go for his gun so I ran and kicked him in the head and his head slammed into the post and he went down as you saw.

Shortly afterwards the news came and was in front of the bank trying to find out anything about what happened. As they were setting up an ambulance pulled up and the paramedics took the gurney and went into the bank. The news tried to follow but were held back by the police. The officer said, "This hasn't been secured yet. No one will be allowed inside.

All of the news channels set up outside and began their broadcast. There were radio station news people there as well. Dominic was in the office working when Jack came in a little riled up. "Dom, didn't Angie go to the bank?"

"Yes, why?"

"The news on the radio said that there was a robbery in progress. I hope Angie wasn't there."

"She left a while ago so she likely missed it. At least I hope she did." He reached and turned on the radio he had in the office.

"We're here at the scene of an attempted bank robbery at Arizona Bank at 7130 N. Oracle Rd. This is the scene of a bank robbery gone wrong. We were told that two gunshots were fired and a bank security guard was hit. There have been rumors of a young girl defusing the situation but the information has been sketchy." As he was speaking the paramedics rolled out the security guard and put him in the ambulance. As it pulled away another ambulance pulled up. The paramedics pulled out the gurney and entered the bank. Everyone waited for additional information.

"Oh my god it had to be Angie!" Dominic said.

The radio news man continued, "They are bringing out someone now that appears to have been beaten. One arm is bandaged up in a splint along with one leg. An officer is getting into the ambulance with this person. There is another person holding an ice pack on the side of his head being helped out with two officers. He doesn't appear to be able to stand on his own. Officer can you give us an update? He just went by and didn't answer. There are many people coming out from the back of the bank along with a few officers that we can see through the windows."

Dominic and Jack were staring at the radio waiting for anything more. The person on the radio continued talking this whole time.

After about 15 minutes the police were letting people leave the bank. Sargent Hernandez told Angie, "Maybe you should leave with the crowd so you don't get stopped by the news. Make sure you go to the station to make a statement."

"Yes sir. I will drive there directly." Angie mixed and left with the crowd.

Johnny of course was out of a job now and was watching TV. He wasn't paying too much attention until they said that there were rumors of a young girl defusing the situation. At that point he was glued to the TV. He was watching as everyone was leaving the bank. "Is that Angie?" he said out loud. "That's her. She did it again. Dam it! She is always on TV." Even though she had not been interviewed or identified he knew it was her. "Why do they keep focusing on her? Dam it!" He stood and almost kicked his TV again. Now he was beyond angry. His face was red and he was looking for something to kick so he kicked the wall and put a hole in it.

The news guy stopped another officer and asked, "Can you give us an update officer?"

"There was an attempted robbery and one of the patrons defused the situation. The bank guard was shot and it is not life threatening. He was sent to the hospital. We have the two suspects in custody."

"Who was the patron that defused this officer?"

"I cannot give that information out at this time."

"They cannot give out that information? Why the hell not? They have done it every other time. It had to be Angie. Who else would it be?" Dominic said.

After another hour and a half Angie was able to go back to the shop. When she pulled into the back lot Dominic ran out to meet her. "Are you OK? You are not hurt? We heard about it on the radio."

"I am fine father, but I was not able to make the deposit because of this." Angie was angry. She got out of the CUDA and locked the door. They walked in together. As they walked in everybody asked her if she was OK. "I am fine." They could see that she was angry.

When they got up front Dominic wanted to go into the office and talk. He closed the door. Right away Angie said, "I cannot believe this, I finally get to make the deposit myself and two idiots have to disrupt it." She reached into her purse and pulled out the bank pouch and handed it to Dominic. "We need to wait until the bank reopens. Maybe tomorrow."

"That is what you are worried about? They said two guys with guns tried to rob the bank."

"It was not a big deal. The first guy wanted everyone to go in the back of the bank and followed pointing his gun at us. As soon as we were out of the sight of the other guy I turned and took his gun away. I do not know what he planned but I did not let him do anything. Then I broke his nose and did a 360 degree reverse roundhouse and his head hit the brick wall and he fell. I dragged him into an office. Then I went and hid around the corner. Everyone went into a back room. Maybe it was the vault room. When the second guy came looking for the first guy the guard came out of the back room and the second guy shot him and his gun went off. I took that as an opportunity to end it and kicked the gun out of his hand. Then he tried to punch me and I broke his arm. He wasn't stopping so I broke his knee. He went down. I ran to the guard and found something for him to hold on his wound and someone else screamed that the guy was getting up. I turned and he was trying to get to his gun so I ran and jumped and kicked him in the head and his head slammed into a post and he went down. Just as I jumped Sargent Hernandez came around and saw me kick this guy. He was shocked."

"I wasn't shot at or was in any danger at the point I stopped these two father."

"Angie, this was a big deal. You are talking about it as if it was just a normal thing."

"It could have been a big deal but I stopped it beforehand. "Maybe he was planning on shooting everyone, I do not know. But I did not want to wait to find out." Angie is beginning to get used to these situations now. She thought they were happening more and more. "Father, I just refuse to be a victim. I will fight until the end if necessary."

"Angie, each time something such as this happens all of us become very worried. I always think, what if this is the time she does not make it?"

"Father I will be fine. If I had waited more people could have been shot. The security guard was too much in a hurry to confront this guy and that could have gotten many of us shot. I waited to be out of the second guy's sight before I acted. I wanted to take them one at a time. This is all part of my training. If I would have been in real danger the guys would not have survived."

"What do you mean by that?"

"If I felt my life was in danger I would have taken them out with the first kick."

"You could do that?

"Yes father. There are certain moves I would use that would kill them instantly."

By the time the evening news came on they had more information about the botched robbery along with the two guy's names and that Angelina Tucci was the one that defused the situation.

The next day, Saturday, Angie went to work as usual. It was late morning when an elderly lady walked into the shop. She walked up to the counter and asked, "Young man, is this the place where Angelina works?"

Jack looked at her for a moment, "Yes ma'am. She works in the shop."

"She works in the shop? What does she do?"

"She is an auto mechanic."

"She is? Her? Could I see please? I can't believe it."

Jack looked at her and thought it would not be a problem to point her out. He walked her around the counter to the entrance of the shop and pointed to Angie. She was bent over the fender of a car and looked up and saw the lady. "Oh, I see. I have something to say to her. I believe she saved my life yesterday and I wanted to thank her if I may."

Jack walked the lady back to the front and asked her to wait. He went back, "Angie, there is someone here to see you."

She looked up and put the tool down she had in her hand and took her gloves off and set them on the bench. She walked up front. "Who is here to see me Uncle Jack?" Jack glanced to the elderly lady. Angie walked over and said, "How may I help you Ma'am?"

"You are very polite dear. I came here to thank you personally for saving my life. I believe if you did not do what you did, we all may have been killed. All I saw was you kicking that last man and I was shocked. I was going to try to help the security guard and I happened to look up and saw you. You are a hero!"

"Ma'am, thank you for your sentiments but I just did what I needed to do to keep everyone safe. I do not believe that makes me a hero. I just stopped anything further from happening."

Dear, you did a heroic thing. At least it was from my point of view. I don't know how you did what you did. It looked like you were from a movie. I didn't know that kind of thing was real. But you did save all of our lives. I just wanted to thank you, dear." She reached out and grabbed Angie's hand and squeezed it. She smiled and left.

Uncle Jack said, "That was very sweet of her Angie. She came here just to thank you. You touch so many people in such unique ways. I hope someday you can acknowledge how many people's lives you have changed."

Angie smiled and went back to work.

Chapter 2

Johnny finally returned to the Dojo in the middle of August 1976. His sensei hadn't wanted him back there until his arm was completely healed and he could fight again. Johnny wanted to learn more ways to fight because of how easily Angie hurt him but his sensei did not agree. Johnny has been training for competition and other training can easily disqualify him. His Sensei does not believe that Johnny would be able to keep other kinds of fighting out of competition.

His sensei concentrated on the same abilities as he has been working on. "Johnny, you work get black belt. This best way advance."

Johnny didn't like this. He was already a brown belt and he felt that to get to black belt in Karate would just be time practicing. He wanted to get Angie back for what she did to him. He was thinking, "How does he know what I need. I need to beat Angie and show her I am better. She deserves this. He continues to become more arrogant bragging about being a champion outside of the Dojo. He was picking fights so he can show that no one can beat him. His arrogance builds fast and by the end of July some of this gets back to his sensei. His sensei pulls Johnny into his office for a talk. "Johnny, hear you try fight outside of dojo. You no pick fight with people. Not what this about. You continue you disgrace Dojo and I. I not teach this. It not right. You stop. Understand?"

"You can't tell me what I can and can't do outside of here. I do what I want." Johnny said.

"You do this you get blackballed here. All I say." He dismissed Johnny. After this talk Johnny began to get arrogant even in the Dojo. He stopped pulling kicks and punches and a few students end up hurt, fortunately not seriously but hurt none the less.

By the first week of August his Sensei calls him into his office again. "Johnny, you disgrace Dojo, I and students. Hurt students for fun. Not good. You leave. You no welcome here. You no train in Tucson. End Karate for you. Go."

Johnny was angry. He left the office and slammed the door so hard the glass window broke. He grabbed his things from his locker and left. "Asshole! I'll show him. He can't do this to me. This is all Angie's fault. It started with her, bitch. I'll show her, I'm going to get back at her somehow." He said out loud as he walked through the Dojo and to his car. He got in and sped away.

Johnny's Sensei was worried. He thought Johnny was becoming very aggressive and he did not like that he was picking fights. He thought about his fight with Angie, the girl from his brother's Dojo. He decided to call his brother to discuss the situation, especially because Johnny left saying he wanted to get back at her. He thought "her" was the girl that he fought.

"Kotomi, Akio, I kick Johnny out. He blackballed. No teach more. I worried he say he get back at girl that that beat him. That Angie. We need work more. Angie need prepared. No want see her hurt, not right."

"Akio, I understand. We work with Angie to prepare. I talk with her."

Johnny told his friend Andy later that day that he wanted to get that bitch Angie for ruining his life. They began to talk about what they can do.

While Johnny was at work the next day, he began to have trouble with his boss and one of his coworkers. Johnny works at a warehouse. He drives a forklift loading pallets of product onto trucks. Lately he has had verbal fights with coworkers but today he was very arrogant and decided he wanted to use a specific forklift. Usually, they just use one that is not being used. But Johnny wanted the one that a Larry was using. He liked this one because it was new.

Johnny walked over to the forklift and told Larry, "Hey I wana use this forklift, get off."

"No, I'm using it now. Use the other one." Larry said feeling a little annoyed. He drove away.

Johnny went after him. "I want this forklift now, asshole."

"What's the problem? Just use the other one." Larry said as he lifted a pallet.

"I want this one now!" Johnny screamed.

His boss heard this and looked over to see what the screaming was.

Larry ignored him and kept working.

Johnny reached over and grabbed Larry and pulled him off of the forklift and threw him on the ground. He got on it and started driving away.

Johnny's boss ran over to Larry and asked if he was alright. He said yes. He was just angry and shocked at what Johnny did.

"What happened Larry?" his boss asked.

"Johnny just came over and said he wanted that forklift and when I said he should just use the other one he pulled me off and took it." Larry said.

"Johnny! Johnny! Come here!" his boss screamed.

Johnny drove over and said, "What?"

"Why did you pull Larry off of the forklift?"

"This is my forklift, that's why. He should know better." Johnny said.

"Johnny, you don't own this forklift. And I don't remember telling anyone that any forklift is theirs. Turn it off and get off now." He called Larry. Larry came over. "Johnny, use the other fork lift. Next time you do anything like this you will be fired."

"Make Larry use the other one."

"I said get off." His boss said.

"No, it's mine." Johnny said in a snotty way.

"OK Johnny, you're fired pick up your stuff and leave now."

"The hell I will." Johnny said.

"I'll call the police then." And he walked away.

"Johnny got off of the forklift, looked at Larry and punched him in the chest. This knocked him down.

"What did you do that for?" Larry asked.

"Fuck you." Johnny said. He went and grabbed his things and left. "Bitch gets me fired now. She is ruining my life. I need to kill that bitch." He said as he was walking to his car.

Johnny's boss went back to Larry and asked, "Are you ok Larry? I saw him punch you."

"I'll live." He got back on the forklift and continued working.

Johnny was livid. He was almost screaming as he drove home. Then he had an idea. He had remembered that one to the TV news reporters joked and suggested that maybe Angelina was psychic. "Yea, we can kidnap the bitch's mother and use her as bait. She will know and come for her. We will be ready and we can kill her mother in front of her and then beat her to death, that bitch. I got to call Andy, Lenny, Rick, Donny and Jake. They will help. Yea. Andy hates her for killing his brother at her dad's shop. I'm sure he wants her dead too. Ha-ha. This is perfect. Just gotta plan this out."